Praise for the novels of
New York Times bestselling author Megan Hart

"*Naked* is a great story, steeped in emotion. Hart has a wonderful way with her characters…. She conveys their thoughts and actions in a manner that brings them to life. And the erotic scenes provide a sizzling read."
—*RT Book Reviews*

"*Deeper* is absolutely, positively, the best book that I have read in ages! I cannot say enough about this book. The writing is fabulous, the characters' chemistry is combustible, and the story line brought tears to my eyes more than once…. Beautiful, poignant and bittersweet… Megan Hart never disappoints me, but with *Deeper* she went above and beyond."
—*Romance Reader at Heart*, Top Pick

"*Stranger*, like Megan Hart's previous novels, is an action-packed, sexy, emotional romance that tears up the pages with heat while also telling a touching love story…. *Stranger* has a unique, hot premise that Hart delivers on fully."
—Bestselling author Rachel Kramer Bussel

"*[Broken]* is not a traditional romance but the story of a real and complex woman caught in a difficult situation with no easy answers. Well-developed secondary characters and a compelling plot add depth to this absorbing and enticing novel."
—*Library Journal*

"An exceptional story and honest characters make *Dirty* a must-read."
—*Romance Reviews Today*

"*[Hart]* writes erotica for grown-ups. She doesn't write sex just to titillate and she holds her characters to a higher standard. *[The Space Between Us]* is a quiet book, but it packed a major punch for me…. She's a stunning writer, and this is a stunning book."
—*Super Librarian*

New York Times Bestselling Author

MEGAN HART

Tear You Apart

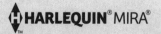

Recycling programs
for this product may
not exist in your area.

ISBN-13: 978-0-7783-1477-6

TEAR YOU APART

Copyright © 2013 by Megan Hart

Excerpt from THE SENSE OF AN ENDING

Copyright © 2012 by Ann Patchett

For questions and comments about the quality of this book, please contact us at
CustomerService@Harlequin.com.

Printed in U.S.A.

First printing: September 2013
10 9 8 7 6 5 4 3 2 1

For all those who have ever lost their will—
good night, and dream in color.

Sometimes love does not have the most honorable beginnings, and the endings, the endings will break you in half. It's everything in between we live for.

—Ann Patchett, from the essay *The Sense of an Ending*

This is a love story.

Chapter One

I came in on the train and then took a cab, but that didn't stop the late March drizzle from destroying everything I'd carefully put together at home earlier this afternoon. My hair hangs sodden against my forehead and cheeks. My clothes cling, damp and heavy and chilled. I stripped off my dark, soaked stockings in the gallery bathroom and wrapped them in paper towels to tuck inside my purse, and my legs feel glaringly pale. Instead of the glass of white wine in my hand, I'm desperate for a cup of coffee, or better yet, a mug of hot chocolate. With whipped cream.

I'm desperate for the taste of something sweet.

There should be desserts here, but all I can find are blocks of cut cheese, sweating on the tray among the slaughtered remains of fancy crackers. The bowl of what looks like honey mustard is probably all right, but the companion bowl of ranch dressing looks like a playground for gastrointestinal distress. Courtesy of the rain, I'm more chilled than the cheese, the dips or the wine.

I haven't seen Naveen yet. He's flirting his way through the entire crowd, and I can't begrudge him that. It's exciting, this new gallery. New York is different than Philly. He needs to make an impression with this opening. He'll get to me eventually. He always does.

Now I hold the glass of wine in one hand, the other tucked just below my breasts to prop my elbow as I study the photograph in front of me. The artist has blown it up to massive size. Twenty by forty, I estimate, though I've always been shit with measurements. The subject matter is fitting for the weather outside. A wet street, puddles glistening with gasoline rainbows. A child in red rubber boots standing in one, peering down at his reflection—or is it a her? I can't tell. Longish hair, a shapeless raincoat, bland and gender-neutral features. It could be a boy or girl.

I don't care.

I don't care one fucking thing about that portrait, the size of it just big enough to guarantee that somebody will shell out the cool grand listed on the price tag. I shake my head a little, wondering what Naveen had thought, hanging this in the show. Maybe he owed someone a favor…or a blow job. The BJ would've been a better investment.

There's a crinkle, tickle, tease on the back of my neck. The weight of a gaze. I turn around, and someone's there.

"You'd need a house the size of a castle to hang that piece of shit."

The voice is soft. Husky. Nearly as gender-neutral as the face of the child in the picture. I pause for just a moment before I look into his eyes, but the second I do, my brain fits him into a neat slot. Male. Man. He's a man, all right, despite the soft voice.

He's not looking at me, but at the picture, so I can stare at him for a few seconds longer than what's socially acceptable. Hair the color of wet sand spikes forward over his forehead and feathers against his cheeks in front of his ears. It's short and wispy in the back, exposing the nape of his neck. He's got a scruffy face, not just like a guy who's forgone shaving for a few days, but one who keeps an uneasy truce with his razor at best. He wears a dark suit, white shirt, narrow dark tie. Retro. Black Converse on his feet.

"And who'd pay a grand for it? C'mon." His gaze slides toward me just for a second or two. Catching me staring. He gestures at the photo.

"It's not so bad." I'm not sure why I'm compelled to say anything nice about the picture. I agree, it's an overpriced piece of shit. It's a mockery of good art, actually. I should be angry about this, that I'm wasting my time on it as if the consumption of beauty is something with an allotment. Hell, maybe it is.

Maybe I actually have wasted today's consumption of beauty on this piece of crap. I study it again. Technically, it's flawless. The lighting, the focus, the exposure. But it's not art.

Even so, someone will buy it simply because they will look at it the same way I did. They'll note the perfectly framed shot, the pseudowhimsical subject matter, the blandly colorful mat inside a sort of interesting frame. They will convince themselves it's just unique enough to impress their friends, but it won't force them to actually feel anything except perhaps smugness that they got a bargain.

"It looks like art," I say. "But it really isn't. And that's why someone will pay a thousand bucks for it and hang it in the formal living room they use only at Christmas. Because it looks like art but it really isn't."

He strokes his chin. "You think so?"

"Yes. I'm sure of it. Naveen wouldn't have priced it if he didn't think he could sell it." I slant the man a sideways look, wishing I could be bold enough to stare at him when he's facing me, the way I was when he was looking at something else.

"Good. I need to pay my rent. A coupla hundred bucks would be sweet."

Of *course* he's an artist. Men who look like that, in a place like this—they're always artists. Usually starving. He looks lean enough to have missed a few meals. Standing this close I get a whiff of cigarettes and corduroy, which should make no sense, since he's not wearing any, but it does because that's how I work. Tastes and smells and sounds link up for me in ways they don't for everyone else. I see colors where there shouldn't be any. The scent of corduroy is par for the course.

"You took that picture?"

"I did." He nods, not without pride, despite what he'd been saying about it earlier.

If he'd been talking shit about another artist's piece I'd have liked him less, even if he was telling the truth. I can like him better now. "It's really not so bad."

He frowns. Shakes his head. "You're a bad liar."

On the contrary, I think I'm an excellent liar.

He looks again at the picture and shrugs. "Someone will buy it because it looks like art but doesn't ask too much of them. That's what you're saying?"

"Yes."

"You're the expert." He shrugs again and crosses one arm over his chest to rest his elbow on as he stares at the photo. I don't miss the stance—it's a mirror of my own. He bites at his thumb. It must be an old habit, because the nail is ragged. "The only reason I did this thing was for Naveen, you know? He said he wanted something more commercial. Not, like, doll heads with pencil stubs sticking out of the eye holes and stuff like that."

I'm a good liar, but not a good poker player. I can't keep a stone face. I know the piece he's talking about. It's been in the back room of Naveen's Philadelphia gallery for months, if not years. Of course I assumed he couldn't sell it, which didn't explain why he kept it hung back there for so long. I joked with him that he kept it for some sentimental reasons; maybe this was true.

"That was yours?"

He laughs. "Will Roberts."

I take the hand he holds out. His fingers are callused and rough, and for a moment I imagine how they'd sound against something silk, like a scarf. His touch would rasp on something soft. It would whisper.

"Elisabeth Amblin."

His fingers curl around mine. For one bizarre second, I'm sure he's going to kiss the back of my hand. I tense, waiting for the brush of his mouth against my skin, the wet slide of his tongue on my flesh, and that's ridiculous because of course he wouldn't do such a thing. People don't do that to strangers. Even lovers would hardly do so.

My imagination is wild, I know it, yet when he lets my hand drop I'm still a little disappointed. His touch lingers, the way his fingers scraped at mine. I'm not soft as silk, no matter how many expensive creams I rub into my skin. And yet, I'd been right. His touch whispered.

"You're Naveen's friend."

"Yeah. You could say that. We have sort of a love-hate thing going on." I pause, judging his reaction. "He loves that I work for next to nothing, and I hate that he doesn't pay me more."

Will laughs. It ripples in streams of blue and green that wink into sparkling gold. His eyes squint shut. He has straight white teeth in a thin-lipped mouth. He shouldn't be attractive in his laughter, the way it changes his face, but there's something infectious about him. I laugh, too.

There's music in the gallery, a string quartet in the corner painfully strumming their way through Pachelbel's *Canon* and *Für Elise*. They must be students, because Naveen would never have paid for professional musicians. I wonder which one of them he used to fuck, because like that painting in the back room and other things here in the gallery, including me, Naveen hangs on to things for sentimental reasons. There's food in the gallery, too, a little lackluster. And there's wine. But there isn't much laughter, and we draw attention.

Will tips his head back for a few more chuckles, then looks at me. "I'm supposed to go mingle."

I want him to linger. I want to keep him from something he should be doing but chooses not to because of me. And I could make him stay, I think suddenly, watching his gaze skip and slide over my body, my damp clothes, my bare legs. He's already touched my skin. He knows how I feel. I want him to want to know more.

"Sure, go." I tip my chin toward the rest of the room. "I have some things I need to do, too."

I *am* a good liar.

"It was nice meeting you, Elisabeth." Will holds out his hand again.

This time I entertain no fantasies of his lips on the back of it. That's just silly. We shake formally. Firmly. I turn away from him at the end of it, feigning interest again in his piece-of-shit-that-isn't-art, so I don't have to watch him walking away.

Naveen finds me in front of a few pieces of pottery on their narrow pedestals. I don't like them. Technically, they're lovely. They are commercial. They will sell. What's good for the gallery is good for me. Still, they reek of manure. Maybe it's the mud they're made from. Maybe it's just the twisted signals in my brain that layer and mingle my senses. Whatever it is, I'm staring with a frown when my friend puts his arm around my shoulders and pulls me close.

"I already have several more commissioned from this artist.

Lacey Johnsbury." Naveen's grin is very white. He smells of a subtle blend of expensive cologne and the pomade he uses in his jet-black hair. Those are actual scents; anyone could smell them.

When Naveen speaks, I taste cotton candy, soft and sweet, subtle. There are times when listening to my friend talk makes my teeth ache. But I like the taste of cotton candy, just as I like listening to Naveen, because we've been friends for a long, long time. He might be one of the only people who know me as well as I know myself. Sometimes maybe better. I run my tongue along my teeth for a second before I answer him.

"I don't like them."

"You don't have to like them, darling, they are not for you."

I shrug. "It's your gallery."

"Yes." Those white teeth, that grin. "And they'll sell. I like things that sell, Elisabeth. You know that."

"Like that?" I nod toward Will's atrocity.

"You don't like that, either?"

I shrug again. "It's a piece of shit, Naveen. Even the artist thinks so."

He laughs, and I'm in front of a Ferris wheel under a summer sky, my hair in pigtails and my fists full of spun sugar. Not really, of course, but that's how it feels. "You met Will."

"Yes. I met him." I look for Will in the crowd and see him in one of the alcoves, flirting with a woman whose hair is not flat and limp, her lipstick unsmeared. She looks as if she hasn't eaten in years. She leans in close to him. He laughs.

I hate her.

I look away before Naveen can see me watching, but it's too late. He shakes his head and squeezes my shoulder gently. He doesn't say anything. I guess he doesn't have to. Someone calls his name, and he's off to schmooze. He's better at it than I am, so I leave him to it.

It's late and getting later, and I should leave. Naveen offered to let me stay at his place. I've done it before. I like his wife, Puja, but their kids are still small. When I stay there I'm treated to lots of sticky hugs and kisses, am woken at the crack of dawn and feel as if I have to give Puja a hand with things like diapers and feeding times. My daughters are long beyond needing that sort of care, and I don't miss it.

"You're still here."

I turn, the sound of his voice tiptoeing up my spine to tickle the back of my neck. "I am."

Will tilts his head a little to look at me. "Do you like anything in this show?"

"Of course I do." It would be disloyal to say otherwise, wouldn't it?

"Show me."

I'm caught. At a loss. I search the room for something I do like. I point. "There. That piece. I like that one."

White canvas, black stripes. A red circle. It looks like something any elementary schoolkid could do, but somehow it's art because of the way it's framed and hangs on the wall. When I look at it, I see the hovering shapes of butterflies, just for a minute. Nobody else would; they'd just see the white, the black, the red. But it's the butterflies that make me choose it. I don't love it, but out of everything here tonight, I like it the best.

"That?" Will looks at it, then at me again. "It's pretty good. It's not what I thought you'd pick, though."

"What did you think I'd pick?"

Will points with his chin. "Want me to show you?"

I hesitate; I don't know why. Of course I want him to show me. I'm curious about what he thinks I'd like. How he could think he knows enough about me to guess at anything I'd like.

Will takes me by the elbow and leads me through the

crowd, still thick considering the hour, but then I guess most of these people live here in the city, or at least are staying close by. There's another alcove toward the back, this one hung with gauze and twinkling fairy lights. The inside of it's curved, which makes it hard to hang square portraits there, and why I didn't look at it tonight. I couldn't face another of those stinky vases.

"There." Will stops but doesn't let go of my elbow. If anything, he moves closer to me. "That's what you like."

The piece is simple. Carved, polished wood. There's no real form or figure, though the piece is evocative of a woman's body. The smooth curve of hip and thigh and belly and breasts, the curl and twist of hair. It's not a woman, but it feels like one. Without thinking, I touch it. She feels like a woman. My fingers curl against my palm as I take my hand away. I shouldn't have touched it. Oils from my fingers could harm the finish. It's not a museum piece, but even so, it's not right to ruin it.

And Will is correct. I like this one. I have no place for something like that in my home, but suddenly, I want it.

"Do you know who did it?" I'm already looking for the artist's card.

Will says nothing. I look at him, thinking he'll be smiling, but he's not. He's studying me.

"I knew you'd like that one."

My body tenses. I'm not sure if I don't like the way he says it, or if I like it too much. Either way, I frown. "You sound so proud."

He glances at the piece of carved wood that shouldn't look like anything but looks like a woman. "I like to figure out what people like. I mean, it's important, you know? For an artist who wants to sell his shit."

"Is that what it's about, for you? Selling things? I thought real artists wanted to…you know. Make art."

He laughs, low. "Sure. But I'm also into paying my rent and eating. Not many people can live on art."

Not many of the people displaying here in Naveen's gallery tonight, anyway. New York City has galleries like this all over the place. Competition's fierce. I told him to keep his Philly gallery, but he insisted on branching out. I'm still not sure this one's going to make it.

"So…you like to know what people like, so you can sell them things."

"Sure." Will's grin is a little sly. "And I was right about you. Wasn't I?"

"Yes." For some reason, I'm reluctant to admit it.

He nods as if I just revealed a secret. Maybe I have. "You like things smooth."

I take a step away from him. How could he know that? Hell. Until a few minutes ago, I'm not sure I knew it.

Will nods again. "Yeah. Smooth. And curved. You don't like sharp things. Angles and shit. You don't like it when there are points."

"Who does?" My voice is anything but smooth.

"Some people do." Will looks again at the carved wood. "You should buy it. It would make you happy."

My laugh snags, like a burr. "Who says I need to be happy?"

"Everyone needs to be happy, Elisabeth," Will says.

Oh, my name.

When he says my name, I see it in shimmering shades of blue and green and gray. Those are not my colors. I'm red and orange and yellow. Brown. My name is autumn moving on toward winter darkness, but not the way Will says it. When he says my name, I see summer. I see the ocean.

Blinking hard, I have to look away from him. My breath catches in my throat. I'm sure I can't speak, not even one word.

"You should buy it," he says again.

"I don't want it." It would make me happy, but my house is corners and angles and sharp points. There's no place in my house for something like that.

"You want it," Will says, leaning in close for just a second. Just a breath.

Naveen saves me. He comes up behind Will and claps him on the shoulder hard enough to rock him forward a bit. Will frowns, fists clenching for a second or two before relaxing as his mouth slides into a smile, so fast it's as if he never looked angry at all.

"What does she want?" Naveen asks with a smile like a shark's.

Before either of us can answer, one of the musicians, a girl with a pixie haircut to match her petite stature, eases her way between us with an overly casual smile for Naveen. She holds up what looks like a scribbled receipt. Her eyeliner has smudged and, yes, I judge her for looking sloppy.

"Can I talk to you about this?"

Naveen gives her a smile considerably less casual than hers and winks at me. He puts his arm around the girl's shoulders, his fingertips denting the soft, tanned flesh of her upper arm, bared by her strapless dress. "Sure, Calysta. Let's talk in my office, okay? Betts, you're good? I'll call you tomorrow?"

"I'll call you," I tell him. "And yes. I'm fine."

Will waits until they walk halfway across the room before he turns to me. "What's up with that?"

I shrug. "Not my business."

He squints, mouth pursed. "He's married, huh?"

"Yes."

"That's not his wife."

"No," I say. "It's not."

Will gives them another look and slowly shakes his head, then lets his gaze slide back to mine. Sly, sideways, full of charm. He reminds me of a fox, I think suddenly. The slight spike at the tips of his ears, the way his hair feathers forward in front of them, the sleek and perfect arch of his brows. He leans close to me again. Sharing secrets.

"How about," he says, "you and me, we get out of here?"

Chapter Two

I thought he meant to take me to a coffee shop. That's what anyone would think when a stranger asks you at close to midnight if you want a cup of coffee. I'm still not familiar with the neighborhood. Naveen's new gallery opened only a month ago, and while I can get to and from it, I don't know about anything else nearby.

Will does. He lives close by, in Chinatown. I love Chinatown. I love shopping for chopsticks and soup spoons I could find anywhere, but which feel so much more authentic here. If I could, I'd have an entire collection of those cats with the waving paws. Money cats. I love them, too. They're usually red and gold, and to me the ticky-tocky motion of their hands always smells like fresh lemons.

I should be surprised when instead of a coffee shop with slices of cake in a revolving case, he takes me to a building made of stone, with ornate metal bars on the windows and a front door he needs to unlock with a keypad. I should hold back, hesitant, when he turns just inside the doorway to smile back at me with that same sly and sideways grin he gave me in the gallery. I shouldn't go upstairs with him, into his apartment, where he again holds the door open, this time so I can step through in front of him, though the space is small enough that I have to touch my shoulder to his chest as I pass.

I should go home.

I think about it. Imagine myself backing off, hands up. Shake, shake of my head and a nervous smile. I imagine myself finding a cab. Taking the train. The entire scenario takes about thirty seconds, and by that time it's too late. I'm already inside.

It's a loft, of course. That's where artists live. It must've once been a warehouse or factory. Wood floors, big beams, brick walls. Living room, kitchen, dining area all one big space, with a hallway leading to what I assume is bathroom and bedroom. There's an actual loft, too, with a spiral staircase that makes my heart ache with envy.

"I want an apartment." I've said it aloud without realizing.

Will looks at me. "So get one."

I laugh. "I have a house. I don't *need* an apartment. I just *want* one."

A place I don't have to share. Built-in bookcases, a tiny galley kitchen I'll never use because I'll never cook. Hardwood floors with colorful throw rugs. A big, soft bed with all the pillows for myself. A quiet place with smooth corners just for me. It would be filled with rainbows and the smell of the ocean sand.

"So get one," Will repeats, as if it's as easy as going down to the apartment store and picking one out. "Hey. Coffee?"

It's late. Drinking coffee now will only keep me from being able to sleep, but of course that's why I need it. "Yes, please."

He has some fancy coffeemaker that grinds the beans and heats the water to just the right temperature. I can't explain why this makes me laugh, but it does. Will slants me a grin as I lean against his countertop—bright, polished metal like you'd find in a restaurant.

"What?"

I shrug. "I just didn't have you figured as a fancy coffee-maker sort of guy, that's all."

Will leans, too, close enough that if he stretched out a leg he could tap my foot with his. "Oh. That. It's not mine. It was my wife's."

Instinctively, I look around his place for signs of a woman's touch, not that I'm sure what that might be. Flowers and throw pillows, I guess. The scent of perfume. He laughs. I'm caught.

"Ex," he emphasizes. "Was. She took the cat. I got the cof-feemaker."

"Oh." The machine spits and hisses, burping out black liquid. The smell is amazing. Just coffee, nothing odd. Still amazing.

He pours me a cup. Then one for himself. He pulls a bottle from a cupboard. Bushmills. "Want some?"

"Um...no." It's nearly one in the morning. I have to leave in a few minutes so I can catch the last train.

I shouldn't be here at all.

"You sure?" He wags the bottle. Tempting me. He splashes his mug with a liberal dose. "It's good."

I'm sure it is. I haven't had whiskey in...well, I can't remember the last time. Have I ever had whiskey? Surely in those booze-addled college days when we drank whatever we could get our hands on, I must've had whiskey.

I hold out my mug. "Not too much."

"No such thing," Will says, and pours in a healthy shot. He raises his mug and waits until I've done the same. *"Sláinte."*

"Are you Irish?" I take a hesitant sip. The coffee's hot and good. The whiskey, better. Both are strong and hit the back of my throat and then my stomach with heat. Or maybe I shouldn't lie. It's the way he looks at me, not anything I'm drinking.

"Who isn't?" He lifts the mug and drinks without so much as a wince. "Come on. I want to show you something."

"Not your etchings, I hope." The joke's not smooth, but since everything about me feels herky-jerky, all rough edges and stumbling feet, why should my words be any different?

Will glances over his shoulder. "Something like that."

I do hesitate then, just for a second. Then another. I'm in a stranger's apartment so late it's soon going to be early. I took his liquor. Would I blame him if he thought there might be more to this?

Would I be disappointed if he doesn't?

In one corner of the vast space, he shows me a desk set up with an impressive desktop computer, stacks of file folders, bits of crumpled paper. A little farther back is a set of red velvet curtains hung on the wall. Next to that is a metal rack holding several rolls of paper backdrops. Also, another table fitted with several lights and a contraption of metal and fabric I've seen before. I forget what it's called. A light box, maybe. Something to showcase items to be photographed.

"This is where the magic happens." He turns on one of the big lights, bathing everything in a golden glow.

I shield my eyes for a second, glad the beam is focused on a battered wooden chair set in front of the velvet curtains, and not on me. That light highlights that chair's every crack and splinter, every flaw. I can only imagine what it would show on my face.

Will opens a folder to pull out an eight-by-ten glossy of a woman seated at a desk, typing at an old-fashioned typewriter. She's dressed like a fetishized secretary. Tight black skirt, white shirt with a bow at the collar, impossibly high heels. Hair pulled back in a severe bun, glasses covering eyes made up with far too much shadow and liner to be appropriate for a real office. I'm confused.

"Stock art." He pulls another shot from the folder, this one of a businessman in a suit and tie, holding a paper take-out cup of coffee and a briefcase. Will waves the photo slowly.

"You took those?"

"I did." He fits them back into the folder. "My bread and butter."

Somehow, this deflates me. "Oh. I didn't know."

"Gotta eat," Will says. "But look at these."

He gestures for me to move closer, and to resist would, at the very least, seem impolite. I stand next to him at the desk, our shoulders brushing as he sorts through another folder to pull out a colorful print of a man and a woman in an embrace. They're wearing historical costumes, her hair flowing. For that matter, his hair's flowing, too. The print behind it is of the same shot, though it's been altered to add a different background and some stylized effects. Also, text.

"Book covers? You do book covers?"

"When they hire me." Will grins and taps the picture. "Love this one. Supersexy, don't you think?"

It is a sexy picture, I have to admit that, though honestly, it's the sort of cover my eyes would skate over in a store. Like whiskey, when's the last time I picked up a romance novel? Have I ever?

He pulls another shot from the pile. This one's darker. A woman in black leather holds a gun, her long hair in a braid over her shoulder. I covet her boots. It's a night for envy, I think, moving closer to him without thinking, so that I can get a better look at the print.

"I've seen that one," I say. "Science fiction, right? They just made a movie out of the book."

"Yep." He sounds proud. "It was a bestseller."

We are standing very close. I could turn an inch in one direction and we'll no longer touch. An inch in the other and

I'll be pressed up against him. I imagine the push and pull of the muscles in his arms if I were to put my hands on them. I do not move.

"Let me take your picture," Will says.

That's it. I back up one step, two, my head shaking. "No. No way."

My reaction's too strong for such a simple request, and I feel instantly stupid. I force myself not to turn tail and run. I lift my chin, square my shoulders. I meet his gaze.

He isn't smiling. Not laughing. Will's studying me with a serious look I can't interpret, and can't match.

"Why not?"

"Why would you want to?" I let out a slow but shaky breath.

"I like to take portraits. It's my favorite thing."

"You don't want a picture of me."

Will looks at the chair, pinned by that bright light. If I sit there, in that chair, that light will be all over me. I'll be all light, no dark. Nothing hidden. No secrets. He'll see all of me, every wrinkle and crevice, every line, every stray and unplucked hair. There is no fucking way I'm sitting in that chair.

Will says nothing.

"*I* don't want a picture of me," I tell him.

He picks up his camera. I know the finished product of art. The canvases, the matted prints. But I know nothing of the tools used to create it. Paints and brushes, f-stops and apertures, lenses, film speed, clay and glaze. I can tell you what it's worth when it's finished, but I have no idea about its creation.

He holds it carefully in one palm, the size of it impressive. I used to have a point-and-shoot until I lost the charger. Now I use my phone to take snapshots, when and if I feel the need to capture the moment. Mostly, I take pictures and forget about them until it's time to update my phone's software, when I upload them to my computer's hard drive and then forget them there.

Will lifts the camera to one eye and points it at the chair. He snaps a shot. Looks at the view screen. He makes some adjustment to something. Takes another picture.

I haven't moved. He hasn't asked again. He just takes another picture of the chair, which also hasn't moved and doesn't speak. One more. Again, he checks the view screen. Fiddles with some settings.

Then I'm sitting in that chair, my heart in my throat and the light so bright it seems as though it ought to make me squint, but I don't have that as an excuse to close my eyes. I see everything. The rest of the room seems cast in shadow, everything but this circle of light in which I sit, my knees pressed tight together, my hands linked just as tightly in my lap. Everything about me is stiff and tense and awkward. I try to breathe, and the air smells metallic. I taste roses.

If he tells me to relax, I will bolt up from this chair and out the door. If he touches me, I will explode. As it is, everything inside me has gone tight and coiled. I want to shake and can't.

It's just a picture.

But he doesn't take it. Will puts the camera to his eye, but nothing snaps. He just looks. Then he puts the camera on the desk and steps back.

"Another time," he tells me.

I blink and blink again. "What?"

Will hands me my mug of coffee as I get up from the chair. "Let me show you something else, okay?"

"Okay." The liquid in the mug should be sloshing, but I guess my hands aren't as shaky as they feel. I sip. It's lukewarm, the whiskey more potent in it.

He sees me make a face, and laughs, takes the mug and sets

it back on the desk. "You don't have to drink it. But here, look at this. Tell me what you think. And, Elisabeth…"

"Yes?"

"Be honest."

I understand what he means as soon as he pulls the sheet off the framed print leaning against the wall below the window. There are others in that stack, half a dozen at least, with a few more dozen smaller frames next to it. The black-and-white shot is of a tree, bare branches like spreading fingers against the cloudless sky. The photographer caught the shadows at such an angle that it looks as if the tree's spindling branches are its roots. It's impossible to tell that sky's color. In the print it's pure, pure white. I imagine it must've been a clear, pale blue.

There should be nothing special about the shot. Ansel Adams took thousands of nature shots, and he's considered a master. This picture has nothing of Adams's vast scale. It's one tree, one sky. It's beautiful. It makes me want to cry.

"Would you hang it in your house?" Will asks. "Would you put it in your foyer to impress people?"

"No." I haven't gone to my knees in front of it, though the picture makes me want to. "If I bought this, I would hang it in a place only I could ever see."

He smiles. I've said the right thing. *This is it,* I think, when he takes my hand and tugs me a step closer. *This is when he kisses me.*

Of course he doesn't. Why should he? We've only just met. I'm no cover model. I'm bedraggled and unkempt and old enough to know better. His fingers stroke my wedding band.

And oh, there's that.

He has a cuckoo clock I didn't see when I came in, and now it whirs into life at the half hour. Two men saw busily at a log while a waterwheel spins. A bird pops out to chirp once before retreating.

"Shit," I say, and recover my hand as if he'd never taken it. "It's late. I have to catch the train—"

"You won't make it."

I knew that when I'd agreed to come here, didn't I? Traffic, distance, the rain. The timing. I could pretend to be upset and surprised, but the truth is I'm only a little upset and not at all shocked.

"Stay here. I have a guest room." He points to the loft. "You can get up early. Catch the first train home. I'll make you eggs in the morning, if you want."

It sounds like a come-on, but I pretend I don't notice. "Oh…I couldn't. I'll go find a hotel room."

"Uh-uh. No way. I'm not letting you wander around in the dark, in the rain, trying to find a place to stay. That would be ridiculous." Will shakes his head. "I have a pair of pajamas that will fit you."

"I really…" I want to say *can't*. I want to say *shouldn't*. The words clog up my throat. Won't come out.

"Do you need to call someone? Tell them you'll be home tomorrow?"

There is nobody at home. The girls are off at college, probably still out at a party or tucked into their boyfriends' beds—not that I like to dwell on that, but I'm not stupid. Ross is out of town. I should know where he is, what he's doing, but though he told me, I didn't pay attention. It didn't matter, beyond knowing he would be gone.

"No. I don't have to call home."

Will smiles. "Okay."

He gives me a pair of pajamas that belong to him, not a pair inherited from an ex-wife, as I feared. Faded flannel pants, an oversize white T-shirt soft and worn from the wash. I should feel awkward wearing his clothes, but he handed them to me so matter-of-factly, along with a toothbrush still in the package, that feeling odd would only make it so, and clearly it doesn't have to be. The bed in the loft is soft, the pillows fluffy. He doesn't follow me up the stairs to tuck me in, so it's definitely not weird.

I sleep right away and wake when the alarm I set on my phone goes off. I've had only four hours of sleep, not enough, but I need to get up and get to the train. Get home.

First, though, I need the bathroom. I dress quickly, not sure what I should do with Will's clothes. I settle for folding them neatly and putting them on the chair at the foot of the bed. Down the spiral stairs in my bare feet, I'm careful not to trip or knock into anything, because the apartment is big and silent and full of echoes from sounds as soft as breathing.

I hear the shower running just as I move to push open the door, which is ajar. I stop, of course. Or in fact, I don't, because my fingertips nudge the door just…a little…wider. The way the bathroom's set up, I have a straight shot gaze toward the claw-foot tub and glass-enclosed shower next to it. In addition to envying the apartment and coveting the cover model's boots, that shower sends a thrill of jealousy through me. Tiles, glass brick, sunflower showerhead. I want it.

Steam hovers between me and the shower, Will inside it, but there's not nearly enough to obscure any details. There he is, naked in the water, head bent as it sluices over him. His eyes are closed. One hand is on the wall. The other's on his dick.

I swallow the noise my throat tries to make, but I'm frozen. Can't move. Don't want to move, let's be honest, because everything about this sight is beauty and glory and oh, my God, he's stroking himself slowly, as if he's going to take an hour to make himself come. Up, down, twist of the palm around the head of his cock. His knees are bent and his fingers curl against the tile, slipping because he can't make purchase.

If he looks up, he'll see me watching. I should go; it's not right to watch something so private. This isn't for me.

His hand moves faster. His mouth opens, water filling it and overflowing when he tips his face into the spray. He fucks his fist with deliberation, and I watch the muscles cord in his arm and back, in that spot just above his ass where the dimples dent his skin.

I want to watch him come. I covet and crave it, as a matter of fact, more than I did this apartment or the boots or the shower itself. I want to see Will jerk and moan and finish, and that desire is what finally pushes me away from the door. Down the hall, to the kitchen where I use the toothbrush he gave me at the kitchen sink. I brush and brush, I rinse and spit and rinse again, my eyes closed and my mind filled with the sight of him.

I know he's there before I turn from the sink, but though I brace myself for the sight of him in a towel, he's wearing a pair of jeans and a white T-shirt like the one he lent me. Wet hair, slicked back. Bare feet I carefully avoid looking at, as though the sight of his toes could possibly be more intimate than the picture of his cock already permanently sealed in my mind.

"Hey," Will says. "You're heading out? I thought I'd make you some breakfast, at least."

"No, that's okay. I'm not a breakfast person, anyway. I have to go. Really, you've done enough already. Thanks for everything." I rinse the toothbrush and hold it out to him, as if he'd want it back.

He takes it, but puts it on the counter. "At least let me give you something for the road."

I want to protest further, but he's already opening the fridge door and pulling out a pitcher of orange juice. The smell sends saliva squirting in my mouth. It will taste like summer.

"Fresh squeezed," Will announces. "The ex left a juicer, too."

He pours me a glass, not a quarter full, not half full, but almost brimming. Our fingers touch when he passes me the glass, but the juice doesn't spill. He watches me while I drink it, and though I think I'll just sip it once or twice to be polite, the second the flavor hits my tongue it's all I can do not to gulp the entire glass. As it is, I finish it faster than is mannerly, and I wipe my mouth with the tips of my fingers when I'm finished.

"See," Will says. "You never know how thirsty you are until someone offers you something to drink."

Chapter Three

I used to greet my husband at the door every night, no matter what time he got home. I'd wait up for him if he was late. I never wrapped my naked body in cling film or had a martini in my hand, and there were days when the smile on my face was definitely forced…but I always met him.

I don't meet him anymore.

The way the earth turns you'd think we'd need to run in place to keep from spinning right off it, but the truth is we all just turn along with it. Ross and I married young, had our children, watched them grow and sent them off to college. Jacqueline and Katherine are twenty-two now. Getting ready to graduate from two different colleges, both hours from home. Jac's got a job all lined up in another state for after graduation, and Kat's waiting to hear on an internship that could lead to a job for her, too.

When the girls started high school, I went back to work. Naveen had been struggling with his Philadelphia gallery for a few years, asking me repeatedly if I'd come work for him and keep him in line. I'd always declined, partly because being a mom had been a full-time job and partly because I thought working with him might effectively kill the friendship that had already suffered more than its share of ups and downs. Still, taking the job with him was easier than trying to find one on my own, and though I didn't "need" to work, I wanted to.

That's when I stopped meeting Ross at the door. Because on the days when he got home first, he never met me. I never came home to dinner waiting for me, or the laundry folded or a glass of wine. Even when the girls were still in high school, I mostly came home to a silent house, dark in the winter, because they had after-school activities or were with their friends. I'd find him in the den, feet up in the recliner, flipping channels on the television set. I would kiss him dutifully while he pretended to listen to my answer when he asked about my day, and I pretended I wanted to tell him.

I don't remember the first day I resented this. I don't remember wondering why all the years I'd made the effort were not reciprocated. Nothing jumped up and bit me or slammed like a door in my face. That's not how it happens. What happens is you get married, you raise your kids, they go off to school, and you look at your spouse and wonder what on earth you're supposed to do with each other now, without all the distractions of having a family to obscure the fact that you have no idea not only who the other is, but who you are yourself.

Today I come home to an empty house that smells faintly of the lilac air freshener the cleaning woman sprays in all the bathrooms when she's finished scrubbing them. My kitchen is spotless. My living room, too, the hash mark lines of the vacuum still fresh in the cream-colored carpet we installed after the girls left for college. In my bedroom I fall down on the unrumpled bed, the comforter matching the pillows matching the sheets matching the curtains matching the carpet. I spread out my arms and legs as if I'm making a snow angel, and I move them slowly back and forth. When I get up from the bed, I've left behind no mark.

I should be leaving for work soon. Naveen will expect me

to call him to go over invoices and details and things I don't want to talk about. At the very least, I should check my email and phone messages to see if anything important happened since the last time I looked. Instead, I go to my closet. I look at my clothes. Everything in there is black or white or gray or beige. When's the last time I wore anything bright? A color, a real color?

In the back, shoved behind a bunch of summer dresses in navy and white, the lines severe but classic, I find an emerald-green blouse. Silk. Shoulder pads and a bow at the front, which should make it clear how long it had been since I'd worn it. I bought it to wear for my first job, when I believed making an impression was important and women needed to wear high heels to office jobs because that's what they did in the movies. The shoes are long gone, as are the black pencil skirts I'd never be able to squeeze into again, but this shirt had been a favorite. I press it to my cheek for a minute, thinking about the rain and the taste of coffee and whiskey. The bright light showing everything.

I know why Will didn't take my picture. Because I'm bland and gray and beige, and he makes art. I put the shirt back on the rack, but in front, where I can see it the next time I have to get dressed.

I scream when I come out of the closet, and Ross laughs. My heart pounds and I press my fingers to it. I feel the throb of it in my chest, my wrists, the base of my throat. Between my legs.

"You're home!"

"Yeah. Decided to swing by here, take a shower, before I hit the office." He studies me. "I didn't mean to scare you."

His hands fit on my hips when he kisses me. Open mouth. Tongue working. No surprises; we've danced this dance many times. When I cup his crotch, though, he pulls away to give me a look.

"Well, well." His brows raise. He's making a joke.

I'm not.

It's easy enough to walk him back a few steps to the bed. He sits. I push. I straddle him, already pulling at his tie and the buttons beneath. His body is tan and firm because he exercises even when he travels. He spends time outside in the yard, on the golf course, biking.

I'm not thinking of Will when I work my way down my husband's body with my mouth and teeth and tongue. There aren't any surprises. I know the dip and curve of every part of him. I know where he likes to be touched, and how. For how long. He's hard in my fist in a minute or so. Then in my mouth. His hands tangle in my hair.

I want to be surprised. I want to find something new. I want this to feel different.

I use my hand in tandem with my mouth. Up. Down. I want to hear him groan in pleasure, but Ross doesn't make much noise when we have sex. He never has. I'm the one who moans and sighs, even if the habit has been lost because of so many years when we had to muffle ourselves so the girls wouldn't overhear. There's nobody to hear us now, and I want him to shout from what I'm doing to him. I want him to shudder and writhe and clutch at the comforter while I mouth-fuck him until he can't stand it anymore. I want him to come saying my name.

There is a surprise when he tugs my hair to lift my mouth from his cock. When he pulls me upward, over his body, to nuzzle and nudge at me through my clothes. Fingers work. We shift, we roll. I'm naked somehow, while he's still mostly clothed. He pushes me onto my knees and slides beneath me to get at my clit with his tongue, his hands gripping my ass.

My hands find the wall above the headboard, my fingers curling against the wallpaper I've never liked but have always been too lazy to change.

Oh, this, this, this. Spread wide, thighs trembling, all I can do is ride his face and let the pleasure take me over. He knows how and where and how long. How many times and in what direction. I come, hard, without making a sound.

I slip down his body and find his mouth with mine. The first time Ross ever went down on me, he was shocked when I kissed him, after. But if I can't stand the taste of myself, how could I expect anyone else to? Anyway, it's erotic, tasting myself on his mouth.

I slide one hand beneath his head, fingers in his hair. The other goes between us to grip the base of his cock and hold him steady as I slide my body onto his. Our mouths seal for just a moment before the kiss breaks on my sigh.

Twenty-two years. That's how long we've been doing this. The first time was in a cheap hotel room after his fraternity's spring formal. He told me he loved me first, and I didn't believe him, but I let him kiss and touch me, anyway.

Ross doesn't say he loves me now. He pushes up inside me. His fingers grip me a little too hard. His eyes are closed. His mouth is open.

He might always look this way when we make love, but it's been a very long time since we did it in the light. I put my hands on his face and trace the lines at the corners of his eyes and mouth with my fingertips until he turns his head to capture my fingers with his mouth. He bites gently. Pleasure surges, and I lose myself in it.

This is comfort. This is compatibility. This is familiarity, and it works. We both tip over into climax within moments of each other, and Ross gives me what I wanted. A hoarse shout. It sounds a little, just a little, like my name.

"What're you up to today?" Ross asks a few minutes later, when I've fallen onto my own pillow.

I'd been teasing into sleep, but this wakes me. I scrub at my face before I look at him. "Work. What are you up to today?"

"Gotta put out a bunch of fires. That jackass Bingham can't do any damn thing right when I'm gone." He yawns.

I contemplate crawling under the covers and going back to sleep for a few hours, but it would be impossible with him in the house. He will turn on the television or bang the dresser drawers. Run the coffee grinder. He will shake me gently to ask me where to find his socks, his keys. "No, don't get up," he'll say. "I can make my own breakfast." But I know he wants me to do it, because I'm here and because he'd much rather not do it himself.

I leave my husband in the bed. In the bathroom, I run the water and splash my face. It's cold, and I swallow it greedily, feeling the chill slip down my throat and hit my too-empty stomach. I fill a paper cup from the dispenser and take it to him.

Ross looks at me as if I'm crazy. "What's this?"

"I thought you might want a drink."

"No," he says with a shake of his head. "I'm not thirsty."

He pats me on the ass when he passes. I hear the shower running, and I sit on the bed with my paper cup of water still in my hands, and I close my eyes against a sudden sting of tears.

From behind me, cradled in its dock, my phone buzzes with an email message. It will be Naveen, I think, emailing me to remind me about the shipments due to the Philly gallery later today. Or it could be my brother's wife following up on summer vacation plans. Or it could be junk mail that has slipped through my carefully constructed set of spam filters and is now clogging my in-box. But the message pinging so cheerfully isn't any of those.

It's from Will.

Chapter Four

Will takes pictures of buildings.

I'm here to carry things or hold them while he points and shoots. Skyline shots, he tells me, are really popular for stock photography. At home, he'll manipulate some of them in Photoshop.

"Post apocalyptic scenes," he tells me with a grin. "Make the city look deserted. Ready for zombies, that sort of thing."

I'm holding his tote bag over one shoulder, an extra-large cup of coffee in one hand. "Uh-huh."

"You don't like zombies." It's not a question. He says it as if he already knows me. He points his camera. Takes a picture. Doesn't even look to see how it came out, just takes another. And another.

"Not really."

He gives me another grin, his eyes narrowing in sunshine that's too bright for this time of year. "Vampires that sparkle?"

"No." I laugh. Shake my head. "Not a horror fan."

"What do you like, Elisabeth? Chick flicks? Rom-com?" Point. Shoot. He aims the camera in my direction and clicks before I can look away.

Sneaky.

"I like action movies. Lots of shooting and muscle cars.

Science fiction, too." I'd put a hand in front of my face, but that would be too obvious. I hate it when women protest with squeals and cooing about getting their pictures taken, as if the world will end. Or their souls will be stolen. It's worse than the ones who pose and pout and primp anytime a camera's within range.

I don't want him to take my picture because then there will be proof I'm here with him. Not that I have any reason to deny it. I'm in the city on business. I had breakfast with Naveen. Stopped by the gallery to handle some things. I met with Will for coffee, that's all. And now to follow him through the city as he takes pictures for his stock work. There's nothing wrong in what I'm doing.

He takes me to a park. We stare together at the giant Easter Island–looking head in the middle of it, neither of us saying much. Just beyond it, a line of people waiting for milk shakes from a stand stretches nearly all the way around the park.

"Those must be some pretty fucking amazing milk shakes," Will says after a minute or so.

I burst into laughter. It's loud. Raucous. Unfettered, that's a good way to describe it, and I stifle it with my hand when he smiles at me.

The weather's so much nicer today than it was the night we met. The air light and clear and warm enough for me to understand why someone might wait half an hour for a milk shake. I want to stretch out on a blanket in the grass and stare up at the sky.

Will takes a picture of the statue, then looks at the digital image on his view screen. "…Art," he mutters. "Jesus."

"You don't like it?" I follow him along the path toward the street again, but spy something that stops me. I bend to pick it up, already grinning. "Oh!"

"I'm just jealous. What's that?" Will says, leaning over me.

The shiny piece of gravel's been broken into a misshapen heart. I lay it flat on my palm to show him. I trace the outline. "See?"

"Cool." He sounds as if he means it.

"I collect them." I study this one for a second or so, then look at him. "Silly, I know."

"It's not silly." Will takes a picture of the rock on my palm. "It means you have a creative eye. Most people would've passed right by that. Never looked twice. I wouldn't have."

His praise warms me. My fingers close over the rock. I feel the press of it against my flesh. Impulsively, I hold it out to him. "Here."

He looks surprised. "What? No. It's yours, for your collection."

"I have a lot and I always find more. You have it." I hold it out again. "Now that you've seen this one, I bet you find them all over, too."

Will takes the rock and keeps it in his hand for a second or so before tucking it into his pocket. We stare at each other the way we'd both looked at the giant white statue of a head. Pondering.

"What else?" I ask him when I can't look at his face any longer.

"I have a commission for some underground stuff. You up for it?"

I can take the train into and out of the city, and I can find my way around once I'm there, but I always take cabs. I've never mastered the subway. I have a secret, not-unfounded fear of getting on the wrong train and ending up lost, and the smells can be overpowering. The sound of the subway, the clatter-clatter, echoing, hurts my teeth and coats my tongue with the taste of gray.

"Of course,"

It's easy for me to imagine H.G. Wells's Morlocks down here under the city, creeping along the tunnels and snacking on innocent tourists in I Love NY T-shirts and fanny packs. Will is serious as he takes shot after shot of the escalators, the curving tile walls, the dirty concrete.

Watching him, I say nothing. I hand him his bag when he asks for it, and hold it when he doesn't. Every so often, he shoots me a grin, and every time he does I'm surprised again that I'm here.

"I'm all done for today," he says at last. "C'mon. Let's go back to my place, see what I got. I'll make you dinner."

"Oh…I…" My mouth tries to make the noises that mean no, but it's useless. I'm already following him. I knew when he asked me to meet him today I'd be going back to his place. "Sure. Great."

Will leads and I follow.

He does make me dinner. Pasta, bread, salad. Wine. I eat but taste nothing. We talk, and I hear the sound of my own voice in answer to his, but if you asked me what it was I said, I'm not sure I could tell you. I watch his hands, fingers on the fork twirling spaghetti. The sleek fringes of hair in front of his ears, against his cheeks. When he gets up to refill my wineglass, I breathe him in and keep myself from touching him by keeping my hands on the table, instead.

Time for me to leave. I stand in Will's foyer, and I look at the door I know I should go through. But first, of course, there's got to be a goodbye.

How do I say it? What do I do? I offer my hand, because what else is there to do for a man who is not my friend, and still mostly a stranger? Will, with a small, strange smile, takes my hand, and I think *that's the hand he uses to jerk off with.*

It happens all at once, so smoothly, how he pulls me close to him. He is going to kiss me. I am going to let him.

At the last second, I turn my face. I can't do it. To feel his mouth on mine would be too much. It's already all too much. Will smiles and everything inside me melts, liquid, running hot. He pulls me closer. He doesn't kiss my mouth.

He kisses my neck, not softly or accidentally, but entirely on purpose. I don't cringe and I don't pull away. I offer myself to him as if I was waiting for this all along, and maybe I was and didn't know it. But the first moment I feel the scratching brush of his stubble on my skin, all I can do is give up to it.

I give up to him.

My fingers thread through the back of his hair, holding his mouth closer to the sensitive skin of my neck as my own lips part on a sigh I cannot contain within the jail of my throat. Then my back is against the wall and Will presses against me, but he didn't push me. I went there on my own. I pulled him against me. His leg eases between mine, his thigh pressing. My heel hooks over his calf. His kiss slides along my throat and jaw, but again, when he tries to kiss my mouth, I turn my head. My hands find the hem of his shirt. *Don't do it,* I tell myself. *Don't.* But I do it, anyway; I lift his shirt and let my fingertips find his smooth, hot skin underneath. His back. His stomach. The flat of my hand slides across him, and it's not enough. It will never be enough.

"I have to go. I really should go." Murmured between kisses against his throat, the words are insincere. No matter what I should do, what I have to do, I'm not leaving.

Will pauses, his breath hot on my cheek. He doesn't move away, and oh, God, I can feel his cock, hard through his jeans, the thick ridge of it against my belly. I am undone.

We stay that way for the in-and-out of three or four breaths. My hands are still under his shirt. I blink rapidly, a puddle of silk ribbons in my brain for a couple seconds when my fingertips skid along the small indents of his spine. Crimson silk ribbons, that's what his skin feels like.

"You should go," he whispers. "You really should go."

But I'm not leaving, I'm following a few stumbling steps toward the small alcove beneath the loft, and the couch there. Leather, overstuffed... I think it's black but it might be brown; I can't focus on the color or the pattern of the pillows. My hands are flat on his chest, and Will lets me push him back onto the couch. Then I'm on top of him, straddling, my dress hiked up around my thighs, and his hands are skimming the edge of the fabric the same way mine did with the bottom of his shirt, and all I can think about is how much I want him to touch me.

Everything is hands and mouth and teeth and lips and tongue. We fumble, and it doesn't matter. Laughter stutters out of me like rocks skipping on a lake. I bend over him, yank at his belt, freeing him. My hair falls in my face, and he pushes it back so he can get at my neck again. My throat. I can not get enough of him.

I push up his shirt, then pull it off over his head. Smooth, smooth skin. Hot. My fingers curl against his ribs. He has a tattoo, a stylized bird over his heart. My thighs grip his. His erection nudges me, thick and hard, and all I can think about is touching him. My hand strokes. His hips push upward. A groan slips from his throat.

I did that.

I did that to him.

I want him bare in my fist. I want him in my mouth. I want Will's cock inside me, but when he sits up with me still on his lap and his hands move beneath my dress, when he once more leans to take my mouth, everything slams to a halt. I tense and freeze, muscles going stiff.

"Not on the mouth," I whisper, feeling instantly stupid. What is this, *Pretty Woman?*

Will doesn't seem to mind. He mouths my jaw instead. His fingers slide along my skin, under my dress, between my legs, just a quick and almost surreptitious swipe against me. It feels so fucking good I want to writhe.

What am I doing, what am I doing, what the fuck am I doing? The thought is like a train, rushing, no end to it that I can see. I curl my fingers over his and push them inside my panties. Against my clit.

"Oh…yes." The words slip out unbidden, but completely sincere. I shift a little so he can push his fingers inside me.

"Oh, shit," Will mutters. "Goddamn."

I wriggle out of my panties as he pushes down his briefs and jeans. Straddling him again, I take his cock at the base and rub the head of him against my slick, wet opening. Over my clit in small, tight circles.

We both groan. I rub myself on his cock, or rub his cock on me, I can't tell the difference anymore. All I feel is his hard flesh on mine and the spiraling, tightening coil of pleasure. I'm going to come before I even put him inside me.

I move up, just a little, one hand on his shoulder, the other still gripping his cock to hold him steady while I fit myself over him. Slowly, so slowly, I ease myself down until he's inside me all the way. I can't move. I can't think. My fingers have left red marks on his skin, but I can't even make myself let go.

Will puts his hands on my hips, under my dress. On my bare skin. He moves. He shifts. He pushes inside me, just a little deeper than I thought he could go. Then out.

We move together, then, perfectly in sync. We find a rhythm, set a pace. Everything is slip and slide, no bad friction. My clit hits his pelvis every time I move, but that's not quite enough, so I use my hand. I know how my body works.

My fingers tweak at my clit, small circles. Then I'm up, up, up and over. Everything tenses. Releases.

Will cries out, low, a murmur of blue and green and gold. The syllables of my name float between us. I have never seen my name that way, in those colors, not from any other voice. I feel him throb inside me. That's never happened, either. It might be my imagination. I don't care. I watch his mouth open.

Everything slows. The beat of our hearts. Our breathing. I lean to press my forehead to his shoulder. I trace the bird with my fingertip and taste salt when I kiss him there.

I get off him. Find my panties and pull them on. I turn to give him privacy as he pulls up his briefs and jeans, but he's still shirtless when he touches my shoulder to turn me. I'm not sure what to say or where to look.

"I really should go," I tell him.

He walks me to the door, where we do not kiss. We don't even hug. I offer him my hand to shake, and he takes it with a low laugh and a quirk of one brow, but he doesn't question it. His hand is strong and warm. It squeezes mine.

Then he lets me go.

Chapter Five

I didn't like Naveen the first time I met him. He was charming and full of himself, a shameless flirt. I guess you could say his sin was that he came on to my roommate before he hit on me, even though I had a boyfriend at the time. That relationship wasn't working out so well, but even so I wasn't supposed to care if other boys tried to make me laugh or not.

I'd just met my roommate, Wendi, that day. We'd spoken on the phone once or twice and exchanged a letter, our conversations limited to what we'd each be bringing to the dorm room. Wendi had a fridge. I had a small TV with rabbit ears. We both liked Little Debbie Swiss Cake Rolls and the color purple, though she was way more interested in coordinating our bedding than I was. We'd already agreed to bunk our beds and switch off who got the top bunk by semester. Wendi was a big girl, buxom and curvy, with lots of red hair and black eyeliner. So far I liked her, even though all the guys at this freshman mixer kept checking her out and ignoring me.

"Hey, ladies. I'm Naveen." He leaned over the registration table, both hands flat on it. Instead of the T-shirt and jeans most of the other guys were wearing, he wore a pale pink dress shirt, open so far at the throat I could glimpse a hint of his nipples. "Have you signed up yet?"

"For what?" Wendi tossed her hair and put a hand on her hip. Bada-bing, bada-boom.

Naveen's eyes tracked her cleavage. "If you sign up for this mailing list, you can get one of these welcome bags."

"What's in it?" Wendi gave the overstuffed plastic bags, adorned with pictures of deodorant and laundry detergent, a suspicious look.

"I'll take one." I scrawled my name and mailbox number on the sheet and took a bag. "It's free stuff."

"Laundry soap, mouthwash, stuff like that. Samples." Naveen looked at what I'd written, then gave me a more assessing look than he'd given Wendi. "Did you put your phone number down?"

"No." I paused. "Why would they need my number?"

"They don't," he said. "But maybe I want it."

In those days before cell phones, each dorm room had a landline with both long distance and cross-campus service, so you could dial a prefix for the building and then the room number to connect. All he had to do was look at the mailbox number I'd put down on the paper, and he could figure it out. That's why I discounted his flirting, why it annoyed me. Because I didn't believe he meant it.

"And maybe I don't want you to have it," I told him with a lift of *my* chin, toss of *my* hair.

Wendi hadn't moved, but she was no longer there. Nobody else was, either. Naveen leaned a little closer across the table, his smile never fading, his eyes not leaving mine.

"If you say so."

"I'll take a bag." Wendi wiggled in front of me, distracting him for a second as she bent over to show him her tits—that is, to fill out the form.

The moment had passed, but it had made an impression. The common room filled with new students mingling and taking advantage of the free food the residence staff had put out. Some kids danced in one corner, others played pool or Ping-Pong, a few gathered at the even-for-then ancient Pacman and Donkey Kong video games. Naveen and I didn't speak, but our eyes met a dozen times over the course of the night. When Wendi left me to go after a guy with spiky blond hair and a pair of round glasses, I went upstairs to finish unpacking.

She stumbled home around two in the morning, turning on the overhead light and knocking into the stack of plastic milk crates we'd set up near the wall mirror to hold our hair dryers and curling irons. I sat straight up in my bottom bunk and whacked my head so hard I saw stars. She wasn't alone. The blond guy was with her, apologizing to me while my new roommate rifled through her suitcase for condoms. With blood trickling down my eyebrow, I assured him I'd be fine, I just needed a Band-Aid. I told Wendi I'd be gone at least an hour. I took a book, the knitted afghan my grandma had given me as a graduation gift, my room key, and tried to find a place to hang out.

The study lounge was no good. The lights were out, but I could still see the shadows of a couple on the couch inside, their slow coupling reflected in the windows. Disgruntled, exhausted and my head aching, I took the elevator to the ground floor and sought the social lounge. It was locked.

I muttered a string of obscenities under my breath—creative ones; my younger brother, Davis, was a marine. I didn't notice the figure sitting behind the front desk in the lobby, and he wasn't yet familiar enough that I should've immediately recognized his voice...but I did. The scent of it gave him away. Cotton candy and sawdust. Naveen sounds to me like a carnival smells. I hadn't noticed upon first meeting him, because of the rest of the noise around us, but in the quiet of 2:00 a.m. it was as if I'd stepped right onto the midway.

"What happened to your head?" He twirled a little on an office chair, his feet propped on the battered desk.

"I hit it."

He made a face. "No shit."

I touched the wound with gentle fingers, wincing at the tenderness. It had stopped bleeding but still oozed a little. "My roommate came home with a friend I wasn't expecting."

"Ah." Naveen nodded as if this made sense. He dropped his feet off the desk with a thump and opened a drawer. "Come around the side, through that door. Come in here."

I hesitated. He looked at me. Gone were the charming smile, assessing stare. He looked me over, all right, but this time it didn't make me feel creepy or annoyed.

He held up a bottle of hydrogen peroxide and a box of adhesive bandages. "Come on. Let me take care of that for you."

I went through the door and settled into the opposite chair with my afghan wrapped around me. I wasn't cold, exactly, but felt on the verge of shivering. I wasn't homesick, but the sudden longing for my own bed, my own room, swept over me.

"Chin up. This isn't pretty." Naveen soaked a cotton ball in peroxide and dabbed at my wound.

Stoic, I didn't wince, not wanting to give him the satisfaction. "Gee. Thanks."

"I didn't say *you're* not pretty," he said in a low voice after a second. "You sure are prickly, Elisabeth Manning."

I was surprised that he knew my name, only for a second before remembering he'd seen it on the form I filled out. I gritted my teeth as he poked and swiped at the cut on my forehead. When he smoothed the bandage over it, his fingers lingered along my scalp line and traced my cheeks and jaw before he withdrew.

We stared at each other without speaking for some long moments before Naveen broke the silence with a laugh and pushed back in his chair to prop his feet up again. Hands behind his head, charming smile pasted firmly back on his face, he winked at me. I frowned.

"Oh, come on. Throw a guy a bone."

"Are you a dog?" I asked him smartly, refusing to smile.

Naveen blinked, his smile fading. "Are you a bitch?"

That was how we became friends.

Chapter Six

"What's wrong with you?" Naveen's voice has lost its cotton-candy sweetness. Now he sounds like licorice. He gestures at the pile of receipts and papers spread out on the desk in front of me, but doesn't touch any of them.

I've been sitting here all morning, passing papers back and forth between my hands. Filing only a few. Finishing nothing, unable to concentrate on anything but the memory of what happened with Will. It's been three days, and I haven't yet felt guilty.

Until now, and that's about ignoring my work and not because of my infidelity. I shrug, carefully not meeting Naveen's gaze. "Nothing. What's wrong with *you?*"

Naveen scowls. He paces in front of the desk, one hand on his hip, the other pressed to his forehead. It's a common enough pose for him, because he likes to make drama. But today, something seems off. He's agitated and anxious, not just dramatic. His dark brows knitted, black eyes narrowed, he won't quite meet my gaze. When he turns suddenly and pushes the piles of paper to the side so he can lean across the desk to grip my upper arms, I'm more startled by the shuffle of the papers falling than how close his face is to mine.

"I'm in trouble, Betts. Bad trouble."

He's gripping a little too hard, but releases me when I look at where his fingers pinch. This close, I can see how his carefully groomed eyebrows need some attention. Red threads the usually bright whites of his eyes. There's a tremor in his voice that for an instant looks like the quicksilver flash of a fish in a dark pond. Surprising, and gone before you really can be sure it was there at all.

"Are you sick? Is it money?"

Naveen always skates on the edge of financial disaster. Backed not only by his wife's trust fund, but her steady employment as a doctor, he's been free to pursue just about whatever he likes without much fear of facing the consequences. Not just in business, either, and I was stupid for a few seconds too long before I looked into his face and understood.

"The girl from the gallery show?"

He shakes his head and moves away, to sit on the edge of the desk with his back toward me. His shoulders hunch as he heaves a heavy sigh so deep it alarms me. This is not the Naveen I'd met in college, the one who'd had a habit of lounging half-naked in my doorway with his pants hanging low on his hips and a wicked smile that made me feel I was on an elevator that had just dropped ten floors. I've known this man for more than twenty years and have seen him cry only once, the night his father died.

I go around the desk to sit beside him, my fingers gentle but firm on his shoulder, not forcing him to turn toward me but letting him know he can. "Someone else."

He's not crying, but his smile is too fierce. "Her name is Francesca. She's Italian. She buys a lot of art."

I say nothing, waiting for him to go on. She can't be pregnant. Naveen had a vasectomy a few years ago, came into the office moaning about ice packs and his swollen balls, expecting me to fetch him coffee and sympathy.

Naveen looks me in the eyes. "I love her, Betts. Oh, God. I don't want to, but I do."

I'm so set back by this that I actually scoot an inch or so away from him across the polished desk. The word *love* has always tasted like the scent of fresh ink and soft paper to me. Like a newly written poem. But hearing it now, in this context, I taste the moldering smell of musty books left unread for years.

"Her husband is older. He travels a lot, so he's gone. He has a few mistresses...." Naveen's voice trails off with a tremor that's not so much like a quicksilver fish this time. More like the slow rise of an enormous shadow beneath the surface of a quiet lake. "I'm crazy about her."

"You're crazy, all right," I tell him flatly. I'm no longer touching him, though I can't remember taking away my hand. "What is wrong with you, Naveen?"

"She makes me...feel," he says, as though that should explain it all.

Maybe it does.

It's my turn to pace, to run my hands through my hair. Naveen's slept with dozens of women that I know about, and I'd guess there are at least as many I haven't heard of. He's never been faithful to anyone for as long as I've known him. I've never asked him if Puja knows about his affairs, nor if she knows about us. The us that never happened, that is.

Jealousy smells like the water in the bottom of a flower vase after the flowers have died. It doesn't taste much better. I recoil not just at the odor and the flavor, but with the knowledge that I am jealous of this woman I don't even know.

This is what makes me sit again to take his hand. Our fingers link and squeeze before I let him go, though his hand still rests on my thigh. "So...what's the problem? She doesn't love you back?"

"She does."

I watch the tips of his fingers trace small circles on the fabric of my skirt. Naveen's nails are a little too long, and I can feel the scratch of them against my skin even through the fabric. I put my hand on his to stop the restless movement. We're close enough to kiss, though I'm not expecting him to try, and I'd pull away if he did. His head dips, eyes closed so his lashes make a shadow on his skin.

"I've been with a lot of women...." he begins, and I laugh. Naveen opens his eyes and manages a smile. "It's true."

"I know it's true, you jerk," I say, but fondly.

"But Francesca is different. I can't stop thinking about her. Everything about her makes me crazy. The way she talks, the way she smells. Her laugh. She's smart and funny and...fuck me, Betts. I love her."

His sincerity is evident in every syllable. I want to pull away, but I don't. "So what are you going to do? Leave Puja and the kids?"

I can't imagine it. Naveen has too much tied up in his family. Pride and money and, despite his philandering, I'm willing to bet a lot of love.

"Francesca ended it." His misery is as bold as his sincerity. "She said she wants to stay with her husband. She said we could be friends—" Laughter barks out of him. He gives his head an incredulous shake. "Friends? Like we're in the tenth grade?"

"If you love her, you should already have been friends." I sound sanctimonious.

Naveen gives me a look. "I'm not sure I know how to be *just* friends with a woman I want to fuck, Betts."

His words are a slap that rocks my head back, just a little. I'm off the desk again, several steps away, before I realize I've moved. My arms cross over my stomach for a second until I realize I'm looking defensive, and I refuse to give him that.

Naveen and I have been *just* friends for a long, long time.

"Shit," he says. "I'm sorry. I didn't mean—"

"So what *are* you doing?" I ask.

He has the grace to look a little sheepish. "I'm being an asshole to her."

Flashback. A memory of my hand, rapping on his dorm room door. I've brought a pizza and some movies to watch in his VCR, and my heart's pounding, pounding, because it's been a week since we last talked and that conversation hadn't ended well. The food and films are an excuse; I've really come to fuck.

The door opens, and he's there of course, chest and feet bare. And behind him, the girl. I don't know her name, but does it matter?

"Hey," Naveen says, as though he was expecting me. He probably was. "I'm sort of busy now. Can you come back later?"

But I didn't, and it took months for us to talk again. I know very well just what kind of asshole Naveen can be. "Of course you are."

He frowns, but doesn't look angry. Only resigned. He shrugs. "I love her. She rejected me. It's what I do, Betts."

"I know what you do." My voice is clipped and sharp and diamond-edged. "Maybe you shouldn't fuck around with married women then. Maybe you shouldn't fuck around at all, you think?"

He looks at first surprised, then wary. For all the years I've shared his secrets, I've never once judged him for any. I can't even look him in the eyes now, though, because for once I have my own secret.

"Will," Naveen says, looking past me, and I think that he knows.

But it's actually Will, standing awkwardly in the doorway, not looking at either of us. One shoulder presses the door frame, one hand cups the back of his neck as he studies the floor. When he does look up, his gaze skims my face before settling on Naveen's.

"Hey," he says.

Naveen pulls away from me. Straightens. His warning look annoys me—as if I'd say anything more, now that we have an audience? My pride might be stung, but it's an old wound. I stand and straighten, too, putting distance between me and Naveen that's meant to look casual but probably doesn't.

When I look at Will, the world stops for the time it takes him to blink and move forward to shake Naveen's hand. They clap each other on the back. Will catches my gaze over Naveen's shoulder, but I can't read it. Then they're out of my office and into the hall outside, talking about some photographs Will's going to be showing next month.

And I'm alone.

Somehow, I find the concentration to finish paying bills and filing invoices, following up on emails and phone calls and chasing down bank statements to prove to artists that, yes, someone really did cash our checks and if it wasn't them, they'd better take it up with whoever had learned to forge their signatures. An hour passes, then another. There's other work to be done, but it's on the desktop in my Philadelphia office, and while I usually bring my laptop and flash drives with everything I need, this morning I was so distracted I forgot. So now I sit and stare out the window at the city and pretend I'm not straining my ears for any sound of Will's voice.

I fucked him.

There is no way around this, no way to make it pretty or

anything other than what it is. I went to his apartment, and I let him put his hands and mouth on me, his prick inside me, and it was not by accident or coercion or because I was drunk and didn't know what I was doing. I fucked Will Roberts because I wanted him.

That's when the shudder hits me, a tremor in my fingers, a twisting in my guts that bends me in half. My heart pounds so hard I press my fingers to it as if I can keep it from beating right out of my chest. I shake and shake and shake. My breath whistles in my throat until I press my lips together and force myself not to breathe for the count of one, two, three.

Calmer, steadier, I open my eyes.

Will stands in the doorway as if it's a line he's not allowed to cross. "Hey. Coffee?"

I should tell him I can't go. I shouldn't *want* to go. But I'm already standing, ready to follow him anywhere he takes me.

Chapter Seven

Because I still haven't learned the neighborhood, we walk around the block until we find a place. Any other street in New York would have a dozen coffee/bagel/pastry shops, but not this one. We settle for a small diner that shows off what looks like decent pastries and questionable sandwiches in the case by the hostess stand. The coffee, as it turns out, is terrible. Will orders a slice of German chocolate cake. I ask for a muffin.

"Sugar?" Will asks, fingers hovering over the small ceramic container in which the sweetener packets have been shoved haphazardly, a rainbow of pastels.

"Two. Please," I add quickly. So polite. So distant. Three days ago I had him naked and inside me, and now I can barely let my fingers touch his when he hands me the packets. I taste the coffee with a grimace and ask apologetically, "Can I have another, please?"

We warm our hands on the mugs and stare at anything except each other. The waitress brings the cake, but tells me they're out of muffins. My disappointment is out of proportion to my need for a shitty diner muffin, and I can't stop the frown. She offers cake, but I don't want cake. Or pie. Really, I think as I watch her rattling off the list of desserts, all I want is for her to shut up and go away. I order lemon meringue and expect to hate it when it comes.

"So," Will says after a second, when she's finally gone and we have no excuse to keep ignoring each other. "How are you?"

"Fine. You?" I sip bad coffee and burn my tongue.

At first, he says nothing. Then he gives me a slow smile, sweeter than the extra sugar I added to my coffee. His smile is the kiss of ocean spray and the keening cry of gulls.

"I wasn't sure you'd be at the gallery today." A pause as perhaps he considers what to say next. "But I was hoping you would be. That's why I stopped by."

Tension eases inside me, and I find my own smile. "I'm glad you did."

Again, he says nothing.

"Will…" I begin, stuttering on the flavor of his name. I can't decide exactly what it is, but it feels gritty. Like sugar. No, like sand. "About what happened…"

An emotion I can't decipher flashes across his face, and everything about him goes very still. His fingers turn the coffee mug. Turn and turn and turn. He leans forward, shoulders hunching, and rests his elbows on the table.

"Yeah. About that."

Before he can say more, my phone trills. I didn't program that ring tone, Jacqueline did, to set her apart from her sister and, I suppose, from everyone else. I'd ignore the call, but the look on his face says he's expecting me to take it. And the truth is, I'm glad for an excuse to stall this conversation, because I'm not at all sure where it's going.

"Hi, honey."

Jac walked at nine months and talked at eleven, and she hasn't slowed down or stayed quiet since. She is my in-charge child, bold and opinionated, capable of compassion but not so great with tact. She resembles me more than her sister does, but she's absolutely her father's girl.

"I wanted to wish you Happy Birthday today, because I'm going to be camping on the weekend. No cell service." She launches into the conversation without much preamble, but I can hear the smile in her voice. "Happy Birthday, Mama! Sorry I won't be home for it."

"It's fine. When you get to be my age, birthdays aren't such a big deal." Ross is the one who believes that, not me. I'd make my birthday a month-long holiday if I could, but it's kind of hard to celebrate it alone. "Thanks, though. Who's going camping?"

"Just me and Jeff. State park. Roughing it." Jac's laugh is almost identical to the trilling tone she programmed into my phone, all burbling bubbles, the warble of a bird. "Tents and everything."

"Sounds fun. Be careful," I add, because I have to and she expects it, not because I fear my daughter will be reckless. She always knows where she's going and how long it will take to get there.

I envy her that.

"Gotta go. Happy Birthday!"

"Thanks."

"Make Daddy take you to dinner or something."

"I will," I tell her, though at that very moment I'm not sure I'll be hungry for a long, long time. "Bye."

Call disconnected, I give Will a small smile. "My daughter."

"It's your birthday?"

"Sunday," I tell him with a small shrug.

"Got any big plans?"

"No. It's kind of a milestone birthday," I say suddenly, revealing something I wasn't expecting to tell him. "Not a big one. Halfway to the big one, I guess."

Will's smile crinkles lines at the corners of his eyes. "Forty?"

I'm so convinced he's pulling my chain, I burst into laughter I hide immediately behind my hand. He looks confused, still smiling, his head tilting a little to look me over. "No?"

"Um, no. Thanks, though. Not quite. I'll be forty-five." It doesn't sound so bad out loud, though in my head I've been testing it out for the past few weeks. "Seems like a lot bigger step from forty-four than it did from forty-three."

The number five to me is the color Crayola used to call burnt sienna and we always called "baby poop brown." It could be why it's my least favorite number. Why this birthday, perhaps, has hit me so much harder than the last few, because when I think of being forty-five, the four—which has always been a nondescript and inoffensive cloud-gray—is overshadowed by that ugly color. I learned not to tell people that numbers had color and flavors had shape, about the prickly sensation in my fingertips when I drank wine. I'd never even told Ross, not really, although I was sure Katherine had a least a little bit of the same thing. We never discussed it, but once when she was a child she'd told me very seriously that the colors on her building blocks were wrong. They didn't "match."

"Wait for forty-eight," he says. "That's when you really look fifty in the face."

It's my turn to be surprised. I'd been sure I was older than him, and by more than a few years. "You're kidding me."

"I could show you my driver's license," he offers, but I wave my hand.

We stare at each other as if this new knowledge has changed things, and maybe it has. We're both too old to behave like kids, maybe that's what we just learned. Or maybe it's that we're both adults who know what they want and how to get it.

"So," Will says after a few more seconds. "About what happened."

The memory of feeling his skin unfurls in my mind like a flower, and I can't stop the hitch of my breath or thump of my heart. Will has no more smile. There's definitely no flirting in the gaze he cuts so carefully from mine. The table between us is so small his knees bump mine every time he shifts, and yet I feel so very, very faraway. When he looks at the plain gold band on my left hand, I know what he's going to say.

"We shouldn't have," Will says.

"Of course we shouldn't have. But we did."

The veneer tabletop is patterned with interlocking circles, orange on cream. It would be retro if it wasn't probably legitimately from the fifties. Will traces the circles, one to the other, making a figure eight. When he looks up at me, his gaze is flat, and I don't know him well enough to tell if this is one of his usual expressions.

He waits a few seconds before answering. "I just don't want you to think I'm trying to cause trouble for you or anything. That's all."

"I didn't think that." Of course I didn't, just as I never dreamed I'd be sitting across from him, watching him struggle with how to tell me he doesn't want to fuck me again.

"Good." Will shifts, clearly uncomfortable and maybe more than a little relieved that I'm not...what? Going to go all *Fatal Attraction* on him?

If he knew me, he'd know that would never happen, but Will does not know me. We are strangers who shared an unexpected intimacy. Nothing more.

"I just don't think that it would be...good." He clears his throat. Awkwardness. I'm blushing just watching him work at finding the right words, his struggle as painful as if it were my own. "Um, you know. Long term. For either one of us. To keep on with this."

"No."

"I don't think married people should fuck around," he says suddenly, harshly enough to set me back.

There's something important I need him to know. To make myself clear. "I wasn't out looking to be unfaithful, Will. It just happened."

"I'm sorry," he says, and I believe he means it.

"Don't be," I tell him, when I get up from the table and put a few dollars down to cover the cost of our order. "I'm not."

Chapter Eight

The restaurant has been our favorite for a long time, since we moved into this neighborhood, which makes it close to twenty-two years. Demetri and his wife, Anatola, make the best gyros I've ever had, along with a homemade Greek dressing so good it should be illegal. I come here for every birthday. It's tradition.

While we wait for our food, Ross slides a box across the table toward me. "Happy Birthday."

I'd not-so-subtly hinted to him that I wanted a pair of black riding boots. Not for riding, of course. For fashion. I'd sent him links, told him the size. This box is too small to be a pair of riding boots.

It's a pair of quilted, ankle-high boots. Not red or even rust, but an off shade of dusty orange. They are not my size. They are hideous. I will never, ever wear them.

"You said you wanted boots," he says, clearly pleased with his purchase. "I picked these up when I was in Chicago."

I slide the lid closed and smile. Big and bright. "Thank you."

Over dinner, Ross talks about work and golf and something his buddies did, the outrageous things another friend's wife was doing, but I'm concentrating on my salad. I chase a black olive around the plate with my fork; it's hard to catch because it has a pit in it, and I can't dig the tines in deep enough. I don't really even want it. I like my olives pitted. But I'll eat it anyway, because it tastes so good, and I'll spit the pit into the palm of my hand and be uncertain about where to put it.

"…She wants the dog," Ross says. "Can you believe that bitch? You don't take a man's dog."

This snags my attention. Lifts my head. "What?"

"She wants the dog," Ross repeats, with a stab of his fork toward me. "Can you believe it?"

"What makes it *his* dog?" I know the friends he's talking about. Kent and Jeanine Presley. We aren't that close, though we've been to their house for parties. I remember the wife. She had round cheeks and a pixie cut that somehow flattered her anyway, and everything about her had made me think of ponies. Not because of the thing in my brain that turned sounds into shapes and colors into flavors, but just because sometimes people remind you of things that have nothing to do with who they actually are or what they do.

Ross stops with a bite of salad halfway to his mouth. "What?"

I've captured the olive, but now I really don't want it. I rub it through a smear of dressing as though that will convince my mouth to take it, but instead of sour olive flesh and the hard pit, my mouth has words. "I said, what makes it his dog?"

"Of course it's his dog."

"Why isn't it her dog, just as much?" I think of the parties we've gone to at their gleaming and spotless house. The hors d'oeuvres on special plates designed for just that purpose. Him at the grill outside, flipping burgers, but leaving all the rest for his wife. "I'm sure she's the one who took care of it most of the time, anyway."

"What difference does that make?"

I put my fork down. "Probably a lot."

"Not to the dog," he says.

I laugh. "But it's not the dog who gets to decide, is it?"

"You don't take a man's dog," Ross says pointedly, and stabs more salad. "You just don't."

"I didn't even know they were getting divorced." I sip water to clear the taste of the dressing from my tongue. It's delicious, it always is, but tonight everything seems to have a bit of sour taste. "What about the kids?"

Ross shrugs, clearly more concerned about the dog than the rest of the details. "He's letting her have the house."

"How generous." Not all words have color, but *generous* has always been a soft powder-blue. It doesn't match the sarcasm with which I've imbued it.

"They're upside down. He'll get out of it, find something better. In this market, he can snap something up." Ross snaps his fingers to demonstrate.

"He can afford to do that?"

Ross pauses in the steady back-and-forth of his fork from plate to mouth. "Well, yeah. She has to buy him out."

"So then he's not 'letting' her 'keep' the house." I don't know why this irritates me so much. I barely know Kent and Jeanine, and they were always more Ross's friends than mine. "She's paying him for it. And I'm sure she did the lion's share of taking care of it. So he's not *letting* her do anything, he's getting out from under a debt and starting fresh."

Ross stares. "Why shouldn't he?"

"Does she work?"

Shrug. "Sort of. Part-time, I guess."

"So how can she afford to buy him out of that house?" It was twice as big as ours, and in a more expensive neighborhood.

"Look, I don't know all the details, okay? It wasn't really

my business. I guess she's going to make payments to him or something. And forfeit her share of the retirement. Whatever, Bethie, what do you care? You don't even like Jeanine."

That's not quite true. I don't know her well enough to not like her. I wince a little at the spurs of burnt umber spiking my name the way he says it. I've never liked it when he calls me that, but he still does no matter how many times I ask him not to. "Why are they getting divorced?"

"People grow apart," Ross says stiffly, in a way that tells me he knows more than he's letting on, but won't share it.

I let it go. I don't really care. My stomach's in knots, and it has nothing to do with the end of the Presleys' marriage.

"So she's saddled with the kids and the house and having to figure out a way to not only get back into the job market to pay for all of it, but she sacrificed her future retirement in order to do it. That's what it comes down to in the end? Money? After how many years together, two kids…" I pause. "A dog."

Ross doesn't notice the layer of sarcasm I put into the word. "Money matters, Beth."

"Only when you don't have enough." The words slip out of me like puffs of black smoke.

He laughs at that. Takes my hand. Strokes his thumb over the palm in the way I told him once, years ago, turned me on. It doesn't anymore.

"You don't have to worry about money, honey. I'll always take care of you." He laughs again. Making light. "Unless you leave me, of course."

Nothing about this feels light to me. Not the birthday hitting me harder than I was expecting. Not the way my world has tipped on end and I don't know how to stand up straight. My fingers curl inside my husband's to squeeze his hand tight.

"What would happen then?" I ask.

Ross kisses the back of my hand, his breath warm and moist

and sending a shiver through me that's not from arousal. "Oh," he says with a smile, to show me he's joking, though I know him well enough to know he's serious, "I'd make sure you get nothing."

Chapter Nine

If there's ever a person who tells you in all their years of marriage they've never wondered what it would be like to walk out, you're talking to a liar. I'd thought it before, when the girls were infants and Ross traveled so much and worked such long hours that I was made a single parent by default. He'd embraced fatherhood with the enthusiasm he had for his golf game. He loved his daughters with everything he had. He simply wasn't there.

Things got better, as they do when children get older and the constant stream of diapers and feedings eases. Ross was still gone a lot, but the girls and I found our rhythm and routine. I was the taskmaster, he was the guy who came around and treated them to ice cream instead of dinner and brought exotic souvenirs for them to squeal over. It wasn't so different from the lives of most of our friends. It worked.

My children are grown, getting ready to graduate from college, moving on to jobs and internships and adult lives. The house that had seemed perfect for the four of us now seems too big, too quiet. Too empty. My husband still travels, still works long hours, still spends his leisure time in pursuits that have nothing to do with me. And…what have I done?

I fucked another man. Without a second thought and, so

far, without remorse. I'd have done it again, if Will hadn't so ungracefully extricated himself from the future possibilities.

I'd thought about leaving my husband before. But am I thinking about it now? Sitting at my kitchen table and staring out at my perfectly manicured yard, then around the room at the nearly new appliances, the cabinets we'd just had redone, the pictures of fruit on the walls, I don't think so.

Ross slides a mug of coffee in front of me. He takes his black, and that's how he always serves mine even though I don't. "Morning. What are you up to today?"

"Work." I've worked for over ten years, and he still asks me—when he remembers. As if I have a long social calendar full of mani-pedi appointments and tennis lessons instead of a job.

"Here or the city?"

"Philadelphia's a city, too, you know," I tell him.

"You know what I mean." Ross looks out to the backyard. "The grass needs to be mowed."

"The service comes on Thursdays." For the seven years we've used the same service, they've always come on Thursdays. Lawn on Thursdays, housecleaning on Mondays. Laundry on the weekends. Always the same. Always.

"Have them take care of the flowerbeds this time, too. Maybe order some mulch."

The flower beds look fine to me, and we mulched in the fall, and why is it my job to do this when he's the one who wants it? I don't say I'll do it, but I don't say I won't. I don't say anything at all.

"You want some more?" At the counter, Ross lifts the coffeepot in my direction.

I haven't done more than take a sip or two of what he brought me. "Not yet. Can you bring me some sugar?"

He turns from side to side, looking around the kitchen as if he's never seen it before. "Where is it?"

"In the cupboard behind you. No, directly behind you. Turn around," I say, when he opens every cupboard except the one I mean. "There's a basket with sugar packets in it."

"I don't see it."

I want to put my face in my hands and cry, or laugh until I cry, I'm not sure which. "Ross. Come on."

He scowls. "Why can't you just tell me where it is?"

"You might have to move something to the side or look behind something."

He turns, triumphant. "Ha! How many do you want?"

"Two." My coffee will be cold by the time I sweeten it. I didn't really even want it, but he brought it to me so I'll drink it. I empty the packets Ross hands me into the coffee and sip it. Not sweet enough. "Can you grab me another?"

He looks up. "Huh?"

"Never mind." I get up to help myself.

He's made himself some toast. At least he was able to find the bread and figure out how the toaster worked without too much trouble. I'll find a trail of crumbs along the counter and embedded in the butter. Now I'm being mean. Ross hands me an envelope from the pile of mail he must've brought in yesterday and left on the counter.

I got all the birthday cards I was expecting last week, and I haven't ordered anything that might come in a mailer like this—rigid but padded, protecting something inside. There's no return address, and my name is printed in careful block letters that have no personality.

"I'll be late tonight. Just letting you know." Ross puts his plate in the sink, though the dishwasher is empty and right beside it. He dusts his fingers and tosses back the last of his coffee. The mug goes in the sink instead of in the dishwasher while I watch, saying nothing.

There's really nothing to say.

I leave behind the crumbs and dirty dishes and irritation, and I catch my husband at the door to the garage. I snag his sleeve, turning him.

"Wait," I say. "Kiss me."

It's perfunctory at best, and it's not good enough. I haven't let go of his sleeve even when he tries to take a step away. Ross, caught, gives me a curious look.

I stand on my toes to kiss his mouth again, taking my time. I cup my hand to the back of his neck, his hair brushing my fingers. I press my body to his and kiss him like I mean it. Like I want to. Like a lover.

His lips part, finally, to allow my tongue, but only for the time it takes him to pull away. He studies me for a second or two. Shakes his head.

"I have to go, Beth."

Spiky brown, orange. Jagged edges. Not smooth.

Of course he has to go. I watch him pull out of the driveway, giving me a wave as he closes the garage door. He always has to go.

And what about me? I think as I go back inside the kitchen, where I leave the dish and mug in the sink without washing them, because I want to see how long it takes before he thinks to put them in the dishwasher himself. If he ever does. Do I have to go?

The envelope on the table comes open with a tug of the small red thread. Inside is bubble padding and two cardboard flats protecting two items. The first, black words in a scrawling hand on a plain white card.

Happy Birthday.

The second, a photograph. It's an 11 x 20 print, scattered

stones on a bed of velvet. Oh, and there's my heart-shaped rock, set off from the others. It's more than just a photo. He's added lines and color to it, little hints here and there. With ink and pen he's transformed a beautiful shot into something unique. Special.

Will has given me art.

Chapter Ten

A handwritten thank-you card seems old-fashioned and intimate and therefore an appropriate response to Will's gift, but I settle for an email instead. Making my reply casual yet polite, pixels and bytes instead of the intimacy of my fingers clutching a pen and moving it along paper. Without leaving an indelible mark, something permanent in the world.

His response pings my in-box only a minute or so after I've sent the message, and though my heart leaps at the sight of his name, I don't open it right away. I minimize the email window and concentrate on researching a specific fabric Naveen wants for the gallery. Gauzy, pale yellow, embroidered here and there with red and orange roses. Green vines. He wants it for one of the back rooms he plans to rent out for parties, to hide the unfinished beams. It's hard to find it by the bolt, and though I've come up with several alternatives, he's insistent on this particular one.

Other than business, Naveen hasn't spoken to me since the day in his office. It's been a week. He's waiting for me to come to him, to apologize, and I haven't yet been able to make myself do it.

Finally, when I've checked off five of the ten tasks I'd

planned for the morning, I give myself permission to look at Will's message.

You're welcome. There wasn't anyone else I could think of who'd appreciate it more.

My fingers type. I could stop myself, but I don't want to. You shouldn't have. It wasn't necessary.

His response is almost immediate. I wanted you to have it.

I have no reply for that but another thank-you, and that should be the end of it. But another message comes through in a few minutes. It's an invitation to a gallery show, not Naveen's, in two days. Will's listed as one of the artists.

I don't answer, but I don't delete it, either. The message should get lost in my in-box, but every time I look it's still there as bold and bright as a neon sign. The next message comes in a few minutes before I'm getting ready to leave for the day.

Please come.

To this I have no ready response except the leap of my heart, the pulse and throb of my blood in soft and tender places. My fingers move, typing a reply I'd never be able to voice aloud.

I'll be there.

Chapter Eleven

Unlike Naveen's, this gallery features only photography, mostly in black-and-white, prints of all sizes framed in identical glass bricks and staggered around a room with black walls. The door frames and windowsills are painted red, and the lighting is harsh and bright. I like it better than the gauzy fabric and fairy lighting of Naveen's gallery, though I'd never tell him so. Even if he ever does start talking to me again.

I see Will's work right away. Among the other shots of buildings and trees, all the same subject matter, his still stand out to me. I study the photos, remembering the way his hands hold a camera.

I don't have to turn around to know he's there.

We stand shoulder to shoulder, not enough distance between us to make this casual. My dress is sleeveless, and his denim jacket brushes my skin. I don't look at him.

"I like that one." I point out a framed series of three nearly identical shots, different only in their distance from the subject.

Will doesn't answer. I shift a little away from him to look at the next piece, a black-and-white shot of what looks like bamboo. There's nothing at all special about that one, and I tell him so.

Finally, he laughs. From the corner of my eye, I see him hang his head. He shrugs, glancing at me sideways.

"Yeah. I know. I only had them put it up here because I was missing a piece."

"What happened to the one you were going to show?"

We turn toward each other at the same instant, eyes meeting. The hem of my dress swirls around my shins, and I imagine the whisper of it against his jeans. It sounds like roses smell.

"I gave it away," Will says.

"Take me somewhere" is what I say back, and though I'm convinced he will smile and shake his head, change the subject, refuse....

He doesn't.

Chapter Twelve

Another diner, more coffee. We both order pie—he likes pecan. I pick cherry. We walked the few blocks from the gallery, and we talked about the weather.

It might be April outside, but in here it's February. I warm my hands on the mug the waitress has filled with hot liquid. "Can I have a couple—"

Will's already pushing two sugar packets across the table toward me. He watches me tear the paper and pour sugar into the coffee. Before I even lift the mug to my mouth, he hands me one more packet. It makes the coffee tolerable at last.

"Thanks for coming to the show."

"I barely stayed long enough for it to count," I say.

"But you came."

I study him. The brush of his sandy hair over his forehead, tufting in front of his ears. The bristle of stubble around his mouth, not quite a goatee. Dark circles press the flesh below his eyes, a little more prominent on the right than the left. He looks tired.

I wait until he looks at me. "What are you doing?"

He could make any kind of answer. Eating pie. Drinking coffee. Talking about the weather.

"I don't know," Will says. "Whatever it is, I shouldn't be."

"No. You probably shouldn't. But I could've just said no."
He smiles. "You could've."

"But I didn't."

"No. I didn't."

Again, we're staring at each other across a table, but this time it feels better. Not quite so awkward, and definitely far more ripe with promise. When he looks at me with that sideways grin, I don't return it. I'm trying to be good.

"You wanna get out of here?" Will gives the diner a roundabout look as he hunches his shoulders, lowers his voice, as if he's trying to keep our escape a secret.

I look around, too. We're nearly the only customers in here. I'm the one who asked him to take me somewhere, but I'm not so eager now to let him do it.

"Where do you want to go?"

He shrugs. "It's New York City. You think we can't find something to do?"

I make a show of looking at the clock, but the truth is, Ross is out of town again, and even if he wasn't, the night is too young for me to have to excuse myself with the lateness of the hour. "You don't want to just sit here and drink shitty coffee?"

"The coffee I could deal with. The pie is crap, too." Will grins.

Slowly I return the smile, reluctant only because I don't want to seem too eager. I stab my pie with my fork, leaving it standing upright in the pool of cherries that spreads like blood across the stained porcelain plate. "Sure. Let's go."

Outside, we walk in silence at first, having already exhausted the weather as our topic of conversation. New York is never dark, of course, but it does look different at night, painted in the white and yellow of streetlights. In this neighborhood tall brownstones tower over us, most of their windows alight with gold.

"I like to look in windows," I admit, slowing as we pass one particularly pretty house. Some of the others have been made into apartments, but this one is still a single residence. You can tell because of the matching window boxes and the glimpses of furnishings in bedrooms on the second and third floors. There are bars on the windows, but I can still see what looks like a nursery complete with blue-painted walls and— "Oh, look! Stars!"

Will pauses to stare upward, across the narrow, one-way street. "Where?"

"In there." I point toward the house, the window of the nursery lined with twinkling white lights. I realize, too late, the stars I saw were from the lights and not anything he might be able to see. "Oh. Never mind."

He tilts his head, curious. "On the wall? Painted?"

"No. I meant the lights. But they're not…" I gesture as we start walking again. "You won't see them as stars."

Will turns to walk backward, staring at the building as we pass. "But you did?"

"Yes," I say after a second. "When I look at Christmas lights like that…those twinkly kind, I see stars."

"Like in Naveen's gallery?"

There the lights are hung in zigzags across the ceiling above the layers of gauzy fabric. They're meant to simulate stars. But that's not what I see. I see actual stars, a halo of light with six points.

"Not exactly."

I don't mean to tell him any more than that—it's not as weird as saying that voices and certain words have scent and flavor and color. But it's still pretty bizarre and something I've shared with only a few people. Trusted friends. My family. Never a casual acquaintance, not on purpose, though there've been a few times when something has slipped out.

"They're real stars," I blurt. "Not like the ones in the sky. It's hard to explain. They sort of…float around the lights. Like…have you ever seen those novelty glasses, the cardboard ones. Kind of like 3-D glasses? When you look through them at the lights, you see a halo sort of thing."

"Like snowmen," he says, catching on. "Or Stars of David."

He gets it. Sort of. It's still too hard to explain. "Yes. Like that."

"Huh." He studies me. "That's kind of cool. Hey. Have you been to Madame Tussauds?"

I laugh, surprised by the question. "Um…no. I haven't, actually."

"We should go."

"We should?"

Will nods. How can I resist? I've never been to the famous wax museum, though I've heard all about it. He leads the way, down one street and another. We find other subjects than the weather. Nothing important, nothing serious. We carefully don't touch for longer than a second or two, not even when he takes my elbow as we cross a busy street. I like how he leads me, almost herding, to make sure I make it across safely.

Madame Tussauds is close to Times Square, down Forty-Second Street. A giant hand creeps up the outside of the building, holding strings as though for a marionette. Inside, red velvet ropes signify a significant queue, but fortunately at this time of night, there's no line. We head up in an elevator and come out in a large room set up like a Hollywood party.

The figures are amazing. Detailed, realistic. Creepy. I think about posing for a picture with some of my favorites, but can't think of how I'd explain the photos to anyone without having to make up a complicated story. We don't have much time to begin with, and every passing second flies by even faster because I'm having so much fun, laughing and pretending to chat with these frozen wax figures. Laughing at Will's jokes and his impressions—he's got a few very good ones, though his impression of Stephen Hawking has me snort-laughing, and I shake my head in mock disapproval.

We wind our way through displays and then through the "scary" part of the museum—Hollywood monsters and serial killers, but it's also the part that leads into the history of Madame Tussaud herself. She got her start making death masks during the French Revolution, according to the information set up all over the place. Turning a corner, we spy a particularly gruesome pile of corpses, with a mural of the Eiffel Tower in the background. It's dark in here, and very quiet but for the soft sound of Will's breathing.

"Elisabeth."

"Yes, Will." His name crunches, the taste of sand and sea.

"About what I said the other day. It was kind of shitty. I'm sorry."

"I told you not to be," I say. "And besides. You were absolutely right. I should absolutely not have done it."

Will scuffs the floor with his toe. "You didn't do it alone."

We're standing in the middle of a room with black-painted walls, the eerie sound of screams piped in from hidden speakers, and gore-spattered wax bodies all around us. This isn't the time or place for this discussion, even if I wanted to have it, which I don't.

"I just don't want you to think—" he starts.

I shake my head. "I don't."

We're standing close enough to kiss, if only he'd lean forward. I have no idea what I'll do if he tries.

"Well," I say, when it's apparent he's neither going to lean or kiss. "We'll always have Paris."

The night air's gone much cooler when we leave the wax

museum. Hint of rain in the air, the far-off rumble of thunder. Neither of us talks about ending the night. Instead, we walk.

New York City is enormous, but it's easy to forget that when the buildings rise so high they block out everything but what's right in front of you. We've meandered through Times Square and the flood of tourists still gaping at the neon lights, even though by now it's getting close to midnight. I know where we are, but not where we're going. I'm trusting Will to lead me, and he does.

We round a corner, and although it had to have been there all the while, I'm surprised to see the Empire State Building, alight with red, white and blue, towering over us. I must've made some sort of exclamation, because Will looks at me. He tips his head that way.

"You wanna go up?"

"It's late." The truth, not an excuse.

He smiles. "It's open late. And besides, the view at night is the best. It's never as crowded."

"Do you go to the top a lot?" I ask as we head toward the ornate art deco doors to what had once been the tallest building in New York City.

Will holds the door for me. "No. Not a lot."

Inside, more queues, also amazingly empty. Will insists on paying for the VIP package, which puts us to the front of the line and gives us access to the 102nd floor instead of just the 86th. Uniformed employees guide us to the elevators, where we go up, and up and up.

Outside on the observation deck, it's more than cool, it's chilly. The wind whips at my skirt and my hair. Goose bumps rise on my bare arms, and I rub them briskly, trying to keep my teeth from chattering.

The view is amazing.

In every direction the lights spread out for miles, bright as day in the city proper and getting sparser and more scattered farther away. The Hudson River gleams, a black satin ribbon dotted with the pearls of boats bobbing on the water. Brake lights and traffic lights, rubies and emeralds, are set in the gold of streetlamps. Down below there might be the stench of urine and cacophony of traffic, but up here so far above the ground, New York City is a jewel box, the treasures inside tumbled out for everyone to see.

Another distant rumble of thunder has me searching the skyline for lightning. This wouldn't be the best place to stand during a storm, but so far the only flashes I see are far away. Probably in New Jersey. The wind's picked up, though. A storm is coming.

Will shrugs out of his jacket and offers it to me. "Here. You're shivering."

"I can't. Then you'll be cold."

"I'll be okay." He drapes the denim around my shoulders and rubs my upper arms for a second.

His touch warms me, but it has nothing to do with the jacket. I pull it closer around me, thinking I should try harder to refuse, but I'm too cold. "Thanks."

We view all four sides of the observation deck and have no more reason to stay. As we get back to street level, the first few frigid, spattering drops of rain have begun to fall. The overhang shields us, but we can't stand there for long. The doorman's already giving us the stink eye. Will dances a little from foot to foot, his hands shoved deep into his pockets and his shirt slowly getting dark with the spray that's started to go slantwise.

"We could go someplace else?" he suggests.

I shake my head. "Where? It's late, and it's raining…."

"We could go to my place. It's not far."

"I don't think that would be a great idea," I force myself to say, although it's exactly the opposite of what I want to answer.

I can't quite read his expression. "Because you don't trust me?"

It's not him I don't trust, oh, hell no. I'm the one who'd cross the line again. As hard and fast as I could.

"If I don't go to your apartment," I tell him carefully, neutrally, aware of the doorman listening to this exchange as if he's got front seats to a Broadway show, "I don't have to trust you."

Thunder booms, making us both jump. We have no place else to walk, not in this weather. And besides, I have a train to catch.

"I'll just be able to make it," I tell him. "Catch the last one."

"Let's share a cab. It can drop me off first, then you, okay?"

It will give me a few more minutes with him, and that's really what I want. Will, proficient New Yorker that he is, hails a cab with a whistle that makes me laugh. I've never been good at that. He opens the door for me and waits for me to slide in across the cracked vinyl seat that catches my skirt and tugs it up too high on my legs. There's plenty of room in the backseat of that cab, but I don't move over more than halfway. He gives the driver directions and leans against the back of the seat.

Our knees bump every time the cab goes over a rough patch in the street. That's a lot. I look carefully out the opposite window so I'm not looking at Will; if he's looking at me, I don't know it. I breathe in. I breathe out. We are sealed in these last few moments, neither of us speaking, but both of us, I think, fully aware of the other.

When the cab pulls to a stop in front of Will's building, I shift a little, moving to give him the room to get out without awkwardly bumping into me. I murmur something that sounds like "goodbye" but tastes like "hello," all bright and summer-yellow on my tongue. We're both turning, turning, he's getting out of the cab, the door is open, the rain and cold are coming in.

Will kisses my mouth. Short, hard, an inelegant and un-glamorous, unerotic peck on the lips, the sort you'd give the prom date you didn't really want but settled for when your crush turned you down. Three seconds, maybe less, and he's gone, the door closing behind him and the cab already pull-ing away, leaving Will standing on the curb and my mouth open in protest.

Wait is the word on my tongue. *Unacceptable. Terrible. Dis-appointing. It was supposed to be better than that.*

And then, sitting back against the seat in stunned dismay, I press my fingertips to the place where he kissed me and think, *He kissed me. Oh, God. He kissed me on the mouth.*

It's not until I get home that I realize I'm still wearing his jacket.

Chapter Thirteen

I should be working from the Philadelphia office today, but I've made the trip into New York on the pretense that Naveen and I need to talk about some invoices. He's still ignoring me. I'm pretending I don't notice. We haven't had a true conversation in weeks. It's the longest I've ever gone without talking to him since that last year of college. Then we didn't speak for six months and got back in touch only when he wrote me a long, sincere letter begging me to forgive him. We had to do it old-school back then, I think with a faint smile. No email. No texting. Long distance calls too expensive. I still have the letter in a box with all my other mementos. I haven't read it in years, but could probably recite at least bits of it from memory, that's how many times I'd read it before I replied to him.

I've brought Will's jacket, folded neatly and in a plastic grocery bag. It sits on the edge of my desk, unobtrusive but always in the corner of my eye. I wait until Naveen is with a client, an interior designer who often purchases entire lots of art with which to fill her customers' foyers. Sarah Roth charges exorbitant rates and never seems to care about the subject matter of what she buys, exactly, only that whatever it is follows the color scheme and "tone" of the place she's decorating. Her hair is never the same color twice. She's pretty amazing, and I envy her style.

In Naveen's office, I scroll through his computer's address book until I find Will's number. I could've asked Naveen for it. He'd have given it to me, if he bothered to speak to me, which he still seems bent on refusing to do. The soft rise of laughter bubbles outside the door, turning my head. It's going to take more than a letter to get me back in Naveen's good graces, and to be honest, I'm not sure I'm ready to make such an effort. He can hold a grudge a long time, and what I'd said was hurtful. Truth, but hurtful.

I punch Will's number into my phone before I can stop myself. Not a call—that would be too forward. Too insistent, somehow, on taking up his attention. What if he's busy? With someone? But an email takes too long, if he doesn't check his regularly, as I don't unless I'm expecting something important.

But a text message, that's just right. Not too intimate or demanding, yet immediate. He can answer when it works for him. My fingertip taps out the message and I hit Send before I can regret it.

I have your jacket.

Then I wait. Unable to concentrate on the busywork I've made for myself, I pace. I drink coffee from the machine down the hall, cup after cup. And finally, just as I'm getting ready to go for lunch, my phone hums.

Meet me?

Oh, yes. Anywhere, I think, but don't type. We arrange to meet not at a coffee shop—neither my bladder nor my nerves could've handled it—but at the Museum of Modern Art, close to where he's been shooting some pictures. I take a cab. The ride's longer than expected, due to construction. We text the entire ride. Simple conversation, weighted with what we aren't saying.

How was your day? What are you working on? Have you seen this movie, read this book? What's your favorite band? Where did you grow up?

Which do you like better, the ocean or the mountains? Will asks.

The ocean, I reply at once. I love the ocean more than anything else in the whole world.

It's my turn then. Have you ever touched an elephant?

I don't know why I asked him that. I'm restless, irritated by the driver's seeming inability to get me where I want to be without encountering every single traffic snarl in downtown Manhattan. It came out of the blue, suddenly, as necessary for me to know as his favorite flavor of ice cream, or the color he likes best.

His answer doesn't come right away. I picture him pondering it, second-guessing his decision to meet me even if it was ostensibly to get back the jacket he'd lent me. I imagine him scratching his head, fingers sliding through that wheat-brown hair to make it stand on end, and I lean back against the seat as heat filters through me at the image my mind built.

No.

The answer surprises me. I've touched elephants at the circus, when you can pay twenty dollars for a ride on their smelly broad backs around the sawdust-covered ring. Once at the zoo during a special behind-the-scenes tour. Once at a Ren faire, where "Lady Wrinkles" would take from your palm treats you could buy from her handlers. Elephants are amazing, beautiful creatures, and it hasn't occurred to me that Will might never have been close enough to touch one.

"We got another block to go," the driver says roughly,

looking over his shoulder. His brows are bushy and wild, his lips moist. His teeth very white. "You want to get out here and walk? It's gonna take another twenty, thirty minutes in this traffic."

"I'll get out. Thanks." I pay him quickly, not giving myself the chance to take advantage of the delay.

I am not dressed for walking. New York women totter along the sidewalks in impossibly high shoes, never breaking stride. I dodge puddles of dubious origin and wobble on cracked pavement in my modest three-inch heels and wish for sneakers. I'd spent an hour in front of my closet trying on different outfits. This shirt with that skirt, this blouse, that dress. Jewelry. More time spent on my hair. I didn't want to look as if I was trying too hard. Now I wished I'd spent even more time, paid better attention to the lining of my eyes and mouth. I'd ended up dressing for a day in the office, not for meeting a lover.

Oh, God.

I see him before he sees me. He's smoking, which shouldn't surprise me but somehow does. He leans against some scaffolding—it's everywhere in New York. The city is forever putting on a new face. Looking away from me, Will takes a long, deep drag before tipping his head back to let the smoke seep from his nostrils toward the sky. He's wearing dark jeans and a midnight-blue henley shirt with the sleeves pushed up on his arms. A series of braided leather bracelets tangle around one wrist. He is so beautiful that I'm frozen in place, buffeted by the never-ending press and rush of people in a hurry.

There's a moment when I could turn around and walk away. Catch another cab. I could be back on the train and on my way home in an hour. I can delete his number from my phone.

But I can't erase the memory of that kiss.

That stupid fucking mouth-on-mouth.

He turns, gaze scanning the crowd but his expression blank. Then he sees me. And everything about him lights up.

Will stubs out the cigarette against the side of a trash can and tosses the butt inside as I cross the street to get to him. "Elisabeth. Hi."

"Hi." I hold out the plastic bag, though the weather's turned much warmer and he wouldn't need it now. "I brought your jacket."

"Thanks." He takes the bag without looking inside.

We stare at each other, and I can't stop my smile. I am suddenly and inexplicably suffused with a joy so fierce I have to duck my head. I don't want him to see it on my face. I look instead toward the museum entrance.

"Should we go in?"

"If you want to." Will gestures a little awkwardly.

"I haven't been here in a long time. Sure. I'd like to."

He leads the way, but steps aside to let me go through the door first; for a few seconds his fingertips press the small of my back. Other than that, we don't touch. We each pay our own way to get in, and move through the lobby toward the stairs. It's not too busy today—the last time I was here it was almost impossible to get through the throng, and I'd had to wait in line for twenty minutes just to get close to Van Gogh's *Starry Night*. It was worth it. It's always worth it.

It's where we go first, though neither of us suggests it. It's as if our feet simply take us there while we chat of inconsequential things, as though we'd never had our texted conversation at all. As if we're strangers. They've changed the location since the last time I was here. Before, it hung on a wall with a bunch of other paintings, but now it's on its own wall, set off from the others to make it easier, I guess, for many people to gather around it.

Will and I stand in front of *Starry Night*. Our shoulders touch. I am moved, as I always am.

"What do you see?" Will asks. "When you look at this?"

Surprised, I glance at him without moving. "What do you mean?"

"Tell me."

I sip a breath. "Well...I love the colors. The bold strokes. It looks like the night sky to me, obviously. But...it's also like... honey. Warm honey dripping off a silver spoon. The flavor of it. The smell, too."

I can't describe it better than that. Will doesn't ask. Slowly, slowly, his fingers curl against mine. Our pinkies link. We are joined.

And then the cavorting squall of schoolkids shows up. Will and I snap apart. He grins at me as he lets a couple kids push in front of him.

"I'm hungry," he says. "You want to get something?"

The café is directly across from the gallery we were in, which is convenient enough to make me wonder if he'd planned it all along. I study the menu, musing at the prices. "Museums should be cheaper," I say in a low voice, not really complaining. Just thinking aloud. I look at him over the hoity-toity menu. "Art should be more accessible."

"I can agree with you because I'll never have anything hanging in a museum," Will says. "Especially not this one."

We laugh together as the waiter comes to take our order. Will gets the cheese plate and some kind of fancy salad. I order a quiche. We both get the MOMAtini, which has raspberries in it. My first sip hits me hard. By the second, I'm pretty sure I'll be on my way to tipsytown.

"That good?" Will says when I tell him this.

"I'm not a big drinker." I take another savory sip. The drink *is* good. "When I drink too much, I always feel like I want to speak French, but badly. Because that's the only way I know how to speak it. Do you speak French?"

"No. But I think you should have another drink."

"I think I need to be a little drunk for some of the stuff in here."

He laughs again and clinks his glass to mine. "You don't like modern art?"

On an empty stomach the drink hits me faster than normal. I study the crimson liquid and take another sip, eyeing him. "I like my art to look like stuff."

His brows raise. He leans back in his chair. I feel the knock of his boot against my foot, but I don't move it.

"You're a realist," Will says.

"Maybe." My tongue runs over my bottom lip, along the sweetness left behind by the liquor.

He's watching me. I shift a little. My cheeks are flushed. I'm too conscious again of how I look, if the neckline of my blouse is a little too low. Or not low enough. If my hair's starting to come loose around my face.

"Not a romantic?"

"Oh," I say, a little too loudly. "No. God, no."

Will studies me for a second. "You like photographs."

"Yes."

"Better than paintings."

"Mostly, yes. Especially paintings that don't look like anything other than four barely different shades of black in a big box or something like that. That shit," I say as I lean a little forward to put my empty glass on the table between us, "is like something a kindergarten kid could do."

Will snorts laughter, either at my language or my slightly slurred description, I can't be sure. "Oh, c'mon."

"I'm serious!" I shake my head, giving him a sideways smile. "Tell me you don't think so."

"Art is subjective, yeah," he says after a second. "If you hate modern art so much, why'd you agree to come here?"

I shrug. "Because I love *Starry Night*. Because you suggested it. I don't know."

Because I wanted to see you, I think. *And it didn't matter where.*

Will gestures to catch the waiter's attention, and to me he says, "You should definitely have another drink in order to get through it, then."

Our food arrives along with a second set of drinks I should decline, but don't. We eat and talk, sharing our food. No longer strangers. He offers me a bite of soft cheese spread on a slim slice of hard toast, and right there in the MOMA café, in front of the world or at least anyone who'd care enough to bother watching us, I take it right from his fingers into my mouth.

"Is it good?" Will murmurs, and all I can say is yes.

I am most definitely drunk by the time lunch is finished, and I don't care. The floor slides a little under my feet, but Will's got a hand under my elbow and I'm not at all afraid of falling. He keeps me close. Herding me again, this time not across a busy street but through the late afternoon swell of museum patrons.

In the restroom, I wet a paper towel and press it to the back of my neck for a few seconds. It does nothing to ease the flush of my cheeks, the sparkle in my eyes. My lips are red and wet, tinged from the raspberries maybe. I pull a curl of hair out of the clip and let it fall over one eye. I slide the top button of my blouse free. I stare at the woman in the reflection, but although I might like to pretend I'm someone else, there's no doubt she's still all me.

"You okay, honey?" The elderly woman at the sink beside me wears bright red lipstick to match her scarlet fingernails.

I admire her leopard print scarf. I've never worn animal prints. They make me feel prickly. "I like your scarf."

She gives it a pleased glance. "Thank you. Do you feel well?"

I stop myself from saying "fan-fucking-tastic" only at the last minute, but make a not-so-subtle swipe at the bands of shimmery color her voice has left in the air. This is why I don't drink, I remember. Because I forget to remember that the rest of the world doesn't see what I see.

"I'm fine." I feign sobriety with another hard look at myself in the mirror. "Just had a little too much liquid joy at lunch."

She laughs. "I've done that myself, once or twice."

Outside, Will waits, leaning against the white wall with his hands in his pockets and one leg crossed over the other. He stands up straight when I come through the doorway. His smile tweaks my own.

"Bonjour," I say, and more words come, slipping out with a flavor of garlic butter and red wine. *"La première fois que je t'ai vu, j'ai eu un coup de foudre."*

"Merci," Will says. "Jacques Cousteau. Escargot. Marcel Marceau."

We look at modern art together, sometimes in silence, sometimes with commentary. Mostly with sideways glances and a few stifled giggles.

"It's pretentious," I say finally, in front of an exhibit that stretches from floor to ceiling. It consists entirely of graph paper on which the artist has traced the lines. "It's not even a pattern. He just traced the boxes. I did that in the sixth grade. Nobody called it art."

"Maybe that's the difference. What someone else calls it." Will rocks on his heels a few times, hands in his back pockets. "Maybe it's not art unless someone else says so."

"Art," I say seriously, "should make you *feel* something."

Will is quiet for a second or two before he looks at me with another quirking grin. "This makes you *feel* angry."

He's right. It's not what I meant, but he's right, and I give him a little bow that makes the world spin a bit. Laughing, he takes me by the elbow again. Down a corridor into another room.

This one is completely black inside, no lights except the film shining against the far wall. Black-and-white, it features a man standing in front of a barn. As we watch, the barn's front wall comes off in slow motion, but the empty window frame is positioned so that it falls completely over him. It's a parody or an homage to an old Buster Keaton movie, I think; I can't quite tell which one. Over and over the front of the barn falls, the man's expression never changing. Over and over, from different angles and distances.

Over and over.

Eventually the film cycles through to the beginning again. Will and I stand in the corner, the darkest spot. We blend into the shadows, and the way the light from the movie reflects off the polished walls and floor, we are almost impossible to see unless you're looking for us. I know this because an older man in a pink polo shirt unselfconsciously picks his nose while he watches the film, and he's only about two feet from me.

I shudder with disgust and bury my face against Will's shoulder to stifle my choking laughter. His arm slips around my waist, pulling me closer. Hip to hip. His thumb moves back and forth against the inner skin of my wrist, held close to my side. Slow, slow strokes. He doesn't look at me.

This small touch, this tender stroke of his flesh on mine, should not be enough to make me shake, but oh, it feels so good, so good I tremble from it. The *shush-shush* of his breathing presses pinpricks of light into my vision. Like sparklers, the lights arch and fade. My eyelids flutter.

Will leans closer. His lips brush my earlobe. His breath pushes at a few stray tendrils of my hair.

"I want to rub the head of my cock back and forth over your clit until you're dripping wet for me." He breathes these words against my ear. I can't move. "Back and forth, so slow it makes you crazy. I want to tease you until you beg me to fuck you."

The shudder of my breath echoes the rattle-tap of the projector noises. I turn my head the tiniest bit toward him. My lips barely move when I say, "I. Don't. Beg."

He takes my hand and puts it on the front of his jeans. On his cock, thick and hard beneath the denim. As slowly as he's done everything else, Will rubs my palm back and forth over his erection, down low enough to curl my fingers around the bulge of his balls. Then up along the ridge.

Up. Down. Just…a little…faster…

His breath catches. In the faint glow from the movie in front of us, his eyes are wide, pupils dilated and dark. His lips are slightly parted, the lower one moist from the swipe of his tongue. The urge to kiss him is like some hungry, furious thing, and it's eating me alive.

A clatter of schoolchildren tumbles into the room, all of them loud and laughing. Pushing and shoving. Will straightens and lets go of my hand. We move deliberately apart, still standing so close I can still feel the heat of his shoulder on mine.

Saying nothing, we leave the room. We leave the museum. We get in a cab and sit without speaking as the tension between us rises and twists, coiling tighter. We ride the elevator to his apartment with hardly a glance between us. Barely a word. And when we get in the door, I push him in front of me, against the wall, hard enough to rattle the pictures in their frames. I kick the front door closed.

Then I get on my knees while my hands, sure-fingered and without fumbling, yank open his belt. The button and zipper. His straining cock pushes at the front of his briefs and he's in my fist before he even has a chance to make a sound.

I use one knee to nudge his legs farther apart as I pull his jeans down to his thighs. His briefs, too. He's mostly naked for me in half a minute. That beautiful cock pulses against my palm as I skim my hand upward, barely brushing the head. Will's hips push forward, and I grip his shaft, keeping him in place. He looks down at me, his gaze dark.

I don't say a word, but he puts his palms flat against the wall on either side of him. Looking up at him, our eyes locked, I open my mouth, let my hot breath seep out over his hotter flesh. He shivers. I brush his prick against my cheek, soft, so soft, the tip of it not quite close enough to press inside my lips. Down a little lower, I breathe against him as my hand works his cock.

I mouth his inner thigh, tasting salt. His skin is pale here, dusted with fine hairs lighter than the coarser hair between his legs. I nuzzle him. I press my teeth to his flesh, nipping hard enough to make him cry out. And still his hands don't move from their place on the wall.

When I run my tongue along the underside of his cock, stopping just before I reach the tiny divot at that head, Will lets out a long, tortured groan. His eyes are closed, his head bent so that his hair falls over his forehead. He shakes again when I let him feel my teeth against him, and when I move my hand up and down, then up a little higher to graze his cockhead. But when his hips pump again, I go still.

Small, quick and flicking flutters of my tongue tease him. My hand moves. Again, I slide my tongue up his cock from the base to just below the head, then up a little higher to let the wet, hot cavern of my mouth hover over the tip. Slick fluid gathers there, leaking. Again, I go still.

Will shudders. His eyes open, looking down at me looking up. He licks his lips and blinks. I do nothing.

"Please," he says at last. "Please…"

At last I engulf him, take him down the back of my throat. I taste him, slippery and a little sweeter than I expected. Greedy, I suck him hard, concentrating on the head while my hand, slick with my saliva, strokes his shaft. My other hand slips between my legs, rubbing and rubbing at my clit through my lace panties. I am wet. I am dripping for him. In fact, my cunt is already clenching when he at last slides his fingers into the back of my hair and anchors them there, pulling just hard enough to make me gasp.

I fuck him with my mouth and tongue, my teeth. My clit is so swollen I don't need to dip inside my panties. Even this indirect pressure is almost too much. I'm coming in long, rippling waves.

And…there are colors.

I taste and smell voices; certain words have color. My brain is wired to connect my senses in a way that most people can't begin to understand, but until now I've never had it happen during orgasm. The pleasure washes over me in shimmering bands of rainbow light and golden stars, and I'm filled not only with the ecstasy of climax but with the wonder of this new sensation.

Will's groan brings me back to my delicious task. I let my jaw go slack to take him deeper. I let him fuck my mouth however he wants. Sweat drips from his face onto mine, one drop, and I smile around his cock. Then I'm coming again, unable to think of anything but this desire. His taste.

He whispers my name. His fingers twist and tangle in my hair. "Shit," he says, "oh, shit this feels so good…I'm gonna come."

I appreciate the warning, but when he makes like he's going

to pull out, I don't let him. He cries out again, wordless. Desperate. His taste floods me, and I take everything he gives me, sucking hard until he's spent and softening in my mouth. I swallow. I stand. I wipe the corners of my mouth.

Will slumps against the wall, his hair damp with sweat. His mouth lax. Eyes half-lidded. I lean in to kiss him at the corner of his mouth, first one side, then the other. Then, sweetly, fully on his mouth. His tongue probes me, and the thought of him tasting himself in me sends another slow ripple of pleasure through me.

"I told you," I murmur directly into his ear, "I don't beg."

Chapter Fourteen

I was five or six years old when I discovered the world was different for me than for most everyone else. My mom's younger brother, Archie, had married a woman I was supposed to call Aunt Dot. That part was fine. Aunt Dot was young and pretty and eager to let everyone know her opinion about everything, from how to make Thanksgiving Day stuffing to whether or not little girls like me should be allowed to sit with everyone else for the meal. Aunt Dot seemed to think kids should sit alone, but since I was the only grandchild at the time, nobody else was in favor of that. Dot, I overheard my mom saying, sure liked to talk.

And that was the problem.

I was too young to understand that what Aunt Dot was saying might rub the other grown-ups the wrong way. For me, it wasn't her words that mattered, but her voice. Fortunately for me, most people's voices, including my own, taste like clear, cold water. Like nothing. My grandma's voice tasted and smelled like apple pie. My mom's is flavored faintly of cinnamon, but without odor. Aunt Dot's voice tasted like sour lemon candy and smelled of mold.

It tasted so bad I recoiled the first time she greeted me, which might've had a lot to do with why she didn't like me.

I put my hand over my mouth and nose. When she leaned in close, talking, her breath smelled of minty gum, totally pleasant, but I coughed on the stench of her voice.

"She stinks," I complained to my mom without any tact. "Tastes bad, too!"

Embarrassed, my mother scolded me thoroughly, though later I heard her telling my other aunt that Dot might not smell bad at all, but yes. She sure did stink. It was my grandma who took the time to come find me in the backyard, where I'd been banished until dinnertime. Bundled in my heavy winter coat, I was doing my best to swing on the tire swing, but I hadn't been able to shove my bulk through the hole in the center.

"To me," Grammy said, "she kind of smells like Swiss cheese. Now, I like a nice piece of Swiss now and again, sure. On a nice ham sandwich. But too much of it just gives me a stomachache."

I scuffed my boot on the hard ground. No snow had fallen, but everything was frozen. "I didn't mean to hurt her feelings."

"I know you didn't, sweetheart. Come here." Grammy hugged me close and kissed the top of my head. "But you know that nobody else can smell how she sounds, don't you?"

It was, literally, as though she'd tugged the pull chain of a lightbulb in a dark room. The glare of understanding made me blink. I thought of the times my mom had laughed at my descriptions or dismissed my comparisons of food to sound. My dad, too. Kids in school.

"But you do, Grammy?"

She nodded, solemn. "Ever since I was a little girl. But not everybody does, honey. And they're going to think you're strange if you say anything about it. So…well. Do the best you can, Bethie. With Aunt Dot. Okay?"

"It's so bad," I told her. "When she laughs, my teeth hurt like they're going to fall out, that's how yucky it is."

Grammy laughed hard at that, covering her face. "Oh, my. Well. Certainly don't tell her that. Tell you what. I'll give you some peppermint candy, okay? You can suck on one of those. That usually works for me."

It was a trick that turned out to work for me, too. I'd taken up the habit of never being without a small package of hard candy—in all different flavors. Peppermint masked only some tastes and smells. Butterscotch was better for others. When I discovered sour apple Jolly Ranchers, it was like the heavens opened up and angels sang. That stuff covers up *everything*. I learned to keep quiet about the way voices smelled and tasted and looked, or the way some words had color.

It wasn't until the ninth grade that I learned there was a name for what I had. Mr. Braverman, my science teacher, was a stickler for class rules. He couldn't have been more than twenty-three or so, impossibly old to a fifteen-year-old. He had thick, messy hair the color of milk chocolate and wore glasses that often slid down the bridge of his nose. He favored oxford shirts in pastels, paired with corduroy pants and thick leather belts. He wore the shirtsleeves rolled up to his elbows, and his forearms, the muscles there, the dark hair, distracted me in class. So did his voice, which smelled and tasted like warm, oozing caramel.

The girl who sat next to me, on the other hand, sounded like an old tuna sandwich. I had no other problems with her— we weren't friends, but she was nice enough. Sitting next to her, though, made me nauseous. I used Grammy's trick of sucking on hard candy, but this caused trouble in two ways. First, one piece of candy was never enough to get through class next to her when she was talking—which was a lot, because she'd been assigned as my study partner for every review session. Second, Mr. Braverman did not allow candy in his classroom. And Mr. Braverman, as I've said, was a stickler for the rules.

I wasn't quite aware of my sexuality enough at that point to understand what fascinated me so about his forearms, but I did like him as a teacher. He made life science easy to understand, and more importantly, fun—even though he was strict. Looking back, I think it was because he was so young, because he wanted to be sure he could handle all of us. It was his first year teaching. He wanted to get it right.

Anyway, I was smart enough to keep my candy habit a secret from my teachers, most of whom, like Mr. Braverman, didn't approve of it. But his was the only class in which I really needed it. Of course, he caught me. Of course he was angry and forbade me to do it again.

Of course, I did.

I've never been a rule breaker by nature, and I wasn't deliberately flaunting Mr. Braverman's rules. I just wanted to keep myself from throwing up all over the desk every day. Still, as subtle as I tried to be, it wasn't enough.

He gave me detention.

I'd taken Grammy's other advice to heart, too. Not to talk about my strangeness, so people didn't think I was weird. It hadn't always been easy—for one thing, I couldn't always be sure what was different for me than other people until I experienced it and noticed they didn't. For another, it can be more difficult to hide ecstasy than revulsion, and while I got used to not recoiling in disgust when someone's voice reeked of sweaty armpits, I wasn't always able to keep myself from reacting to the sparks of golden light or sparkling stars that often appeared at random in conjunction with certain colors or shapes or faces.

I didn't tell Mr. Braverman why I needed to keep sucking on peppermints in his class. But even after getting detention,

I kept doing it. And of course, he caught me at it again. He was angrier than he'd been before, and I understand why. I was making him look bad. He yelled and slammed a book on the desk. The class grew quiet, sort of scared. I'm sure most of them were confused.

He gave me detention again, this time for a week. For the first three days, I was under the stern eye of Mrs. Fields, who taught Latin. But the last two days, Mr. Braverman had detention duty. Four to six after school. And on the last day, that final Friday, when I'm sure we were both straining toward the weekend and he was probably regretting not assigning me only two days, he and I were the only ones in the room.

I'd finished all my homework, and I wasn't allowed to read for pleasure, so I'd settled for writing letters in my notebook. My best friend, Andrea, and I had composed a code for passing notes, not a very complicated or even a very good one. We simply wrote nonsense sentences in which the first letter of every word made up the message. We'd gotten so good at it we could string the words together almost as fast as if we'd been writing the sentence itself. I busied myself with telling Andrea about my latest crush on a senior on the wrestling team. She thought it was the grossest sport ever. I couldn't explain to her that the color of his eyes made me feel all swimmy inside.

"Heaven indicates sunshine, never around my evergreen. Iguanas see big rivers inside another noodle," I wrote. *"Affordable nirvana designates illicit leverage on verifiable editions, horrifying irate matrons."*

Caught up in my woe-filled confession, I didn't think much about the scratch of pen on paper. It smelled of ink to me, and that was fine. But from outside came the low, dull roar of someone cutting the grass, and that noise tasted like microwave burritos. The last time I ate them, I got food poisoning. Without thinking about it, not paying attention, I slipped a mint from my pocket and into my mouth. I didn't even look to see if Mr. Braverman was watching, which of course, he was.

I almost choked on the mint when my teacher slammed the flat of his palm on my desk, making my pen skid across the page. I yelped and backed up in my seat, but the desks in this room were attached to the chairs, and I couldn't move more than an inch or so. Mr. Braverman looked furious.

He leaned very, very close. "What the hell is your problem?"

As far as curse words went, it was far from the worst I'd ever heard. Still, coming from a teacher, it was pretty bad. The anger in his voice turned his sweet caramel into something more like scalded milk. Not a terrible smell, but not as delicious as caramel, either.

"I'm sorry—"

He slapped the desk again. "I asked around, Elisabeth. None of your other teachers have such a problem with you. So. Why me?"

I shook my head, trying not to cry. I wanted him to back away, but he kept leaning closer. "I'm sorry, Mr. Braverman, I just…it's the smell!"

He blinked and retreated half an inch. "The smell of what?"

I'd said too much, but couldn't stop now. I didn't look him in the eye. "Just give me another day's detention."

"I don't want to give you detention, Elisabeth. You're a good student. You're doing well in my class. I just…" He straightened and pushed his glasses up on his nose. "You can't eat candy in class, that's all. I could see if it were medically necessary or something, like if you were diabetic. But you're not."

"No." I shook my head.

"The smell of what?" he asked again, softer this time. "The chemicals from the lab?"

"No." I chewed my lower lip. "It's the sound of Theresa's

voice. It…it smells like bad tuna. The only way to really ignore it is to suck on peppermint candy."

For what seemed like forever, he said nothing. "When Theresa talks, you…smell something? You don't hear it?"

"I hear it," I said miserably. "But I smell and taste it, too."

"Do you smell and taste everything you hear?"

I shook my head again. "No. Mostly voices, but not all of them. And not when they're singing to music."

"A cappella?"

"Yes."

"You don't sing in the chorus."

My lip curled, just a little, and I shuddered. "No. Even if the voices are good, it's like…well, it would be like if you really like pizza. You might like it with mushrooms or pineapple or pepperoni and onions, right, but you wouldn't necessarily like it with chocolate pudding and green beans and candy corn."

"I don't like candy corn at all," Mr. Braverman said kindly, and I burst into tears.

He handed me tissues from the box on his desk and watched me carefully as I sobbed into my hands. He didn't say much. It seems to me now that probably Mr. Braverman wasn't quite sure what to do with a semihysterical teenage girl. That, more than my seeming defiance, or the rowdy boys in the back of the class, was probably the most eye-opening experience of his maiden year teaching. He did a decent job with me, though, patting my shoulder sort of awkwardly and not trying to soothe me with lame phrases. Maybe he'd had sisters.

"I'm a freak," I said in a tortured whisper after a minute or so. "I'm sorry, Mr. Braverman, but if I don't eat the candy while I'm sitting next to her, I'm going to barf."

"We don't want that, for sure."

I risked a look at him. "I'm sorry. I like your class. I wasn't trying to be a pain."

He let his butt rest on the edge of the desk across from mine. "You're not a freak, Elisabeth. But I can't believe nobody's ever talked to you about this before."

Grammy had. My parents knew. My brother knew. We just never talked about it.

"Let me show you something. Come here." He beckoned me into his small office, a closet, really, tucked into the back of the room. Floor-to-ceiling shelves overflowed with books and lab supplies. He pulled a thick volume from a shelf and settled it on the desk, flipping through the pages. He tapped one. "Look."

That was the first time I saw the word *synesthesia*. "A neurological condition in which stimulation of one sensory or cognitive pathway leads to automatic, involuntary experiences in a second." I read the definition. I looked at him.

"It's a neurological condition. Probably genetic," he offered.

I thought of my grandmother. "I inherited it?"

"Yes. Most likely." Mr. Braverman motioned for me to move closer until we stood shoulder to shoulder in the cramped space. "Look, Elisabeth. Here are charts and lists of all the different ways the people in this book manifest their different...well, I hate to say symptoms, because that makes it sound like a disease. And it's not, really."

I wiped my nose with a tissue and leaned over the book, then looked at him. This close I could see that behind the glasses, he had pale blue eyes framed by thick black lashes. Suddenly, I felt swimmier than my senior varsity wrestler crush had ever made me. Small gold sparkles like stars flashed and twinkled along the arches of his eyebrows before they faded. I focused on his arm, leaning on the desk beside me. That was no help.

"This person lists tasting shapes." I laughed a little. "Weird."

I ran my fingertip down the columns, skimming the information. Mr. Braverman tapped on a photograph. Underneath it was a small chart showing what colors corresponded to which numbers. That person also saw letters as having personalities and gender—*A* was feminine, for example. I couldn't grasp that.

On the next page, I started to read aloud. "'Mary Sheeran says the colors are like watching fireworks, alternating bursts of pattern and light that expand and contract along with the rhythm of music.'"

I knew just what that was like, though mine was connected with facial features. The curve of brow or jaw, the lift of a smile. "For Mary, alcohol intensifies the experience, as does sexual activity. She says during or-orgasm…"

I stuttered on the words, blushing hard. Something palpable hovered between us, and I was afraid to look at him. Not worried that I'd see something nobody else did, but that he would see something in me I didn't want revealed.

Mr. Braverman broke the uncomfortable silence by closing the book with a solid thud and pushing it back on the shelf. "Everyone has something unique about them, Elisabeth. I wish you'd just told me about the candy, instead of acting like you were doing it just to be bad."

"My grammy told me not to tell anyone about it. That people would think I was crazy."

"Well," Mr. Braverman said, "you're not."

Chapter Fifteen

Since that day in Mr. Braverman's class, I've never forgotten that Mary Sheeran, that lucky bitch, literally sees fireworks when she comes. Orgasms are pretty spectacular all on their own, but to see bursting and shifting patterns of color—that's always seemed like an extra bit of luck. And now it's happened to me.

It doesn't escape me that of all the lovers I've ever had, Will's the first to make me come so hard I literally saw stars. I look at his photo on the computer screen, not even embarrassed to be cyberstalking him, because it's been over a week since the day he took me to MOMA. I haven't heard from him since, not an email or a text. And fuck him, I left his apartment with him still coating the back of my throat, so he can very fucking well text me first. I'm not going to go chasing after him as if I have no self-control.

He has a Connex account, but it's for his business and not personal, so it's not set to private. I scroll through his pages of pictures, most of them his work or the book covers that have featured his photos. There are a few of him, though.

In one he wears a dark shirt, skinny dark tie, his hair a mess, all pushed in front of his ears and over his forehead, a little slick with sweat. The lines at the corners of his eyes are very distinct in this shot, maybe because of the light or because he's squinting. Not smiling. He's not smiling in any of the pictures, and I wonder if it's because he wasn't happy in any of them or if it's because, as a photographer, he knows that smiling makes his eyes squinch up like that.

I love the way he looks when he smiles.

In this picture he's pointing at something out of range, a cigarette held between his first and middle fingers. Brow furrowed. Familiar black Converse sneakers. And oh, there, that braided leather belt. I know that belt, the length of it, the feel of the leather in my palm. The click of the metal buckle as it's undone.

My clit pulses. I shift in my desk chair, crossing my legs. Uncrossing. I'm wearing a pair of yoga pants I picked up on sale, thinking I was going to start doing something crazy like Zumba. Be like the wives of Ross's coworkers, speed-walking around the block listening to recipe podcasts. I should've saved the money and bought a couple cartons of high-end ice cream with the money. At least I'd have enjoyed them.

The fabric, though, is clinging, soft and so thin the first tickle of my fingertip over the bump of my clit is almost as if I'm touching myself bare. Almost better, since the fabric barrier blunts the sensation enough to be teasing. I rub in slow circles as I study another picture of him. Someone caught him in profile, a half hint of a smile, his gaze bright. He has one hand around the waist of a tall blonde in red lipstick, both holding sweating drinks of clear fluid. The flash is reflected in the ice cubes.

They're lovers. He and that woman, at least in the moment captured by this picture. I can see it in the way his fingers curl so slightly, denting the material of her sheer blouse. How she leans into him, how her gaze has fallen on his face. Her mouth is open a little, showing a glimpse of white teeth and pink tongue, as if she's getting ready to lick her lips at the sight of him. I understand completely. I can't even be jealous of anything except maybe how lovely she is, lithe and blonde and young, and that she had that moment with him and I've had hardly any.

Did he take her home that night to his apartment? Did he put her on that couch? No. His bed. Did he push up her dress, run his fingers over her long, lean thighs? Did he slide inside her cunt?

Up and down, my fingers press. I'm wet all the way through the scant lace of my panties. The yoga pants. My head falls back as I rub, rub, rub. So close already, just from thinking of Will fucking another woman. I shouldn't like that, should I? Maybe it should even make me jealous, but instead I imagine him pushing her onto a bed, the sheets a tangled mess, the pillows scattered.

He tugs up her dress and finds her bare beneath. A woman like that would keep her pussy smooth. My fingers slide past the waistband of my pants at last, beyond the lace, to stroke the soft curls between my legs. I groom, but I'm never bald. My clit's a hard, tight knot under my fingertip. All I have to do is press, just a little, and the walls of my pussy clench. One finger slips inside my heat. My body bears down on the intrusion.

I think of him pushing her legs apart. Crawling up the bed to get to her cunt with his mouth and hands. His tongue, the slick, hot swipe of it against her flesh.

Oh, fuck.

My back arches, my head pressed to the back of my chair. Both hands, now, one with my fingers deep inside, the other lightly pinching my clit in time to the rocking of my hips. I haven't touched myself this way in a long time, so long I can't remember the last time desire hit me so hard in the middle of the day that I had to relieve it.

I want Will between my legs. I want his tongue on me, his fingers inside, stroking upward while he sucks my clit. I want, I want, I want. At the base of it, that is what this is.

Desire.

The leather of my chair creaks as I rock against it. Soft, breathy moans escape me. Then some a little louder.

Everything inside me goes tight, tangling and twisted. When I come, I taste him. Not my synesthesia, but true memory, and it floods me. All my muscles twitch and jerk, until at last, spent, I melt into my chair with my arms and legs sprawled. I'm coated in sweat, tangy when I lick my lips. My hair is stuck to my forehead and small wisps cling to my cheeks. I feel as if I've run a mile with hungry zombies hot on my trail.

I'm starving.

"Mrs. Amblin?"

Startled, I spin in my chair, face even hotter than it was a minute before. "Maria. Hi."

Our weekly housekeeper pauses awkwardly in the doorway. "I wasn't expecting you to be home today."

"Oh. Yeah, I'm working from home." I carefully do not turn around to close the Connex window, still showing the picture of Will and the blonde. I rub my fingers along the soft fabric of my pants, glad I took my hands out of my panties. "I was going to work out."

Maria has been with our family for a long time. Now she tilts her head a tiny bit to look around my office. It used to be the smallest bedroom, the spare room, but since we finished the basement with a guest room and full bath, I took it over. Ross has the house's official "office" on the first floor, and yet he never works from home.

"You need me to do anything in here?"

"No, thanks."

We look at each other.

"You all right?" Maria asks.

"Me? Fine." I give her my best broad smile. "How are you? How's your granddaughter?"

Maria is always happy to talk about her granddaughter, and today's no different. She chatters while I casually shut down my laptop and lead her out of the room. In the kitchen, she disappears into the laundry room while I pour myself a tall glass of orange juice and gulp it so greedily it makes my stomach hurt. I could've left the glass in the sink for Maria—Ross would've. But I rinse it thoroughly and put it in the dish rack.

My knees are still weak. I want a shower. I need the kiss of sunshine, though, the caress of fresh air. Outside, I pull catalogs and bills from the mailbox and wave at my neighbor Sandra from across the street. She's weeding her flower beds. I nod at a couple walking their dog as they pass, and send another wave toward Ed from next door as he gets out of his car.

If I sank down onto the green, soft grass in my front yard right now, if I rolled in it and pressed my face to it, what would any of them do? Would they run to help me up, feel my forehead, call an ambulance? My husband? Or would they watch me wriggle and writhe without a word?

My world has changed. Upside down and inside out. I am not the woman who brought macaroni salad to the neighborhood potluck picnic last year, or the one who passed out Halloween treats in a witch's cap and pointy shoes. I'm not the one who picked out this oversize mailbox so the mail carrier wouldn't have to leave packages on the front porch, or the one who chose the color of these shutters and the front door when it came time to paint them.

I am someone different now, and I don't quite know who.

Inside, Maria gestures at my purse on the counter. "It was ringing."

Expecting Ross or one of the girls, I thumb the screen. One recent call. One missed call. One voice mail.

Will.

I delete the message without listening to it.

Chapter Sixteen

Saturday is laundry day. For me, anyway. For Ross it's golf and beer with his buddies day. It used to matter more when the girls were small and I was overwhelmed with ferrying them where they needed to go, when I needed a break. Now the break is Ross spending the entire day away from the house instead of hovering over me while I try to read or do anything else.

I could have Maria do the laundry, but it's been hard enough for me to allow her to clean our bathroom. Having her handle and fold my underwear is just too much. So, though it's not a task I enjoy, it is one I've refused to delegate, and therefore, one about which I try not to complain.

Ross has no problems about complaining. He's very particular about the state of his whites. They have to be washed separately, using a special extra stain treatment, and sometimes even soaked for a while first in a bucket of diluted bleach. He only wears white business shirts and will throw them out if they're not pristine.

I don't mind going to the extra effort for his laundry—so long as he separates the whites from the rest of his laundry. Which he consistently doesn't do. Today, looking at the jumble of shirts and socks and briefs among the rest of the clothes, I can't face it. I cannot sift through his dirty clothes, I cannot turn the pockets inside out and check for change or receipts or anything else.

Everything goes in the washer together in double handfuls, shoved until I can't fit anything else. I add detergent, choose the temperature. My fingers fumble on the washing machine's controls, as if I've forgotten how to use it.

All I can think about is Will.

This is me, on my knees, where I want to be. Hard floor pressing my skin, maybe I'll even bruise, just a little. That's okay. Later I'll look at the bruises and remember what I've done.

He has the most beautiful cock I've ever seen, but I haven't taken him inside my mouth. Not yet. I want to take my time. Make this last. I want to measure and map him with my hands and tongue and teeth before I consume him. I want to taste and tease him. When I slide his cock into my mouth to nudge the back of my throat, I want him to already be weak-kneed and throbbing, ready to spill.

When I look up, he looks down. His hand has found my hair; his fingers tangle but don't pull. I put mine over his and tuck them in deeper. I encourage him to tug. To push my head, just a little, toward the sweetness of that cock. I want him to beg me to put it in my mouth, and in another minute...

"Please," he says. *"Please just—"*

The house phone rings, pulling me out of my fantasy. I don't answer it. I blink and shake my head to chase away the images, but I can't manage to rid my mouth of his remembered flavor. My mouth is dry, but even gulping orange juice straight from the bottle can't quench my thirst.

I try to think if I've ever wanted someone this way, and can't remember it if I have. I take myself off to the den with the book I've been trying to read forever, and settle into the couch with a glass of iced tea, and my iPod shuffling up songs I'd forgotten I had. I read the same page four times before I give up and let my head fall back against the cushions. I stare at the ceiling. There are cobwebs.

I open my mouth and slide him in. All the way, balls-deep. My tongue caresses the head, my teeth scrape, just gently. Then out, my hand at the base, sucking a little harder on the tip while he shudders and mutters my name, and his fingers go tight in my hair, this time hard enough to hurt. Just a little.

I want it to hurt, just a little.

His ass is resting on the edge of the desk. His pants around his ankles. My hand's between my legs, fingers in my panties, and I'm wet and slick. My clit's hard under my fingertips. I pinch it gently, making my hips buck, and for a second or two I lose my concentration on his cock because the pleasure in my cunt is just too much....

The phone rings again, and this time I twist to look at the handset on the side table next to the couch. It's Kat, so I snatch it up and connect just before she gets sent to voice mail. "Hi, honey."

"Hi, Mom. You're home. I've been calling your cell. And I called here earlier, but you didn't answer."

I turned off my cell so I would stop checking it obsessively. "What's up?"

"Just wanted to see how you were doing."

I'd spoken with her on my birthday, but not since. This wasn't unusual. Jac's the one who keeps in almost constant touch, texts, phone calls, emails, posts on my barely used Connex wall. Kat is more reticent and independent.

It's impossible for my daughter to know what I've done, but that's the first thought that springs to my mind at her question. How am I doing? I've been better. Then again, I suppose I've been worse.

"I'm fine. What's going on with you? Everything okay?"

She sounds quiet when she answers, but not upset. "Yep.

Everything's fine. Just trying to finish up everything here. Did you have a good birthday?"

"It was fine. Thanks for the gift card. You didn't have to do that."

"Did you like it? What did you get?" She sounds brighter now.

I list the music I'd downloaded so far. A couple songs I'd been thinking about but didn't own. I love music, but it can be hard for me to find songs that don't smell or taste bad. Kat understands, while Jac does not. We talk about music and books for a few more minutes, then Katherine says abruptly, "How old were you when you got married?"

"Twenty-two."

"Did you think that was too young?"

"I didn't at the time," I tell her. "But now? Yes. I think that maybe it was too young."

"So…why did you get married?"

I laugh. "Because I was in love with your dad, and he asked me, and it seemed like a good idea at the time."

More silence from her. Something is…maybe not wrong. But it's not right.

"What's going on, Kittykat?"

At least I've made her laugh, even though I know she hates the nickname. "Nothing. Just thinking about things, like what I'm going to do when I'm finished with school. Life stuff."

"Ah. Life stuff." Silence for a few breaths. "Anything you need to talk about?"

"Not really." She sighs. "I'm okay, Mom. Just a lot to think about."

"And you're my thinker." We both laugh. She starts to tell me about a video link Jac sent her, and the conversation leaves serious behind.

We disconnect and I spend another hour or so going from

link to link on the internet, laughing at the *Wrong Number Texts* and *Damn You Autocorrect* blogs until my stomach hurts. It's been a while since I spent the day doing nothing of importance, and it feels lazy and indulgent, but also somehow necessary. Relaxed, humming, I sort the piles of magazines and mail that never seem to be filed.

I find the envelope Will sent me, and the song I was singing lightly under my breath eases into a sigh. I let my fingers trace the letters of my name in the address, seeing the soft shades of gold and brown and orange my name has always evoked. The picture needs a frame, and it will need a place to hang, and right now I have neither, so the envelope gets wrapped up carefully and tucked into the basket I'll fill with clean clothes and carry upstairs.

I've left the laundry go too long in the dryer. Most of our clothes get hung, but there are a few things, T-shirts and pajamas mostly, that get folded. In our bedroom, I press my face to the still-warm and wrinkled clothes I've tossed onto the bed. They smell fresh, they smell clean, but it's nothing like clothes that have been hung on a line to dry in the sunshine. When I was growing up, my mother always hung the laundry in the backyard. All the neighbors did. The worst trouble we kids ever got in was when we played "maze" in the back-and-forth lines of hanging sheets on laundry day, marking the clean fabric with streaks from our Popsicle-stained fingers. The smell of sun-dried laundry is irrevocably tied to the sound of my mother's muffled voice singing her favorite Simon and Garfunkel or Bob Dylan songs around the clothespins in her mouth.

Will's envelope rests on my plum-colored bedspread until I pick it up and think of where to put it until I can frame it. Or to keep it safe if I decide never to look at it again. I can't stop myself from opening it once more, sliding the photo out carefully, with the tips of my fingers against the thin white border.

It's not the heart-shaped rock or the black-and-white scheme or even the touches of swirling color that make me smell the ocean. It's the thought of Will. His name. His eyes. I close mine, rocked suddenly by the rush and whoosh of waves and the spray of foam on my cheeks. Tactile, sensual memory that has become somehow irrevocably linked to no longer just the sound of his voice, but the thought of him.

"I'm home," Ross says from the doorway.

Embarrassed, still touching the picture, I turn as I slide it back into its manila prison.

"What's that?"

"Oh. Something one of Naveen's artists sent me." I hold up the envelope as though I'm offering to show him, because I know my husband. He doesn't care. Won't look. Mention art to him and his eyes glaze over. I put the envelope carefully into the top drawer of my dresser, where I keep other important papers I never look at. "How was golf?"

I don't care about golf any more than he wants to talk about art, but he talks anyway, rattling off something about par and birdies, details I'm not paying attention to. Still talking, he heads for the shower. Minutes later he's out, towel around his waist, hair dripping. Still talking.

I am overcome with the need to touch him, to somehow anchor myself to this man. We have made children together. We have spent years building a life, a very good life, and I do not want to lose it.

"Come here," I say in a voice not much like my own. "Kiss me."

Ross looks faintly surprised and doesn't move from his place at the dresser, where he's rooting around for a pair of briefs. "What?"

"Come and kiss me." I crook my finger and walk backward toward the bed. A little hair toss, a bit of a grin, a sparkle. I make myself shiny for him.

I remember when we'd spend an hour kissing and touching before we got down to fucking, but that doesn't happen today. My husband kisses me roughly, too much tongue, his hands groping and squeezing too hard. His cock rises while water still beads on his skin.

I want him to undress me, spend some time. I want him to kiss my mouth and throat and work his fingers between my legs until I can't stand it anymore. That doesn't happen, either.

Ross gestures. "Take your clothes off."

It's easy enough to do, though not very sexy, since I'm wearing comfy around-the-house clothes. Naked, I lie back on the bed next to the pile of unfolded laundry as he crawls toward me. I think he's going to kiss me, but instead he reaches over me to pull open the drawer on my nightstand.

"Use your toy." He presses my vibrator into my hand. "It's faster."

It's small and smooth and curved to fit my palm. It could be exciting and erotic to use my vibrator while we fuck—because let's be honest, I think, as Ross kneels in front of me, jerking his cock to get it hard enough to fit inside me, we're not about to make anything like love. It could be sexy, but he wants me to use it so he doesn't have to work as hard to get me off.

I've been feeding myself sex thoughts all day long, so it wouldn't be that hard for me to come. But of course, Ross doesn't know that. I press the button on the vibe and slide it against my clit. The buzz is almost too strong; it makes my hips buck. When Ross moves over me, ready to push inside, I put a hand on his chest to hold him back.

"Wait." I was ready before, ready all day long, thinking about another man, but now I need more time.

I can remember how watching Ross stroke himself used to turn me on, but it's not working now. He's paying attention to his dick, not to me. He keeps looking at the clock.

I get on my knees, cheek pressed to the mattress so I can hold the vibe on my clit as Ross pushes inside me from behind. I'm wet, and yet he still sticks and stretches before he's all the way in. I don't complain. I push back against him, wanting him to fuck harder. A little faster. I want to be in sync with him the way we used to be, when we spent hours making love, and it didn't have to be a gymnastics show.

My orgasm is fragile and elusive, slipping away. I'm not going to come, not even with the vibrator, and while there have been plenty of times Ross and I have had sex that I didn't have an orgasm, I've never felt this desperate about it. He thrusts faster. He's getting closer; I know him so well I can hear it in the shift of his breathing and the way he groans, by how tight his fingers are gripping my hips. Usually these signs trigger my own pleasure, but not today. Nothing is working today.

"Wait," I breathe again.

He slows, but it's not enough for me, and I guess it's too much for him, because he lasts at that pace only for a few seconds before moving faster again. The vibe slides against me, and it feels good, but not good enough. I turn it off and push up on my hands, relieved to get the pressure off my neck from my face pressing into the mattress.

I thought he was going to finish, but he keeps going. We move together. And finally, gradually, the pleasure builds again. I relax into it, both of us working toward the finish.

And then Ross presses his thumb on my asshole.

It could be a mistake, except that he does it again a second later, this time pushing harder. No more orgasm for me, not even close. I jerk at the intrusion, breaking the rhythm.

Surely he should know better, right? Certainly he should remember all the other times he's tried to shove something up my ass, and I said I didn't like it? He couldn't possibly have forgotten the times—more than once, because I wanted to be a good sport—that I let him try to fuck me in the back door and how much I hated it?

"Jesus fucking Christ, Ross!" I cry when he pushes against my asshole again. "What the fuck?"

My writhing and protests send him off. He grunts and thrusts and pounds me so hard I lose my balance and fall forward onto my face. Graceless. Irritated. And definitely not aroused.

"Some women," he says when we're disentangling ourselves and I'm reaching for a handful of tissues to clean up with, "like that."

"I don't like it."

"I thought you might," he says.

"What the hell gave you that idea? All the other times you've tried it and I've said no way? Stay the hell out of my ass, Ross." I'd laugh, but I'm too annoyed. "Christ."

"Sorry for trying to please you," Ross says in that pouty, put-out tone that tastes to me like pickle juice.

"Pay attention to me for once!" I shout. "Just...listen when I tell you something."

"I listen to you all the time."

"Well, apparently, you don't hear me." I get out of bed on knees gone weak not with passion, but anger. In the bathroom, I pee, I wash my hands, I splash my face with water to relieve the burning in my eyes.

In the bedroom, Ross has put on briefs, while I have to find my scattered clothes, somehow lost although I didn't toss them aside in anything like wild abandon. He's in my way, digging through the pile of laundry on the bed. He doesn't fold any of it, just tosses it aside while he looks for what he wants. Instead of waiting for him to move out of the way, I go instead to my dresser to pull on a clean pair of panties and a T-shirt.

"Did you wash all this stuff together?"

I turn to see him holding up a white dress shirt and a fleecy pullover, one in each hand. "Yes."

There's nothing on the white shirt but a few strands of fuzz from the fleece, but Ross stares at it as if it's full of holes. "It'll have to go through the wash again."

"What?" I take it from his hand, look it over. I pluck the fuzz from the sleeve and a bit from the collar and shove it back toward him. "There. All fine."

"I thought I asked you to wash my whites separately," Ross says. His voice isn't pickle juice now, it's that softer, wrinkly tone, that patronizing and falsely calm voice he uses when he's angry and trying to act as if he's above that sort of thing.

"And I told you that I'd be happy to, so long as you separated them from everything else."

He stares at me as if I'm speaking a foreign language. "I don't understand what the big deal is."

"The big deal," I tell him, "is that if you're going to ask me to do something for you, and I ask you to make it easy for me to do it, it would be great if you actually did."

"Why can't you just do it for me?" Ross asks.

There are always choices. Peace we keep with words we don't say. Things we don't do. But losing my fury just then isn't a choice, it's not something I decide. It simply leaks away from me, replaced by a bone-deep despair and utter exhaustion. I have no words. I have no actions. I have nothing left for him, and I push him gently to the side to get at the laundry on the bed. I sort through it, pulling the whites and tossing them into an empty basket while he watches. They fill barely a quarter of the space, and washing them again will be a waste of resources and my time, but I can't fight with him about it again. If I do, I will say things I don't want to say and do things I don't want to do.

If marriage is compromise and working together, sometimes it's also just biting the fuck out of your tongue to keep yourself from ending it all over a basket of laundry.

Chapter Seventeen

"It could've been worse," Andrea says. She's been my best friend for so long I think I know what she's going to say, but she surprises me. "At least he was having some kind of sex with you, even if it was shitty."

I pluck at the bread stick in the basket between us and give her a look. "Really? You think shitty sex is better than none? I don't know about that."

"Jonathan hasn't had sex with me in four months," my friend says flatly.

I don't know what to say. Andrea shrugs and punches her salad with her fork until it submits to being eaten. She chews and swallows, washing it down with iced tea.

"He can't keep it up," she adds.

"Ouch. I'm sorry." I ordered a half sandwich, but have no appetite for it or the soup that came with it. Will hasn't called back since the day I deleted his voice mail. I was an idiot for not listening to it. I can't stop thinking about what it might've said. But I focus on my friend now. "Wow. Can he take something for it?"

"He won't." Andrea lifts her chin, though her bottom lip wobbles. "He says it's just a passing thing, stress from work, or that he's tired. Or that I need to lose a few pounds. If I worked out more, he'd be more turned on."

"What?" Outraged, I slap the table. She's thinner than I've ever seen her. It also explains the salad. "What a dick!"

She shrugs again, not meeting my eyes. "I put on some weight. It happens. Everything gets harder when you're over forty."

"Except Jonathan's dick, apparently," I say before I can stop myself, and feel instantly terrible about making fun of what is obviously not a humorous situation.

We didn't get to be best friends because we don't understand each other, though. Andrea looks first surprised, then begins to laugh. In another minute we're both cackling like grackles, turning heads at the other tables, but we don't care. It feels good to laugh like this, so hard we both end up in tears.

"I tried to be understanding." She wipes her eyes. "But it makes me feel like crap, Elisabeth. I mean…I've tried everything except wrapping myself in plastic wrap and greeting him at the door with a bacon sandwich."

I twirl my spoon through the soup I don't want to eat. "You shouldn't have to. Have you at least tried to get him to the doctor? Maybe there's something else going on?"

She shrugs. "He won't go. He's a stubborn asshole. His dad died of a heart attack when he was just a few years older than Jon is now. I think he's just trying to ignore anything that could be bad."

"Like that ever works." Impulsively, I reach for her hand to squeeze it. "I'm sorry, honey, that sucks. A lot."

"Yeah. It does. I haven't had an orgasm in, like, a year. Even when he was still sleeping with me, it wasn't very good." She stabs her salad again, and I can't blame her. I'd murder more than lettuce if I hadn't come in that long.

I'm surprised enough to blurt, "You don't take care of yourself?"

I've known this woman since we were virgins who thought French kissing was going to be gross. (Sometimes, it totally is.) We've shared stories about our periods, childbirth, boyfriends, husbands, our hopes and dreams and fears. There isn't much I could think of that Andrea and I haven't dissected and torn apart over the years, but all at once I realize that we haven't ever talked about masturbation. I assumed she does it, but the look on her face tells me I'm way off base.

"Andrea!"

She shakes her head, looking embarrassed. "I…just…no. I just don't do that."

"Why?" As far as I know, she's not religious or ashamed of sex or anything like that. She's certainly had orgasms.

"It just doesn't work for me. I mean, I've tried it, but it's just not the same when I do it myself." She makes a familiar face, the same one she'd make if I tried to get her to drink straight tequila.

It's not nice to laugh at her, but her expression tips me into a giggle. "That's terrible!"

"Right?" It's good to see her smile. Better than the way she looked when we first got here. "I'm going crazy!"

"Don't you have a vibrator?"

Another embarrassed grin. "No."

"Andrea. You have to get one." I lean forward to keep the conversation between us.

She gives me a raised brow. "Yours didn't make it any better with Ross that last time, did it?"

"Ugh. No. But when I use it alone, it's great." I use it alone a lot more than I do with my husband.

"I like…you know. I need something—" she makes a discreet hand motion "—inside."

Just like that, we're laughing again. Snort-laughing this time, hard enough to turn heads. We laugh so hard the waiter comes over to ask us if we need anything, and all either of us can do is shake our heads and wave him away.

"You can get something for that!" I whisper through my guffaws. "Check Google!"

Andrea's laughter fades. She wipes her eyes with her napkin, but they still glisten. "It still wouldn't be the same, Elisabeth."

My heart breaks for her a little, and new words slip out before I can really think about what I'm saying. "So, find yourself a man."

Neither of us is laughing now. Andrea is quiet for a moment, toying with her fork but no longer eating. I cover the silence by taking a long, long drink of water.

"I could never," she says finally. "I mean…first of all, who'd have me?"

I've never had much of an opinion about Jonathan one way or another, but right now I hate him for making my best friend feel she's not fuckable. "You would have no trouble finding someone. None."

She sighs. "Sure. Right. But even if I did, I could never cheat on Jonathan. It would be wrong. I'd feel too bad."

What can I say to that? It's not as if I disagree with her. Just a few months ago, if we'd been sitting across from each other like this and she'd been the one to suggest such a thing to me, I'd have responded the same way.

This time when the waiter comes back, to ask if he can bring me a box for the lunch I haven't touched, I shake my head. "No, thanks. But we'll take a dessert menu."

"Oh, no," my friend begins, but I wave her to silence.

"Shush. If ever there was a day when we needed chocolate lava cake and a shot of Bailey's in our coffee, it's today. And lunch is my treat."

She protests, but I insist. I've missed her so much, it's terrible and unbelievable we let it go so long. Over cake and coffee, she tells me about her job, boring but with great benefits, and how she could get a promotion if she applied for it, but there'd be too much travel to Europe involved.

"Wha-a-at?" I let the word drag out, the Bailey's and laughter giving me a little boost. "Are you crazy? How cool would it be to get paid to visit Italy? Andrea, c'mon! Your kids are grown. What's stopping you?"

Her look tells me everything. I feel awkward. She shrugs.

"I just don't like to be away from him," she says. "Even with the problems. I know you'll probably think I'm crazy for that, too. But I hate it when I have to go to sleep without him. When he's gone on business, I miss him like crazy, and that's me being in my own house. I can't imagine what it would be like to miss him and be homesick, too."

I wish I could say I understand, but I don't. I nod anyway, because how can I say out loud that I don't miss my husband when he goes away? That, in fact, I've come to prefer it when he's gone?

"But you," Andrea says suddenly. "We've talked all about me. What about you? What's going on with you? How were the girls' graduations?"

"Both of them told us not to come. And they didn't want a big party, either, since both of them had to be at work right away after graduation." I'd wanted to have them both come home for a weekend, but it hadn't worked out.

Andrea's kids are a few years younger, still in college. She shakes her head. "I can't believe they're old enough to be out of college."

"That means we're old," I tell her, though sitting here I feel as if we're both still sixteen, scribbling notes to each other in class. "Remember our code?"

For a second she looks blank, then slaps a hand to her forehead. "Oh. Wow. Yes. Holy cow, that was so long ago. How did you remember it?"

"I guess I've been remembering a lot of things." I can't keep myself from sounding sad.

Andrea gestures for the waiter. "Bring wine."

We sit in that restaurant for another few hours while I tell her about my frustrations with Ross. They are stupid things. I know it. Dishes in the sink, boots in the wrong size.

"I couldn't even exchange or return them," I tell her. The wine has made me eloquent with my hands, if not my words. "He got them on clearance!"

"He tried," she offers helpfully.

"He tried," I agree. "But he did not listen."

Andrea is silent for a moment or so. Then she reaches to squeeze my hand. "It will get better, Elisabeth. You're just in a rut. Maybe you should go away together, the two of you. Or try a date night…?"

I would have to plan a trip. A night out. With his schedule it's practically impossible to do either, and when it comes right down to it, I realize something I won't admit to her—I don't want to. I do not want to go away for the weekend with Ross. I do not want a date night.

I want to tell her about Will so much. I want to unburden myself, not of the guilt I still don't feel, but of the anguish over not having listened to his message. I want to tell her everything, not to lift it from my shoulders, but so that I can remember and relive it. But because Andrea is my friend and I love her, because I don't want to put her in a position where she'd feel uncomfortable, I seal my mouth on my secret.

"Yes," I tell her. "A date night. Sounds good."

We part with hugs and promises to get together soon, though I think we both know it will probably be another six months before we do. In the last moment before we walk in opposite directions to catch our separate trains, my best friend since forever grabs me in a last-minute hug.

"Thanks," she says against my cheek. "For listening."

"Anytime." I squeeze her hard. "Of course."

Andrea pulls away with her eyes bright again, and I hate that she's so sad. For that matter, I hate that I am. "You know I'm there for you, right? If you need to talk about anything, ever."

"I know." And my mouth opens again to spill out everything that happened with Will, how I can't stop thinking about him. But I remember what she said in the restaurant, and I know there are some things even best friends can't share. "Same here. If you need to talk, keep me updated, whatever. I'll be thinking about you. It's going to be okay," I tell her, in a burst of optimism that feels utterly fake.

She makes that tasting-tequila face again. "It's just sex, Elisabeth. Nobody ever died without it."

It's not the lack of sex that's killing her, it's feeling unloved and unattractive and unfuckable, and I'm so angry at her husband that I'd gladly kick him right in his inoperative junk right now.

"We take our cars to the shop when they need the tires rotated. We get our hair done when we want to look nice, get massages when our muscles are sore, and go to the chiropractor when our backs hurt. Why the hell can't we go somewhere and just get laid when we need it?" I say, suddenly vehement without meaning to sound so harsh. "I mean, it's just sex."

"But it never would be," Andrea says. "Just sex, I mean. It would always become something else."

"Why?" I demand. "Why does it have to?"

Andrea makes that face again. "I don't know. But it would. For me, I know it would."

"Maybe not."

She laughs and hugs me again, shaking her head. "It would be disaster."

"Maybe," I tell her, "it would be a beautiful disaster."

"No matter how pretty it is," Andrea says, "it would still be disaster," and then we both have to run to catch our trains.

On the way home, I stare at the passing scenery and wish I hadn't had so much to drink. My stomach is upset now. My head aches. My mouth is dry. I close my eyes but that makes it worse.

I pull my phone from my purse and thumb open Will's contact information. I don't have a picture stored for him. Just his number.

And then, because I'm stupid, I type in a text. My brain's too fuzzy to make a sentence out of nonsense words. All I can manage is three letters, one for each word I want to say.

I M Y

And though I wait and wait, Will doesn't text me back.

Chapter Eighteen

Other friendships had come and gone in college, but the one I'd forged with Naveen that first day always stayed. He drove me crazy. We fought, sometimes like brother and sister. Sometimes like the lovers we'd never quite managed to become. He told me he loved me one night while he was drunk and sick, in between heaves. I told him I loved him over the phone, when we were apart for the summer and the boy I'd been dating dumped me without warning.

Tempestuous. That was the best way to describe our relationship. Up and down, love and hate, lust and affection. Yet it endured through boyfriends and girlfriends, breakups and makeups.

He'd begun college a year ahead of me but had failed a few classes, which meant we were slated to graduate the same year. It was a tough one for me because I was determined to graduate "on time" even though it meant carrying an extra-large class load, including a killer accounting class that threatened to destroy my GPA. I was constantly on edge about my grades and also about my relationship with Ross, which had been steady for close to a year, but which had recently gone "on a break." Naveen, for the first time in all the four years I'd known him, was without a girlfriend of any kind.

We'd kissed a few times over the years, usually after we'd been drinking. We'd shared a bed more than once, though we'd never even come close to having sex. He was my best friend, my rock, the one man I could count on to make me feel beautiful when I needed to. And finally, after four years of on-and-off flirting and drama, Naveen asked me to be his girlfriend.

We had been drinking, but weren't drunk. We were in Naveen's room with the lights off, squeezed into his narrow bed with The Cure playing on repeat. Finals loomed on the horizon. Then graduation. And after that…neither of us was quite sure.

"But I want to be with you, Betts," he'd said. The cotton-candy of his voice soothed me. His hand had been warm in mine. "At least try it, right? Give it a shot."

I was anxious about my grades and my future. I'd been waiting forever, it seemed, for Naveen to ask me for something more than the hookups I'd always managed to turn down. And now that he'd asked me…

"I don't know what to say."

His mouth had brushed my ear, then my lips. The kiss got deeper as he put his hand flat on my belly, but poised to move lower. "What is there to say? We're meant to be together. C'mon, Betts. Let's do it."

"Be together?"

"Yes." There was a short silence. "Let's fuck. Please. I want you."

The thought of it was exciting and scary, the end of something I'd come to cherish. Even if it meant the beginning of something else, I couldn't say yes. So instead, I told him I needed time to think. I got out of bed and left him there, and a week later he greeted me at the door of his room with another girl behind him and a smirk on his face that to this day I haven't truly been able to forgive.

We never talked about that night in his room when he told me he wanted us to be together. Naveen flirts with me all the time. He's good to my kids and polite to Ross. He's made me a part of his family, given me a job. He's still my best friend.

And he still hasn't forgiven me for what I'd said to him about Francesca.

It's been months now since his confession, and he has barely talked to me about anything but work. Today he's meeting with a small group of women who all seem to be related. They want "something sexy but not trashy" for someone's apartment. They all look a little trashy to me—lots of makeup and jewelry, high heels with designer jeans. Fake nails. Naveen, of course, is in his glory. Practically preening. I wonder what the love of his life would think if she could see him flirting and trying to upsell these women who wouldn't know art if it gave them a boob job. Then I remember he told me that was how they'd met, when Francesca came in to buy something. Maybe he's auditioning a replacement.

I've been used to my friend's flirting for so many years that it had stopped bothering me, but today it sets my teeth on edge. It could be hormones, my body hurtling me without brakes toward menopause, and in the meantime turning me upside down in a maelstrom of what Ross liked to call "lady emotions." It could be the lack of sleep I've had for the past week or so. I haven't been able to fall asleep, and when I do, my dreams have been bad.

Or, I admit uneasily, as I watch Naveen drop a wink to one of the women and let his hand rest way too low on another's back, his fingertips skimming the top of her low-slung jeans, it could be jealousy.

He leans too close to murmur something in an ear, and I

can't watch anymore. I get up from the desk to close my door. Hard. I need my friend, but I know that makes me nothing more than selfish. If I didn't have my own burdens, I'd still be letting him stew without a second thought.

He's the only person in my life who would understand this, though. The only one I'd tell. I couldn't even reveal this to Andrea, my best friend since forever.

I don't answer the knock on my door, but Naveen opens it, anyway. He holds out a thick envelope and a package tied with brown string. "Can you deliver this for me?"

"Don't you have a service for that?"

His dark eyes glint, but he doesn't smile. "It's some things for Will. Prints that didn't sell, and a couple of framed shots he's decided to keep."

Does Naveen know? I say nothing. He puts the packages on my desk.

"I'll give you his address," Naveen says. He could be pretending he doesn't know I've been there.

I decide I don't care. I've been his secret keeper, his enabler, his alibi. I stand to grab my coat. Naveen hasn't moved. In order to get past him, I will have to push. We stand that way for what seems like a long time until at last he sighs.

I put my arms around him without thinking. Hold him close. I stroke a hand down his hair, the curls at the base of his neck. It takes him a few seconds to put his arms around me, but when he does, he turns his face to bury it against my neck.

"Why did I ever let you go?" he murmurs against my skin.

"You never had me, remember?" Sometimes, even old and oft-repeated conversations never become too familiar.

"I should have."

"We'd have killed each other, and you know it."

We stand that way for another minute. His fingers squeeze

my hips. I rub his back in small circles, much the way I used to comfort my daughters when they were upset.

Naveen pulls away to look into my face. "I love you, Betts. You know that?"

"I know you do. I love you, too. Can I go deliver these packages, or are you going to sob all over me?" I tug gently at his hair and let him go.

He takes another few seconds before he moves away with a small, quirking smile. I could ask him if he knows, or guesses, but I don't want to know if Naveen thinks Will and I are having an affair. He kisses my cheek.

"Don't bother coming back to work," he says magnanimously, as if he's my boss or something. "Take the rest of the day off."

A raise of my brows is all the answer I give. He chuckles, glancing over his shoulder at the tinkle of laughter coming from the women in the other room.

"No, really," he says, looking at me. "Don't come back to the office."

Chapter Nineteen

I've brought pastries and coffee, and the packages are growing heavy while I wait in front of Will's door. I haven't been able to convince myself to knock. If I don't do it soon, I'm going to have to put something down to ease the ache in my muscles.

He might not even be home. I purposefully didn't call—I didn't want him to tell me not to come. I'm so stupid.

At last I knock, faintly because of my full hands. So softly he might not even hear it, and I can turn around and walk away. I can have a service deliver the packages, or Naveen can take care of it, after all. I'm not his errand girl....

The door opens.

"Hi," Will says, not looking at all surprised to see me.

I hold up everything in my hands. "Naveen sent me. But I brought goodies."

He steps aside to let me in, and closes the door behind me. He isn't alone. Sitting at the large island in the kitchen is a small boy about three or four years old, his legs swinging from the stool as he finishes a plate of something chocolaty. Beside him is the blonde from the Connex picture.

"Thanks for bringing this." Will takes the packages, peeking into the top of the envelope. "I can do something with these. Better than having them sit around the gallery, right?"

"Right." I clear my throat, unbalanced now that I'm holding only the bakery bag and paper holder of coffee cups.

"Come on, Misha," the blonde says brusquely, barely giving me a glance. She has a hint of an accent I don't recognize, and her voice is colorless and without flavor. "I've an appointment."

Her voice is low and husky. She tugs the little boy's shirtsleeve, and he reluctantly slides down from the stool. His mouth is outlined with crumbs.

"Can I come next week, Daddy?"

The word stuns me. Will ruffles the kid's hair and reaches to pick up a small backpack I hadn't noticed, one emblazoned with robots. He presses it into the blonde's hand. She slings it over her shoulder and finally gives me a tight nod.

"I'm Elisabeth," I feel compelled to say. "I work with Will. Rather, at one of the galleries that feature his art."

She couldn't care less, that's clear enough. Maybe I don't rate. Maybe she's stopped caring about women in Will's apartment. Whatever it is, she gives me a tight nod and him a grim face.

"Next week I'm out of town," she says. "Misha will be with me."

"Okay, so when you get back, buddy." Will bends down to the kid's level, holding him by the shoulders. "I'll see you then. You can come for the whole weekend, okay?"

It's not enough—I can see it in Misha's face—but he nods. Much like his mom. He looks like her far more than he resembles Will, though there is something of him in the shape of his brows. It could be the flavor of his voice, an echo of Will's, though Misha's is more like a placid lake than the ocean.

"We'll see." She doesn't offer her name. She takes her son by the hand and leads him to the door, glancing once more at me without expression or seeming interest. She pauses to give Will a harder look. *"Je vais le faire appeler. N'oubliez pas que vous me devez l'argent pour son école."*

There are a few beats of silence when he closes the door behind her. He stands for a second or so, palm flat against the panel, shoulders a little hunched, before turning to me with a wry grin. Will shrugs and edges toward me. For the first time in my presence, he looks as if he's wishing for a cigarette.

"I thought…you didn't speak French."

He smiles faintly, takes the pastry bag and coffee from me and puts it on the island. Peeks inside. "Yum."

"I should've called first," I offer, and hesitate, my words fading. I feel stupid.

He gives me a shrewd look. "You think so? Why?"

"Well…"

His gaze flickers at the packages, over me, toward the door, around the kitchen, before finally settling on mine. "You're just dropping off some stuff for Naveen. Right?"

He'd called me once, and I didn't answer, and I'd texted him once with the same result. We haven't spoken since the day I walked out, after sucking him off against the wall I could reach out and touch if I took only a few steps in that direction. I want to scuff my toes along the tile floor, but keep myself still. I straighten my shoulders. Lift my chin.

"Yes. So. I should go."

"Okay," Will says mildly. "Thanks. See you."

He doesn't walk me to the door. My fingertips skid on the metal frame before I find the handle and turn it. Then I'm pushing it open and walking through it. Into the hall, bare concrete walls, the far-off sound of sirens filtering in through the wire mesh covering the open window at the end of the corridor. The elevator is directly in front of me. I'll be in it in a minute, the door closing behind me, beginning the rattle and shake of ancient gears and wires that will take me all the way down.

I put one hand on the concrete wall, next to the elevator call button. The concrete's rough and raw enough to scrape my skin when Will's voice makes me turn. Blood beads in the wrinkles of my fingers.

His mouth is on mine so fast I shouldn't be ready for it, but the truth is I've been ready for Will to kiss me since the second I walked through his front door. Our mouths open, tongues meet. His hands anchor my hips; mine grip his shoulders. Then higher, to clasp behind his neck, to toy with the softness of the hair there. His kiss travels from the corner of my mouth, along my jaw to my neck, and I am lost.

I was lost before I got there.

I turn my head to give him full access. His teeth are sharp, but the soft heat of his tongue soothes any sting they've made. A hiss escapes me, not because he's hurt me, but it must sound that way, because he pulls back and looks up and down the hall.

"My neighbors," he says after a second. "They're kind of nosy."

They're also very quiet, but I guess just because I haven't seen or heard anyone else in this building doesn't mean they're not there.

"We'd better go inside," Will says, kissing my mouth.

As if I'm going to say no. I laugh into his mouth, tasting his smile, and let him lead me step by step toward his front door. He hasn't stopped kissing me when we cross the threshold, or when he kicks the door closed and pushes me up against it. Not even when he presses his thigh between my legs, nudging upward against the barrier of my dress. We're tangled.

Breathing hard, he breaks the kiss to look into my eyes,

searching them for…what? I don't know. I don't care, just then, what he hopes to find or expects to see.

I put my hand on his shoulder and push, not gently, but not cruelly, either. I push him until he edges back a few steps, and I move past him without breaking eye contact until the last possible second, when I turn and walk backward so I don't have to look away. One step. Another. Three, four, five, and I'm in the hallway leading to his bedroom.

Will doesn't move.

I retreat another step. He stays still. We don't move, long enough for me to watch the motes of dust dancing in the shafts of light coming in the windows overlooking the street.

It's now or nothing; I either take this next step or I go home.

I turn my back, but glance over my shoulder as I do. His room is to the left, toward the back of the apartment. The door's cracked open, and when my fingers brush it, it groans. Inside, his bed is neatly made, the headboard of dark scrolled metal, the dresser and matching armoire a surprising and delightful art deco style. The far wall is a bank of floor-to-ceiling windows, all the blinds raised, the sun shining in so blinding it's impossible for me to see if anyone is in the building across the way.

Behind me, the door creaks.

And then his mouth is on mine.

I'm not ready for it. Teeth crash. I would pull away if I could, but he's molded to me and backing me up, fast, toward the bed. All I can do is take the kiss, all the way. Deep. My head spins at the taste of him, and I hold on to him even harder so I don't fall down.

When the backs of my knees hit the bed, Will holds me, so we ease onto it instead of tumbling. He's on top of me for only a few seconds before we're turning, rolling, and I'm straddling him with my dress pulled up, out of the way. My knees grip his hips. The scarf holding back my hair slips so that strands fall in my face, and he pushes them back so he can get at my mouth. I cannot get enough of him.

His hands move over my breasts, cupping me, before one slides inside the neckline of my dress. Under my bra, lace and satin, not new but definitely chosen with him in mind. He finds my nipple, already hard, and rolls it between his thumb and forefinger. My mouth is on his throat when he does that; I bite a little too hard. I don't mistake his hiss for anything but pain, although he doesn't complain. I lick the spot anyway, remembering how it felt when he did the same.

Will makes quick work of the buttons at the front of my dress, pushing it open. I sit up straight so he can get at my breasts. The bra fastens in the back and he deftly unhooks it. The fabric falls forward, and I put a hand up to catch it before I'm completely exposed. Everything is hands and mouth, distraction, yet I can't quite let myself be half-naked in front of him.

His mouth moves gently along the curve of my jaw. "No?"

"I…" I shouldn't want to. "I can't."

Will pulls away to look at my face. How could I have lived my entire life without knowing this man? His eyes are gray and green, and I smooth my fingertips over the arches of his brows. I touch the sleekness of the hair that falls in front of his ears.

"Because of this." He touches my left hand. The ring.

"That's not why. It should be." I didn't think I'd be able to speak, but the truth slips out with a taste like sunshine on water. "But it's not."

"Then…what?"

I would pull away, but he's got me held tight, with his hands on my hips. Somehow we've managed not to fall off the bed, though he has one foot on the floor and one leg stretched out toward the pillows, and I'm on his lap with a leg curled around him and the other half bent behind me. Awkward and a little uncomfortable, which neither of us noticed before this pause.

"I'm…I haven't…" I haven't been with another man since I was twenty years old, skin unblemished, stomach flat, breasts that had never nourished twins. I'm forty-five years old, and while I don't hate what the mirror shows, I'm not sure what I'll do if he doesn't like what he sees.

Will brushes my hair from my face again with an expression so tender it makes me want to weep. Without shifting me from his lap, he tugs the scarf from my hair. He holds it up.

It was a Mother's Day gift from Kat when she was in elementary school. Ugly. It has horses and horseshoes on it, a pattern of black and gray, but I love it because it was a gift from my child. It's soft and oversize, and it feels like her gap-toothed grin and the soft brush of her hair when she hugged me as I opened it.

The fabric slides through his fingers when he holds it up. "Use this."

I don't understand. "What?"

Will wraps the scarf around his neck, the ends dangling, and grips my hips again. "Use the scarf on me. Blindfold me."

Startled, I laugh. "What? No!"

He smiles. "Yes."

Neither of us move. His erection presses against me. I look into his eyes.

"Why?"

"Because you're worried about how you look to me," he says. "I don't want you to worry."

The idea roots like a weed, growing into a blossom in a heartbeat. *Vanity,* I think. *Thy name is Elisabeth.*

Will takes the scarf before I can. He ties it over his eyes, arranging the material so he'd really have to strain to peek,

It tufts his hair in the back and covers most of his face except his mouth, which is slightly open. His pulse throbs at the base of his throat.

He's waiting for me to touch him.

And I do. Slowly at first, just a brush of my fingers over his shoulders. Down his arms. Over his chest. The way his tongue slides over his lower lip makes me bold, and I slip my hands beneath his shirt again to find the tight pebbles of his nipples with my palms.

Will sinks back against the tossed pillows, his head tipped back, and I imagine his eyes have slid shut under the barrier of the scarf. I push his shirt up, watching his face carefully, but though his lips part and a soft sigh escapes him, he doesn't move or protest. I shift on his lap a little to get better access to his body.

He's lean, but not wiry. No fake tan for him. Pale, smooth skin on his ribs and belly. Over the jut of his hip bones, I run my fingers. Across the soft brush of hair below his navel.

"Sit up." It's not a request, and he doesn't hesitate.

I pull his shirt up and off, careful not to dislodge the blindfold. His chest hitches a couple times as I toss the shirt aside. His flesh pebbles into goose bumps. When I run my hands over his shoulders and chest, he smiles. I can feel the steady but fluttering thump of his heart beneath my palms. I touch the bird tattooed there.

"What's this?"

"It's a crane," he says.

I let my fingertips trace the lines of it. "Why?"

"It's a symbol of good fortune."

I want to lick it. I want to kiss and lick and bite every piece of him, and I start with his throat. I press him against the cushions again, my teeth taking his flesh harder than before. I don't want to hurt him...but suddenly, I do want to mark him.

This thought makes the breath catch in my throat. I sit up. My heart pounds, and I press my hand to it, as though I could make it slow down by doing so. I have to close my eyes when the room threatens to spin, but only for a second or two.

This is the truth. I have been in love. I have been in lust. I have made good choices and bad ones, I have been smart and I've been stupid. But I have never in my life felt the way I do now, here, with Will.

I don't think. I move. I tug at his belt, then the button and the zipper beneath it. In moments my hand is in his pants, inside his briefs. The angle's wrong, I can't really stroke him the way I want to, but I don't care that it's awkward, because the feel of him in my palm is enough to make my clit pulse.

He makes a noise, and for a second I think he means to stop me, but then he relaxes again against the pillows. His chest rises and falls. He licks his mouth, and I can't resist leaning to kiss it. Deep and long, tongues stroking the way my hand now strokes his cock.

Then I'm moving, tongue and teeth leaving a trail along his throat, over his chest. The crane tattoo. I count his ribs with my kisses, then move lower. His belly muscles jump under my mouth. I'm tugging at his jeans, over his hips, down his thighs, but his briefs stay up. They don't matter. I tug at the elastic so I can see him. All of him.

He is so beautiful. So perfect. I'm no connoisseur of cock, but I don't need to be an expert to know what I like. I ease his briefs down, freeing him. Finally, I can touch him the way I want to. My fingers curl around his shaft, stroking slowly upward. Then down. I'm mesmerized at the sight of my hand on Will's cock. How it fills my palm. How the shades of his skin change from the head to the base.

Will's hands are at his sides. He grips the mattress when I stroke him. Then a little harder, fingers denting the comforter. His chin tips up. He bites his lower lip. Fascinated, I watch the flush creep from his throat to his face.

He can't see me, but I see all of him. I have never felt so powerful or in control. When I shift, the tug and pull of the lace between my legs is delicious torture. I'm wet; I can feel how slick I am beneath the fabric, though I haven't done so much as even tap a finger there.

All I can think about is how he will feel inside me. I rub myself on his thigh, back and forth, the pressure on my clit just enough to make my mouth fall open with the pleasure, but not nearly enough to get me off. Will pushes his cock harder into the circle of my fist.

Again, I lean to kiss his chest. His throat. I tug his earlobe with my teeth, and his cock throbs. I move my hand slowly, so slow, and still he shakes a little with each stroke.

"I want you inside me." The words slip from my lips into his ear.

He turns his face toward me. His breath caresses my cheek. "Yes."

But first, I slip open the rest of the buttons on my dress. The thin belt at the waist. I pull it off in a tangle over my head, not caring if the sleeves are inside out or if it will wrinkle when I toss it to the floor. My bra. My panties. Will doesn't move through all this, doesn't even try to tip his head and peek from under the blindfold. His hands fist in the comforter. I swear I can see his heart beat in his prick.

I ease myself over him. He shudders at the soft brush of my pubic hair against the base of his cock. He pushes upward, just a little. My cunt's so wet I slide against him without friction. I rub my clit along his length, just like he once promised to do until I begged him to fuck me.

With the blindfold covering most of his face, his mouth is both desperately sexy and vulnerable at the same time. His tongue flicks out to touch his lips, as if he's tasting something sweet. Tasting me.

I shake at the sudden image I have of climbing up his body to press my clit to that tongue. Of his hands on my hips, moving and shifting me against his eager mouth. But I could barely take my clothes off in front of him. I might have no problem with going down on him, but putting his face between my legs is too intimate, too strange, too fraught with complications and emotional baggage. I settle for rubbing myself against his cock again.

Straddling him, I take one of his hands, then the other, and put them on my body. Over my hips, up my ribs. My breasts. The fullness of every curve. I give up everything to his touch. I put his fingers against my clit, then lower, inside me.

"Oh, fuck," Will says.

I guide his hand while I watch his face. He has learned me so quickly. I'm on the edge as fast as I would be by myself. I could come from his fingertips, the press and bunch of his thigh muscles under my ass. But I want more than that.

All I have to do is move a little, shift an inch, raise myself the smallest amount, and he's inside me. All the way. His cock's sweet curve hits me so perfectly I'm not sure I can move without coming. The best I can do is shudder and squeeze my knees to his sides. My hands go flat on his chest. I lean forward to kiss him.

Will fucks into me, not too fast, not frantic. It's hard to kiss him now. Hard to concentrate on anything but the way he's sliding in and out of me, and the press of my clit against him with every thrust. I want to pay attention, to kiss him, to make this good for him, but all I can do is let the pleasure sweep me away. I bury my face in his neck, my mouth full of the salt flavor of him that is echoed in the ocean spray taste of his voice when he says my name.

I might've been self-conscious about the bounce of places that shouldn't jiggle, but he can't see me. Only feel. I push myself upright and ride him, spine arched. My hair tickles my back. He fucks upward as I roll my hips, and then I'm coming so hard my teeth snap closed with the force of it. Will's cry is short and rough, the tumble of sea-smoothed glass. The slap of water on rocks.

Neither of us say anything when it's over, though our breathing is very loud. I ease myself off him and onto my back, at his side. Will makes no move to take off the blindfold. His hands fold on his belly. Turning my head, I watch the rise and fall of his chest as his breath slows.

Carefully, I run my finger along the edge of the blindfold, across his cheek and over the hair in front of his ears. Gently, softly, a whisper of a touch. He barely turns his head toward it.

"Did you like that?" I'm too sated to be offended if he says no. I know he liked fucking me; it's the blindfold I'm curious about.

"You have to ask?"

"This," I say, and touch the scarf again.

He's quiet at first, and I'm not sure he's going to answer. "Yeah."

"What about it?"

"I liked when you took my hands and moved them over your body. When you let me see you that way. And when you showed me what you like, how to touch you." He paused to lick his lips. "You wanted me to touch you."

It is the most erotic thing anyone has ever said to me.

"It kept me focused," he adds after a second, with a small laugh. "And I couldn't be sure what you were going to do, exactly, so it was a little uncertain."

I find words. "What did you think I might do?"

His mouth parts on a small gust of breath, but he takes another second before he says, "…Well, you could've done any-thing you wanted to. Couldn't you?"

I pushed up on my elbow. "And you liked that."

"Yeah," he says in a low voice. "I guess I did."

I tug at the blindfold to ease it off his eyes. Will rolls to look at me. I'm not so worried now about my body, though honestly, if he was going to judge, it would be now, when his dick isn't hard. His confession moved me, though. If he could reveal that to me, I guess I can let him see what I look like naked.

"Hey," he says.

I smile and let my fingertips skate along the curve of his face before putting my hand flat over his heart, which is still skipping a little. "Hey."

"By the way," Will says, "I missed you, too."

Chapter Twenty

I'm unaccountably nervous, cooking in Will's kitchen. I shouldn't be—I'm only making a pesto dish with sautéed vegetables. Simple. Yet my fingers fumble with the knife when I pull it from the holder.

I've cut myself, I think with a small sense of wonder as the bright blood wells up. I suck my finger automatically. The blood tastes like autumn leaves burning.

"You okay?" Will pauses in pouring me a glass of wine.

"Fine." And I am, the wound so scant you can barely see it, the blood gone. I wash my hands thoroughly, anyway.

He passes me the glass, along with a kiss that tastes of wine. He nuzzles my neck for a moment and I revel in that touch. I find his mouth again. I can't get enough.

He praises my dinner as if it came from a four-star restaurant, so much that, laughing, I have to tell him to stop. "It's only pasta."

"Nobody's made a meal for me in a long time, that's all. Food always tastes better when someone else makes it for you," he says, and refills my wineglass.

"I like to cook. I used to cook a lot." I sip the wine, letting the flavor roll around on my tongue while I think about all the meals I'd made over the years. Dinnertime, even when the girls were heavily active in sports and other activities, had always been important. I couldn't remember the last time Ross and I sat down to a home-cooked meal.

"Not anymore?"

"With my daughters out of the house, no. Not so much." I shrug, twirling my fork through the strands of pasta, though I'm no longer hungry.

Will leans back in his chair. "You have daughters."

"Yes. Twins." I think about telling him their names, how old they are, where they go to school, but somehow giving him that seems like too much information. "And you have a son."

"Yeah."

I let the wine make waves in my glass. "And his mother? She's the ex who left the coffeemaker but took the cat?"

He looks uncomfortable. "Yes."

"Things aren't good between you two?"

"No," he says. Shakes his head. Fiddles with his fork, his attention on the plate as though it's suddenly important. "No. Not very good."

"I'm sorry. That must be hard for you. I mean, you share a kid. No matter what happened between the two of you…" I trail off, realizing I have no idea what happened between the two of them, and it's not any of my business.

Will looks up with one of those shrewd gazes I've seen him give the city skyline. Framing me. "What about you?"

"What about me?"

"Your husband," Will says. "What would he think about this?"

It's not funny, but I laugh. "I'm sure he wouldn't like it."

"I didn't know if maybe you had an agreement or something."

"Oh…no." My brows raise at the thought. "God. No, not at all. I'm just…"

We both fall silent. I'm not sure how to finish the sentence, anyway, because I'm not sure what I'm "just" doing. The shining silver thread of silence stretches out between us until finally, I find the words.

"I was thirsty," I tell him. "And you gave me something to drink."

Will gets up abruptly from the table, plate in hand. He puts it in the sink with a clatter while I watch without moving from my place at the table. His shoulders hunch. He grips the counter edge. He doesn't look at me.

He doesn't move when I stand, or when I step so close to him, although he has to feel my body heat, even though we're both fully clothed. I want to touch him, but I don't. I wait.

He turns.

"I haven't…been…with anyone since I broke up with my ex," Will says.

I think he means a relationship, but then I understand. I'm flattered. I'm also scared shitless, but can't make myself move away, not even a step. My fingers curl against my palms.

"How long?"

"Since before my son was born."

Three years? Four? Either way, a long time.

"At first it was because I thought maybe she'd take me back. I thought, we're having a kid together, you know? Surely she'll give me another chance. We'll figure out how to make it work, at least for the kid's sake. And then after…when I knew it was never going to work again, we were never going to be together, I just didn't want to. It was all so much work and effort and just…" He grimaces, shuddering, shaking his head. He looks at me, his expression raw and honest.

I'm not sure what to say. "I hope it was worth it."

He reaches to twirl a finger in the hair framing my face. His fingertip brushes my cheek and I can't stop myself from turning toward his palm, from pressing it against my mouth. Then I'm in his arms, against him, my face against his shirt. I feel the press of his lips against my hair.

"I'm not trying to cause you trouble, that's all," Will says.

My shoulders lift and fall with the force of my sigh. I close my eyes. I breathe him in—the scent of his laundry detergent, his soap, his skin, the sea-smell of his voice.

"He doesn't know. He won't find out," I say.

Will's laugh is short and sharp. "Famous last words."

My fingers hook in the hem of his shirt and find the heat of his skin beneath. "My husband does not pay attention."

More silence. We breathe together. Will pushes me gently until I look at him; his gaze searches mine. I think he means to speak, and I stop him with a kiss.

"I have no intention of leaving my husband. Does that make you feel better?" I ask. "Or worse?"

Will hesitates. "Better, I guess."

"I've never cheated on my husband before, Will. Believe me, it's not something I went out looking for. I just…well, I turned around and there you were. I don't know why. I'm not sure I care, to be honest." I push onto my toes to brush a kiss across his mouth again. "But don't worry. You will not be the reason my marriage ends, if it does. Okay? I will never let you be my reason."

He nods, just once, looking both relieved and unconvinced. "Okay. Thanks."

I kiss him again, slower this time. Lingering. The press of his growing erection against my belly sends a thrill through me.

"Fuck me," I whisper.

"Again?" he asks, as though the idea shocks him, even

though he's already inching my dress up to my hips and his mouth is slanting over mine.

"Oh, yes," I tell him. "Again."

Chapter Twenty-One

I'm on a train.

I don't know at which stop I got on or where I'll get off; I only know the train is going, going fast, and the world outside becomes a blur. The trees and sky mesh and meld and become something else. I'm on a train and I should get off, but I don't.

The universe is playing a cosmic joke on me. Here I had my life, a good life with everything a woman could need, and suddenly, there is something more I didn't know I could have or even want.

"Here," the universe says, "here is a chance for you to not simply be 'fine' or 'all right' or 'resigned.' Here is a chance for you to be satisfied and content and maybe even on occasion deliriously, amazingly, exuberantly happy and full of joy. For you to have everything you didn't know you needed, but always felt was missing."

So this is where I am, on a train that's out of control, and I am not just a passenger. I'm the fucking engineer, I'm the operator, I'm the one shoveling the furnace full of coal to keep it going fast and faster.

I do this.

This is me.

It doesn't seem to matter, owning this, knowing it. If I

could make myself believe it all happened by chance and I couldn't help it—that I've been swept away, it's not my fault, it's fate, it's cosmic interference, whatever that might be—would that be easier?

Everything is always pretty in the beginning. I know this. I've been through it a few times, after all. But this...oh, this is something different than I've ever known. There shouldn't be time for it, but I carve out opportunity. I make the space for him because this is more than infatuation.

It's the way he says my name and looks at me when I talk, as if what I have to say is important. How our eyes meet and lock and we lapse into silence, speaking with just our smiles. It's his hand on my elbow as we cross the street, making sure I'm safe. It's the taste of his skin, the brush of his hair on my face when he kisses me, the press of his tongue in my mouth. It is his beautiful, delicious cock. It's the way he can't make up his mind about which pair of jeans to wear, when to me they all look the same. It's the songs he sends me to listen to, the books I tell him to read. And yes, it is the fact he pays attention.

When we are together, everything shines.

The truth is, I didn't know I was looking for this until I found Will, but I must've been, all this time. And now it is not random, it is not fate, it is not being swept away.

This is my choice.

And I don't know how to stop.

I don't want to stop.

Chapter Twenty-Two

I can't spend too much time away from the gallery; Naveen does expect me to work for my paycheck, after all. And though I suspect if I went to him and told him the real reason I want to sneak away for an hour or so at lunchtime, he'd smile and give me a thumbs-up, I don't want him to know. I don't want anyone to know.

I carry the weight of my secret like a stone, and hold it in both my hands because I don't want to let it go.

The ping of a text woke me this morning. Will, playing at being casual, inviting me to watch him shoot some pictures in a warehouse. Professional. Neutral. Distant.

He wants to pretend this is all accidental, but for me it isn't a game. I haven't simply let it happen. I'm falling because I jumped, and not because I tripped. This is on purpose and I own it, even if he won't. But I let him pretend we're meeting so I can watch him take pictures of empty rooms and peeling paint, and not so that he can fuck me.

But oh, I have every intention of making him do that.

He takes a lot of pictures using natural light. I have to lean in close to see what he sees through the lens, and I take a long, slow breath of him when I do. The feathers of his hair tickle my cheek. I want to nuzzle against his skin, and stop myself only at the last minute. And then only just.

His phone buzzes from his pocket. We pull apart while he answers. It's the model who's supposed to be here, posing for some urban fantasy romance cover. She's sick. Will's expression goes dark as he listens to excuses that sound like bullshit even in the small bits and pieces I can hear through his speaker.

"She's not sick," he says when he disconnects. "She's hungover, or she ate too much for breakfast and she's determined to barf it all up."

"That's such a cliché."

He slowly smiles. "Yeah. It is."

"Maybe she's got the flu. You're so cynical."

We're standing very close together. I can count his eyelashes and the bristly threads of his brows. I can see the glint of silver in his hair when he stands in the light coming through a window from which all the glass has been broken out.

And then I can't stop myself from touching him. My fingers curl in the front of his shirt and pull him even closer. He holds his camera to the side, out of the way. Our mouths are very close, but we do not kiss.

We talk every day. Silly things. Jokes and comments on the weather. We talk about our kids; it's been such a long time since my girls were small that his stories of crayon-colored drawings for the fridge make me feel both nostalgic and relieved I'm no longer in that place. We share our favorite colors and flavors of ice cream and television shows and music, but we never talk about what this is.

He doesn't lean toward me, but he doesn't pull away. And I…I stand there for another half a minute with my lips so close to his all it would take is a whisper and we'd be kissing. But I don't do it. I pull away and walk toward the window, glancing over my shoulder at him to see if he's watching. He is.

"Great view," I tell him.

Outside the window is the vast expanse of the East River. Below us, busy streets. This warehouse is slated to be turned into expensive condos pretty soon, and I'll admit that I don't have the vision to imagine it as anything other than a giant box of filthy wooden floors and cobweb-strung beams. I spin, arms out, to make the hem of my skirt flare.

He's taking pictures of me, and I should protest but I don't. My spinning makes the dust fly up, motes dancing like stars in the shafts of light. This is it, this is me. I am made of stars.

I've made myself dizzy so that I stumble, but Will is there to catch me. Together we look out the broken window to the world below, and at last, at last I think he's finally going to kiss me. That's when the sound of boots and voices distracts him.

"Shit," Will says. "Security. C'mon."

"Wait, what?" I follow him toward the stairs on the opposite side of the huge room. We'd come up on the elevator, a gigantic, creaking thing that gave me visions of plummeting to our deaths.

Will holds the metal door open for me to step through. "Security. I didn't get permission to shoot here."

"Oh. Shit." I pause and wait for him on the landing. There are windows here, thank God, or else we'd be in darkness.

Will eases the door closed to keep it from slamming. We make it down only one flight when the door we came out of opens. Voices, two or three, echo in the concrete shaft. Will pushes me against the wall, out of sight—unless they decide to come down the stairs, in which case we're screwed. My hands skid along the metal railing. They are on the landing directly above us. In a minute I smell the familiar tang of pot.

I start to laugh. We can't move from under the landing or they'll see us, though honestly, stoned security guards can't be that much trouble, can they? Will lowers his camera bag gently to the gritty concrete and puts a finger to his lips.

When I can't stop laughing, he covers my mouth with his. His hands anchor at my hips, pushing me back. I'm holding on to the railing, the metal cool and gritty under my palms.

He kisses me hard and harder. *It will always be like this,* I think, before the slide of his tongue on mine makes it impossible to think about anything but that and the creeping tickle of his fingers against my inner thigh as he pulls up my skirt and eases my panties down. Always hard and fast and delicious like this. We will never grow cold.

His fingertips circle, and I'm already close to the edge when he eases off. I mutter a protest into his mouth, but only for a second, because he's turning me to face the wall. Behind me, Will puts his hands over mine on the railing, curling my fingers tight on the metal. He nudges my feet apart as he pushes up my skirt, and I hear the click and clack of his zipper, but the moment I let a moan slip free he's got his hand over my mouth again.

Above us, the guards are talking about their girlfriends and getting laid, but it sounds more like bragging than truth. They're complaining about their boss, and that sounds more real. They're talking about rousting out bums who like to sleep in the warehouse, and how they'll happily beat the shit out of anyone they find inside, and though we aren't bums and I'm pretty sure they wouldn't actually hit us, my heart beats faster and I struggle a little against Will, who digs his fingers into my hip until I go still.

With his hand covering my mouth, he bends me forward. I grip the railing tighter when he pushes inside me, and it's a good thing he's stifling me because I can't stop myself from moaning again. I spread my arms apart, not caring about dust or rust as my fingers skid on the metal. Holding the railing lets me angle my body to take him in deeper, all the way to the verge of pain.

The colors begin their swirling dance, bursts and flashes. He's not saying my name or anything else, but the faint cry of gulls and the rush of the ocean fill my head. I push back against him, but the slap of our flesh is too loud and he holds my hip to keep me from moving. Slowly, slowly, he eases inside me and slowly, slowly, retreats.

The guards are still above us, and I no longer hear what they're saying as anything more than a long stream of jumbled sounds. I don't care about them. All that matters is the maddeningly slow press of Will's body into mine.

He curves himself over me. I feel his breath on the back of my neck and taste salt from his hand. When he bites the soft flesh exposed by the scooped neck of my blouse, I come. Hard but soundless, biting back cries that would surely be too loud even behind the guard of his palm. The metal railing rattles as I shake, but I can't stay still enough to keep it quiet. Will moves a little faster then. Deeper. The hand that had been gripping my hip shifts forward to press against my clit.

I'm not quite there, and honestly don't expect to get there again. Really don't care. I'm still shaking from the first one, unable to catch my breath, my legs weak. But Will's still moving so slowly, so quietly, that every time he thrusts he pushes my body forward, against his hand. And that slow, steady pressure builds and builds until I'm tipping over. I've bitten him on purpose before, but now I sink my teeth into his hand by reflex.

He shudders.

Blinking, I return to the world with an ache in my fingers from gripping the railing too hard, weak knees, strained toes from pushing my body into the right position. He pulls

out and away, and I relax all at once, still quiet, still furtive.
I start to laugh again.

I try to hold it back, but from upstairs I hear one of the
guards remark confidentially to the other that "sometimes,
man, I just don't know what it all means," and I can't keep it
in anymore. My shoulders shake and I bite my tongue, but I
can't stop.

Will is laughing, too, and he pushes me back against the
wall to cover my mouth with his. The kiss presses in my giggles, and then, without thinking, I have my arms and legs
wrapped around him, my face buried in his neck, my ass resting on the railing and the concrete wall digging into my back.
It's not comfortable, but I'm not laughing anymore. I'm clinging to him like a baby monkey, trying to get as much of myself around as much of him as possible, and now I'm stifling
something closer to tears.

Upstairs, the metal door creaks and clangs shut, leaving behind only echoes and the faint, drifting scent of their smoke.
Neither of us move. Will is supporting me, arms around me,
his face pressed against my skin. We breathe and breathe, and
finally, I have to move. I extract myself from him one limb
at a time until I'm standing in front of him. Panties around
my ankles, slickness coating my thighs, my clothes and hands
filthy. I've left the marks of my fingers on his shoulders. I
hold his face for a moment, forcing him to look into my eyes.

We say nothing.

By the time we've gathered our things and taken the stairs
all the way down to the street, Will is making jokes that de-
flect attention from what we did in the warehouse. I'm quiet,
looking out the window of the cab we share back toward the
gallery, where I'll get out and he'll keep going. We have a
history in cabs, I think, and wonder if he'll kiss me again or
if he'll just keep pretending we don't do that sort of thing.

At the gallery, the driver stops and I pay him, but before I get out, I slide across the seat and take Will by the front of the shirt. Not hard, not grabbing. He could pull away, if he wants to. I offer my mouth without saying anything, just a tilt of my head, a parting of lips. I wait. Wait, wait, wait.

And then, just before it would become awkward even for the cabbie, Will leans in to brush his mouth across mine. It's a sweet kiss, brief and perfect and exactly what I wanted. I smile into it. He smiles back.

"Talk to you later," I tell him. Not a request.

I get out of the cab and don't look back to see if he's watching me from the window, but I figure he probably is. Inside, I head for my office, avoiding Naveen, who is tied up with some clients, anyway. At least until he comes to find me and I'm busy doing my best not to fiddle with my hair, which I'm sure is just-fucked messy, or my lipstick, which is just-been-kissed smeared.

"Hi." I'm casual.

Naveen isn't paying attention. He hands me a stack of invoices and folders, sending receipts fluttering to the floor like errant butterflies. He's blathering on and on about some sort of show he wants to put on at the end of the year, how the gallery will need to be redesigned to accommodate some bigger pieces, blah, blah, blah.

He stops almost in the middle of a sentence I'm not really paying attention to, because I'm so busy reliving the feeling of Will entering me. Startled, I realize Naveen's asked me a question. "Huh?"

Not a question, though he's looking at me expectantly, as though I'm supposed to provide an answer. "Next week. On Thursday."

If I ask him to repeat himself, he's going to be pissed off, and also wonder why I wasn't paying attention, which could ultimately circle around to why I'm distracted, a subject I want to avoid. "Thursday is probably...fine?"

"So you think I *should* see her."

I get it now. "Oh, Naveen. You have to ask me that?"

"Yeah. I should tell her to fuck herself."

I roll my eyes. "Shut up."

He looks distraught, running a hand through his hair to mess it up, then smooth it. "She said she has something to tell me. Something important."

"Well," I say slowly, understanding now why he's so nervous, because it's about that woman he told me he was in love with, and not some random bang, "I guess you just have to be prepared for what she might say. What do you think it could be?"

"She's leaving her husband," he says confidently.

"Would that be a good thing for you?"

His mouth works. He shrugs then. "No. I don't know." He gives me the old, helpless look that used to melt me. "What do I do?"

"I don't know. I wish I had an answer for you."

He sighs, shoulders lifting. "Fuck, it's so complicated."

"Yeah," I say. "That. Twice."

Chapter Twenty-Three

We talk every day.

A call in the morning if I'm on my way to work at the Philadelphia office, maybe a video chat if I'm working from home. If I'm going in to the New York gallery, we meet for lunch, and mostly, just eat lunch. We talk again on my train ride home, and those couple hours are never long enough.

We talk, and talk and talk. About everything from alien abduction to the zombpocalypse—I'm uncertain about the former and adamantly opposed to the viability of the latter, while Will's a believer in all of it, including Sasquatch and the Loch Ness monster. On the existence of God we are both torn.

We message each other throughout the day. Silly quotes. Commentary on whatever it is we're doing. He sends me pictures of what he's working on and I reciprocate, though of course his are always artistic and beautiful and mine are stupid, out-of-focus snapshots. I have an entire gallery of the work he sends me, hidden in a folder on my phone.

He makes me laugh.

Oh, God, how he makes me laugh.

He tells me the dumbest jokes, or subtly imitates the lady on the bus with the shopping bag or the guy behind the counter at the corner grocery—never unkind, never mocking, just perfect mirroring of gestures and phrases. He replays them for me late at night in front of the computer while we sneak in a video chat, and I have to be quiet so as not to alert Ross, sleeping in the room down the hall. I hold both hands over my mouth and laugh, and laugh and laugh until my sides are sore.

And then…there is nothing.

I wait for my early morning message, and when the hours pass without one, I start to wait for the lunchtime invitation. When that doesn't come, I break down and call, leaving a short message on his voice mail when he doesn't answer. Just before I go home for the day, I send another instant message. Ignored.

At home, I find dirty dishes in the sink and crumbs on the counter, a pile of laundry by the washer and the sounds of the television coming from the den. That's where I find my husband, firmly ensconced in his favorite recliner with a beer in one hand and some kind of sports on the big screen.

Maria will clean the kitchen, of course, if I decide to live in filth and leave it for her when she comes in a few days. That's why we hired her. That is why my husband thinks it's perfectly okay to live in our house like it's a hotel. But I don't want to live this way, housekeeper or not, so I pull out a dishcloth from the drawer and attack the counters as if they've done me wrong.

I'm not hungry, but I make myself a bowl of soup, anyway. I eat it at the counter with my silent phone next to me. It refuses to buzz or beep or chirp. I refuse to look at it.

Later in bed, Ross rolls over, groping expectantly. He doesn't fumble. He knows just where and how to touch me, but I'm instantly tense, waiting for him to make it all go wrong. He doesn't. He eases me into arousal even though I don't want it. His fingers stroke and probe, and his mouth finds places to tease. We find one of the tried-and-true positions, me on my back with him on his side. It should work.

I'm wet, he's hard, his fingers toy with my clit as he fucks into me…but it's not working. He finishes, and I'm left with a vague sense of loss. That's what this has become.

Loss.

Dozing, Ross sounds like a chain saw. His arms and legs are still tangled with mine. He's sweaty. I need to pee. I cannot fall asleep this way, so I do what every wife learns to do—I shove him until he rolls off me, and mutter, "Turn on your side, you're snoring."

He does, and I stare up at the ceiling for a few minutes before I manage to get out of bed and go to the bathroom in the dark. I wash my hands, also in the dark. I grip the sink while the water runs to cover up the sound of my sudden, gasping sobs.

Back in bed, fully dressed, covers pulled to my chin, I cannot sleep.

There used to be nights when Ross and I stayed up late talking. Not just in the beginning, when we were dating and everything was new and sweet, and staring into his face was as delicious to me as ice cream. Later, when the kids were small and the only time we had together were these late-night conversations under the blankets. There were times when we fought in fiercely hissing whispers, and times, too, when we giggled ourselves into hiccups. Now I can't remember the last time Ross said anything that barely raised a smile, much less made me laugh so hard it was as good as having an orgasm.

There are a lot of reasons to stay in a marriage, and I've learned that love can be the least of them. Debt. Family. History. Laziness. Those can keep a person from leaving.

Fear can, too.

Lying beside my husband now, I want to turn and kiss him the way I used to. I want us to laugh under the covers again.

At least, I try to want those things, but the truth is…I no longer really do.

I give in to the embarrassingly obsessive and desperate urge to check my phone, but there's still no message from Will. No reply. I'm still awake when the sun comes up. *Everything changes,* I think.

Everything ends.

Chapter Twenty-Four

I won't chase and I won't beg. More days pass without a word, and eventually, I stop checking. So there's this sense of relief, this lifted weight, and I face the day with confidence that everything will be okay. I go out to the yard, to the flowers and the grass, and I put my face toward the sun and close my eyes against the brightness. I smile. I spread my arms, not caring what the neighbors might think. I spin.

I spin.

Inside the house, I face the disaster of my kitchen and, determined, roll up my sleeves as I put on some music—loud as I want. There's nobody here to judge if my choice runs to teeny bop pop I heard on the radio, or classic rock I've loved forever. With my iPod set on shuffle, I get to the business of straightening and wiping and scrubbing and organizing.

And then…I find myself standing at the sink staring out the window for a long, long time as the water runs over my hands, gone red from the heat. They should sting, but I don't notice. I stand and stare as the iPod plays one song after another, plays one of the songs that make me think of him.

They all make me think of him.

And I haven't danced at all.

Slowly, slowly, I push the faucet to turn off the water. I stare at the suds in the sink, the dishes I was washing. How long have I stood there, staring at the grass and flowers through the glass, but seeing only Will's face? Too long, that's the only answer. One minute, one second, one breath is too long to have spent dwelling on this, and still I stand and stare, until I sit with a cup of coffee I don't want, and stare at my hands, laid flat on the table, and remember how it felt to touch him.

It's the middle of the day and I don't care that I get into the shower with the water as hot as I can stand it, or that I curl into a ball on my side and close my eyes and pretend that the rush and hiss of the pounding shower is the roar of the ocean in the way he says my name. I don't care that I pretend my hands are his when I touch myself, or that when I come I'm thinking about the way he tastes. I should be ashamed of this hungry, aching desperation, but I'm only sad and empty and disappointed.

And then, that tiny ping, that subtle notification sound I've almost forgotten. Like Pavlov's dog, I jerk and twist beneath the water, certain I've imagined it. But no...when I get out without even taking a towel to dry my sopping hair, when I lift up my phone from where I left it as an afterthought on the edge of the tub, there it is. The small red "1" of a notification.

The sour taste of anger coats my tongue when I thumb the screen to check the message. All it says is Hi, how are you? I want to throw the phone across the room, while simultaneously flipping it the bird with both hands.

I think about ignoring it; he'll be able to see I read the message and that I'm not replying. But just as I don't chase and I don't beg, I do not fucking play games, either. I type in an answer as neutral and meaningless and stupid as his: Fine. You?

And he doesn't reply.

For hours.

By the time I get another ping, my stomach is full of acid-eaten holes and I've called him every name I can think of, including motherfucking prickblister, pus-encrusted douche-nozzle and cock-kicking fuckpucker. I'm kind of proud of the last one. I've called myself worse, because I know I'm stupid and undone, and I've made this too important. Given him too much power. I hate it, but when I hear that tiny, sly ping I'm snatching up my phone as if I'm on fire and it's going to put out the blaze with piss.

Hi, how are you?

Fine, I type, and it's a good thing there's no way to hear tone in a text message, because mine is bitter and full of fury. You?

Good. Just finishing up some editing on a couple pics.

To this I have no reply. I think of lots of things I could say, but all of them will come out sounding angry, and I refuse to give him that. I will keep my crazy in my basket, thank you very much. He doesn't deserve to know I've spent one single fucking second thinking about him....

Lunch tomorrow?

My fingers type then, moving on the phone's touch keyboard so fast I make a message full of autocorrected typos that would completely dilute the scathing, furious words I intend to send. I delete it all. I type some more, knowing he can see that I'm replying, and hating even that, because fuck it all, I'd like him to think I'm just blowing him off. I delete everything again. Then once more. And then his next message appears.

I M Y

"Fuck you," I say aloud. "Fuck you sideways and upside down with a red-hot poker covered in broken glass, you fuck-ing fuckety fuck."

But my fingers press the spaces on the keyboard that make different words than that, because they are both smarter and more stupid than my mouth or my head or my fucked up heart. I type and do not delete. This time, I say, What time?

Chapter Twenty-Five

He's standing outside the restaurant smoking, not looking my way, and do I imagine myself walking away without speaking to him, leaving him standing there for an hour, or for forever, waiting? Hell, yeah. Do I imagine myself running across the street and leaping into his arms, cling to him like a baby monkey, like a fucking barnacle?

Oh. Yes.

When I cross the street to face him, he turns to me with a smile so wide and bright and genuine that I want to kiss his face off. I want to run my hands through the mess of his hair and smooth my fingertips over those brows and trace the curves of his ears with my tongue. I want to eat him up like a peach until the juice drips down my hand and wrist and arm and I lick it all away.

Instead, I give him the barest hint of a smile. "Hey."

"Hi." He moves as though to hug me, but I step back so deliberately there can be no mistaking my message.

Do. Not. Touch.

"You look…great," Will says.

I don't answer that. I look at the restaurant menu in the window instead, though honestly, I don't give a fart in a high wind what they serve. I won't be able to eat. I plan on ordering the most expensive thing they have and making him pay for it, though. Maybe I do play games, after all.

He opens the door for me, and the solicitous hand at the small of my back as he lets me go in front of him should not make my knees weak. We take a booth near the back, in the shadows. It's curved, which means I slide in first, but I put my purse on the seat between us so he can't sit too close.

We order drinks. We order food. We make small talk that sounds like pebbles rattling in a pie pan. At first, Will is animated and effusive, but as he watches me pick at my salad and give him brief answers without smiles, he sits back in the booth.

"If you don't want to be here," he says, "maybe you should just fucking go."

My fork shakes a little against the edge of the plate before I set it down very, very carefully. I wipe my fingers on my napkin. Then my mouth. I put my hands on the edge of the table, fingertips barely touching the smooth, polished wood. And I say…nothing.

He shifts in his seat with a frown. "That's it? I get the silent treatment?"

"I'm being careful with what I say, that's all. I want to make sure nothing comes out that I can't take back."

"Maybe you should just say whatever you think," Will says with a sneer. "You think I can't handle it?"

My fingers slip on the smooth wood. "I don't want you to handle it. I don't want to say anything I'll regret, that's all."

"If you're pissed at me, you should just say so."

"Should I be?" I press my lips together and rub my tongue slowly on the inside of my teeth to keep my voice low. "Are you?"

I think of Glenn Close in *Fatal Attraction,* telling Michael Douglas how she will not be *ignored.* But that's exactly how it felt those long weeks when Will stopped talking to me. Ignored.

"I would never just stop talking to you," I tell him, whispering only so I don't scream. "I would never just disappear like that. That was a shitty thing to do to me, Will."

"I was busy," he begins, and I've had enough.

I need to get out of this booth, and now. But the other side is blocked by a tray of food waiting to be served, and the only way out is past him. "Move."

He doesn't, even as I'm grabbing up my purse and sliding along the smooth vinyl toward him. I bump against him. "Move!"

He won't. I don't want to cause a scene. And sitting this close, I can feel his thigh on mine. I can feel the heat coming off him. When he slides a hand between my legs beneath the cover of the table, all I can do is let him.

"Everyone's busy," I tell him.

His fingers press, press, press. "My ex went out of town. I had my kid. I was busy, Elisabeth."

To anyone looking at us, we simply appear to be deep in conversation. There's enough distance between us, the angle is just right to hide the fact he's inching up my skirt to get inside my panties. At the last minute, I clamp my thighs shut, trapping his hand before he can.

"Then you should've told me."

There's more to it than that. I can see it in his face. He twists his wrist a little, but I don't give him even a quarter of an inch.

"I told you—"

"Bullshit." I lean a little closer when the waiter passes by, lowering my voice to keep it from attracting attention. The heat of Will's hand against my bare skin is beginning to burn. "It's an excuse, and a shitty one. You think I wouldn't understand if you told me you had to take care of your kid? You think I'd be some kind of bitch about it?"

Steadily, he works his hand a little higher. His knuckles brush my panties before he twists again to press my clit. I do not move except for the rise and fall of my shoulders when I take a breath. My muscles ache from the effort of keeping him away. When I relax the tiniest bit, he takes advantage, pressing harder. Twisting so infinitesimally that nobody would be able to tell.

He can't see the golden stars beginning to creep into the edges of my vision, but I'm sure he must see something in my eyes, because his hand moves just a little faster. His pupils are so wide-open his eyes have gone dark. His tongue slips out to touch the center of his bottom lip.

"I don't owe you anything," Will says, but low and under his breath.

I do not want to let him see how good he's making me feel, because I don't want to be feeling it. But when I put my hand over his, it's not to push it away. I grip his wrist tight, holding him closer.

"Yes," I tell him. "You do."

I am close, so close, but not going over. The waiter shows up then with a dessert tray, and I pull away. I shake my head at the pies and cakes, and decline a box for my leftovers as I slide toward the other end of the booth, now cleared by the busboy. I assure the waiter everything was fine, though I can see by the way he eyes my plate that he takes my uneaten food as a personal affront. I get out of the booth and push past him and out of the restaurant to the New York City street outside, and I breathe in exhaust and heat and the scents of puke and piss, and I blink away the last flutters of gold Will's touch gave me.

I'm halfway back to the gallery when he catches up to me. He falls into step beside me without saying anything. He follows me through the door I don't bother to hold open for him, and down the hall past Naveen's blessedly empty office and into my own. Then, when I whirl on him to tell him to get the fuck out, he shuts my door. The lock clicks.

We sweep my desk clean. Paper clips scatter. Then he's inside me, and nothing else matters but this.

After, with his forehead pressed to mine and the taste of his sweat on my lips, Will says, "I was ignoring you on purpose."

I cup his face in my hands and kiss him. "I know you were."

We disentangle, comb and straighten. He fills a paper cup from my water cooler and drains it, then crumples the cup. I pull my hair back with a spare elastic from my drawer and swipe my face with powder. Fix my lipstick. Will is glancing at the door, ready to make his escape, when I finish. I recognize the look.

"You don't have to talk to me every day," I tell him carefully. "If it's too much. But you can't just abandon me, Will. That's not fair. I deserve better than for you to just disappear. Frankly, you deserve better than to be that sort of guy."

"I came back," he begins, and stops when I don't smile.

"You can have a life. I expect you to have a life. I have one, too, you know."

His brow furrows. "Yeah. Believe me, I know."

And that's the problem, isn't it? I don't have an answer for it. So much to say and nothing seems right, so we stare at each other, too far apart to touch.

"Did you…really miss me?" I almost don't ask, in case the answer isn't what I want to hear.

He nods.

I shouldn't feel so relieved. I shouldn't feel anything for him, but there's no holding it back. No stopping it. I sag against the desk a little. "Good. I want you to miss me. A lot."

"I worry this is going to make trouble for you."

"It might." My chin lifts. Shoulders and spine straighten. "But that's my problem."

"It would be mine, too." Will rubs at his mouth with his first and middle fingers. "Sometimes, I think we should stop. Before it's too late. Before we do something that we can't take back."

"It's already too late," I tell him. "We've already done it. It's done, Will. We can't take it back. That's the way stuff like this works."

He won't move, so I do. I pull him closer, step by step, until he takes me in his arms. We fit just right, Will and I, and I don't want to let him go.

"You're my kryptonite. I don't know why." My words are muffled against his neck. I can't stop myself from nibbling, just a little, and I can't stop myself from telling him the truth. "But if you don't want to talk to me anymore...if you don't want to see me..."

His arms tighten, just a little, around me. "Are you breaking up with me?"

I look at him. "Are you breaking up with *me?*"

We both smile at the same time.

"Just don't ever disappear on me again. If you have to stop talking to me—"

"I don't *want* to stop talking to you."

"Then...don't. We'll find a balance." I say this more confidently than I feel, but it seems the only thing to say.

Then I kiss him, kiss him, kiss him until neither of us can breathe.

Chapter Twenty-Six

Find a balance. That's what I'd told Will we should do. It was certainly what I believed I wanted when I said it, but sitting here alone on a Friday night with nothing but a carton of ice cream and a spoon to keep me company, I'm feeling decidedly…unbalanced.

We've been cautious with each other. Not talking every day. It isn't like it used to be. There's a distance. I don't like it, but I understand it. We haven't seen each other in what feels like forever, and though I'd told him I would be alone this weekend, he'd already planned to have his son.

I try to miss my husband instead. Isn't that what good wives do? Pine for their mates when they're away on business trips? It's what Andrea would do, and even though she's my best friend, I shudder at the thought of ever being like that.

Still, I try. I thumb his number into my phone. Ross picks up just before the call gets shunted to voice mail. "Hi."

"What's up?"

"Nothing. What's up with you?" I keep my voice light, just a little teasing.

"Working," he says, after a hesitation that's just a little too long. "Finishing up some stuff, then heading out for dinner."

He's in Arizona. I forgot about the time difference. "Oh, right. Where are you going?"

"There's a Ruth's Chris Steak House here. We're going there."

"Out, after?" I know how those guys work.

"With clients."

"Have fun," I say, and add impulsively, "Maybe some pretty girls will ask you to dance."

"What's that supposed to mean?"

I hadn't meant anything by it, actually. Just teasing. "Nothing, Ross. It means nothing. Have fun, that's all."

"You think I'm out having fun? It's taking clients out, that's all. A few drinks, some sports on TV, maybe some pool or something. Jesus, Elisabeth. You act like I'm out stuffing dollars in a stripper's g-string!"

"I wouldn't care if you were," I counter. "It sounds like that would be more fun than pool, anyway."

Another short but weighty silence. "Dinner and drinks, that's all. Jesus."

"I was teasing you!" I snap, and bite my tongue against anything else that tries to slip out. I take a breath. Try again for sweetness and light. Be a good wife, a good wife. "Anyway, I'm jealous. Ruth's Chris. Yum."

"Did you get the letter about the home insurance payment?"

I think for a minute of the stack of mail on my desk. "…Yes?"

Ross's voice is muffled as though he took the phone from his ear. I can hear him muttering to someone else. Then he's back, voice clear. "Did you take care of it?"

I taste burnt sugar. Bitterness. "Yes."

"Because you know we don't pay that. You have to send that to the mortgage company."

"Yes, Ross, I know that," I say around the stinging flavor

his voice has pressed against my tongue. "I've been paying the bills now for…oh, eighteen years or so. I got it."

"Well, sometimes you ask me about it. You have to send that to the mortgage company."

"Yeah, I got it." A sting in my palms alerts me to the fact I'm about to ruin my manicure from pressing my nails into my flesh. I relax my fingers. "Thanks."

"It's not a bill," my husband starts, and I lose it.

"I got it! Okay? I understand all about how the home insurance is paid, Ross, I take care of it every year. I've taken care of it every year since we bought this house. I'm completely and totally capable of making sure it's all taken care of," I say tightly, without taking a breath. "And stay the hell out of my stuff."

"What's that supposed to mean?" he cries, wounded.

"It means that you wouldn't even have known about the letter if you hadn't been sifting around through the mail on my desk."

"What, I'm not allowed to look at the mail?"

"If there's something you need to see, I put it on your desk. The rest of the stuff is mine, and I take care of it. You're more than welcome to start paying all the bills and balancing all the accounts and making sure everything in this goddamned house is taken care of, Ross," I say, too loud, too harsh. Too angry. "But since I don't see that happening, just leave my desk and everything in my office alone, and stop acting like I need you to hold my hand through every little fucking thing."

"We never got a letter like that before," he cries. "I just wanted to make sure you knew!"

I rub my tongue against the back of my teeth to scrape away the flavor of his voice, and force myself to calm down. "We get a letter like that every year. Just because it's, like, brand-new to you doesn't mean I don't know how to handle it."

Ross says nothing.

"Go to dinner," I tell him, and disconnect the call.

Friday night alone, ice cream and a fight with my husband. It's no wonder I'm ripe for seduction, and still I'm surprised when Will pings me. He says his ex won't be dropping the kid off until tomorrow, and yep, I hate her.

At least there's video chat.

"I'm just your little lady in the box," I tease. "Your genie."

"You gonna grant me a wish?"

I wish I could. "Depends what it is."

Will laughs, and his phone shakes a little. "I'm getting ready for bed now. Come with me?"

"Do I have a choice? I'm in the box. I go wherever you take me."

I watch my laptop screen carefully as he lifts his phone. The sensation is disorienting; for a moment I can imagine I am actually in a box, being carried in his hand. That I am tiny, that I am small. That I am made of magic.

I've been in his bathroom before, of course, but the angle is different and everything is off-kilter. Will props his phone on the sink and bends to look at me.

"Hi."

"Hi," I reply.

We're both grinning like idiots, like dogs in August, as my grandmother would say. She had a lot of folksy sayings, most of which I never understood. This one, I do. We grin and grin because there are no words, because joy is manifesting itself in my face.

Will runs the water in the sink and brushes his teeth, making a show of it. Eyeing me once in a while while he makes a grand display of scrubbing. Suds foam from the corners of his mouth. I'm totally charmed, incapable of doing anything more than watch raptly as he mugs for the camera.

With an audience, I discover, Will is a showman.

He rinses. Spits delicately. Looks at the camera.

"See what you'd be in for," he says, "if you had to face that every day."

But I want to, are the first words that come to my lips, and of course they're bitten back. *I'd love to. I want you.*

I say nothing.

I smile and he smiles, and he leans again across the counter, his face immense, and then only his smiling mouth is on my laptop screen. I wait. He retreats a little, peering into the lens as though he's looking into my eyes.

"What next?" he says.

"You tell me," I say, then boldly add, "I think you need a shower."

"Do I?"

"Oh, yes." Excitement quickens in my stomach, the beat of my heart, the pulse and throb of my blood in my throat and wrists and cunt. "Definitely."

Will gives the shower, which I can just catch a glimpse of in the corner of the screen, a sideways look. Then back to me. A quirk of his grin. "You think so?"

"Yes. You're filthy."

He straightens, brow furrowed as though considering. His hand taps, taps on his stomach, fingers inching his shirt up to tease me with a hint of his belly, but so casually, so nonchalant, as though he has no idea what he's doing to me. He looks again into the camera.

"I'd have to take my clothes off," Will says seriously. "Be naked."

"That's how one usually takes a shower." My voice is serious, too. Cool. Almost disinterested, if you didn't know me, but of course he does. Too well. Better than anyone ever has, I think.

Will reaches to tug his shirt over his head. I'm breathless, watching. He takes his time, easing the shirt up, up, bunching the fabric in his fist and revealing himself to me one torturously slow inch at a time.

I was dressed for ice cream gluttony and bedtime, and there's no hiding the sharp jut of my nipples through the thin fabric of my tank top. I could cross my arms, but I force myself to keep my hands on the table in front of me. I want him to see what he does to me without even touching me.

Chest bare, Will straightens. His fingers slide along his ribs before he puts both hands flat on the counter. He bends again to look into the camera.

"Now what?" Will says, but his fingers are already hooking into the waistband of his jeans, tugging them a little lower. I can see the hint of the hair just below his belly button. "I guess I should take these off."

I make my eyes wide. "Oh, not that. Anything but that!"

His fingers flip open the button. The zipper parts a single metal tooth at a time, just a few before he pauses to look again into the camera, serious as a heart attack. "I can't take a shower with the jeans on, Elisabeth. I have to take them off."

I clasp my hands in front of me like Brer Rabbit pleading with Brer Fox not to throw him in the briar patch. "Oh, please, oh please! Anything but that!"

Will smiles. "Don't you try to briar patch me."

"I wouldn't dream of it." I smile, too, leaning forward as though getting closer to the screen can get me closer to him.

The zipper is down the rest of the way and the jeans pushed past his hips, pulling his gray boxer briefs along with them just enough to tease me with a glimpse of his erection. Then he moves out of sight, kicks off the jeans and stands straight again, his cock pushing at the front of his briefs. His hand curls around the length, stroking gently through the fabric. He's already hard. I'm already wet.

"Elisabeth, Elisabeth, Elisabeth," he murmurs. Even through space and time and the barrier of metal and glass, the sound of my name in his voice sparkles and dances in glittering blue and green and gold. "What am I gonna do with you?"

"Whatever you want," I breathe. My hands are on each side of the laptop screen, easing it closer. "Anything you want."

He's not smiling now. Will's entirely serious, his hand on his prick, mouth slightly parted. I've seen that look, the one that goes from teasing to need. The lighting isn't good enough for me to count the colors in his eyes, but I know them well enough by now. His pupils are large and dark. His hand moves gently up and down until he stops, gripping.

"Take them off," I whisper, not sure if he can hear me through the computer, but unable to say it louder.

Still, he hesitates. I've seen him naked now so many times, and yet I understand. What is natural in person seems harder this way. I'm fully clothed and still feel totally exposed.

Will hooks his fingers into the briefs and pushes them off. At this angle, he's a little too close to the phone. I can see him from midthigh to just below his mouth. When he straightens, that beautiful cock is perfectly framed. Helpless, ridiculous, I reach to touch. My fingertips skid on the laptop screen.

When was the last time I touched him?

Too long ago, but a few minutes would seem too long at this point. I remember how he feels. Smells. Tastes. I withdraw my hand, fingers curling into my palm, where the flesh still stings from where I earlier clutched it. Will stands without touching himself. His penis is so fucking pretty I can't stand it.

"Touch yourself." The words are mine. But the voice…my voice is low and husky and shredded on the jagged edges of my desire. "Touch yourself for me."

My cunt clenches at the noise he makes, deep in his throat. His tongue comes out, licks his bottom lip. His hand hovers, not quite touching his cock, not yet.

"I want to watch you," I tell him. "I want to watch you jerk that beautiful cock until you come."

Words have power. They can wound, elate, subdue. Arouse.

When his fingers close around his cock, both of us groan. I've had him in my cunt and in my mouth, but this is the first time I've seen him do this since that first night I stayed in his apartment.

He takes a moment to widen his stance, hips pushed forward. He strokes his cock from the base to just below the head, not palming it. Short, fast strokes, knuckles nudging the rim. I can see a little more of his face. He's not looking at me, but down at himself, though every now and then his gaze flicks upward. He's standing in front of the mirror, I realize. Watching his reflection. Then his eyes close and his head tips back a little. He bites his lower lip.

Something changes. Instead of him stroking, now he leans with his free hand on the counter and fucks into the curled fingers of his other hand. He looks at me, still biting his lip, his gaze intense. His hair's fallen over his forehead.

"You're right here," he murmurs. "I'm fucking you. Right like this."

I manage an incoherent mumble. My nipples are diamond-sharp, my cunt aching and toes curling, clit pulsing. I haven't even touched myself.

"Let me see you," Will says.

I understood his hesitation in getting naked for me, but I don't let myself think about it. I strip out of my tank top, the air suddenly too cool. I shimmy out of the pajama bottoms, aware of the slick leather under my bare ass and how ridiculous I must look sitting naked at my desk. With Will's gaze on me, I cup my breasts, flick a thumb over the tight nipples.

"I want your mouth right here." My words are thick and sweet. I pinch my nipples lightly and sigh. "Fuck. I want all of you right here."

"I am right here," Will says. "Sit back. Show me your pussy. I want you to feel good, too."

The chair moves easily on its wheels as I push it a little farther away from the desk. I spread my legs for him, forcing myself not to think about anything but giving him what he wants. Not how it's impossible to keep my stomach flat in this position, not how I haven't shaved and plucked and waxed myself bare like a porn star. I watch Will watching me, and every other insecurity fades away.

"Yes. That," he says, when I slip my fingers inside me to get them wet. When I circle my clit, his pace stutters. His fingers curl on the countertop, while his other hand grips his cock tighter, this time sliding up and over the head.

I know how and where to touch myself. The right amount of pressure, the perfect pace. But it's been so long, I've been so shut down, I can't quite get the rhythm. And the sight of him distracts me. I need to close my eyes and concentrate on my pleasure, but I can't make myself look away from the mesmerizing beauty of what he's doing. I push my fingers inside myself again, bring them out slick and hot, find my clit and stroke it between my thumb and forefinger. I'm echoing him, the way I found myself mimicking his phrasing and the cadence of his voice…but it works. When I touch myself the way he's touching himself, it feels even more like he's touching me.

"Shit," he breathes. "Feels so good."

It does feel good, and finally, there it is. The sweet spot. Everything inside me tenses…. *I'm going to lose it,* I think, as my fingers slow. He's getting close, and I'm easing off.

"Talk to me," he says.

I don't even think about what to say. Does it matter? "Fuck me."

"I am fucking you," Will says.

"Harder." Sex talk, ridiculous. But it works. I push my fingers inside myself, curling upward. There's that spot, the one his cock hits so perfectly. The heel of my hand presses my clit. Everything moves in time. "Fuck me harder."

"I love it when you come," Will says. "I love that noise you make when I pull your hair—"

Just the thought of it's a trigger. I cry out. He groans. Closer and closer, we work together, even though we're so far apart.

I let go.

I'm mindless again, without words, though not without voice. Hoarse and low. All I can do is breathe. The crush of waves on sand, that's what I taste and smell and hear, and feel on my skin when Will's pleasure comes out through his voice. We come together, and it takes forever, and then I'm aware of my skin sticking to the chair and the chill in the room and the clatter of Will's phone when it falls over and shows me nothing but the speckles in his countertop.

"Sorry," he says after a couple seconds, and tilts it upright again. His hair is messed up, and he has that sleepy-eyed look, that slow smile I recognize. "Hey."

"Hey."

We don't say much as we both tidy up. I put my pajamas back on and take my laptop from the desk to the chaise longue, where I curl under a blanket and rest it on my knees while I wait for Will to come back into view. He's wearing his pajamas, too, when he returns—the blue ones with the sailboats that I bought him one day in the farmer's market as a joke, because he normally sleeps in his briefs.

Suddenly, I want to cry.

He takes me, his little woman in the box, into the bed with him and puts me on the pillow, so when he turns onto his side, one arm beneath his head, it's almost as though I'm there beside him. I turn, too, stretching out on the chaise with my pillow tucked beneath me.

We can't stop staring at each other. Saying nothing, nothing to say. I trace the curve of his jaw and throat, the sweet spot below his ear, with only my eyes, because he's too faraway to touch. We stare and we stare and I can't stop myself from smiling, because he's smiling, too. We don't have to speak to have this conversation; in fact, the only way to have it is by not using words.

And then, although it's more than silly, it's stupid, it's ridiculous, I pull the laptop closer to me so I can pretend it's Will I'm holding, not some box of metal and wire and glass. Only for a few seconds, long enough to hear the sound of his breathing as close as if it was in my ear. But I can't feel him and I can't smell him. I want him to talk so I can at least have that last sensation, yet when I pull away to look at him, Will's eyes are closed, his breathing heavy.

We've never slept together, and this is nothing like it would be if we ever did. But it's the closest we will ever get to it, I think, as sleep weights my own eyes. I listen to the soft shush-hush of his breathing. Then the shuffle of blankets as he shifts. I look at him. He's looking back.

"How are we going to say goodbye?" Will asks in a sleep-furry voice.

He means now. I mean forever. "I don't want to."

His sleepy smile slaughters me. If I was standing, it would've sent me to my knees. Will yawns.

"We have to, at some point. Can't stay online all night," he says.

Of course he's right, but that doesn't change how I feel.

He gets up on his elbow, propping his head in his hand. He studies me.

"If you knew this was the last time you'd talk to me, what would you say?" I ask. It's too late for this kind of conversation, the sort I promised myself I'd never have with him. But I want to know.

Will laughs, and it's uncomfortable, not genuine. "C'mon. We'll talk again."

I'm not so sure. "I just assume every time will be the last, that's all."

"That hasn't happened yet."

"No," I tell him carefully. "But it's going to."

He leans closer to the camera. "Do you want it to?"

"No."

Another yawn, sleep in his eyes. "Go to sleep. It's late."

I like him telling me what to do as much as I like anyone else doing it, which is to say not at all. He must see it in my face, because his voice softens. His smile is supposed to win me, but I'm not sure it does.

"C'mon." Will's whisper is the grit of sand in my teeth. "We're friends, right?"

"Yes." I can't make myself smile, but I choose to let him win me.

I choose it.

"Good night, Elisabeth," Will says, but I can't force myself to say the words. He laughs a little. "Want me to count to three?"

I shake my head. I let my fingertips trace the outline of his face for a second or so. "Good night, Will."

Before he can count or move or do anything at all, I slide my fingers across the touchpad and disconnect the call. His image is frozen there for too short a second, a blink, before the laptop beeps and all I see is my own face. My hair's a mess and my mascara's painted shadows under my eyes. I turn my head from side to side, wondering exactly what Will sees when he looks at me.

How could I have ever believed he and I would be "just friends"? We will never be "just" anything. There's too much of us.

Chapter Twenty-Seven

I keep telling myself this is just infatuation. That it's not real. That we are built of sand, not brick.

I sit at my desk and stare out the window, but I don't see anything. I don't hear anything. I tell myself that if I stop seeing him, this all will pass. It will fade.

Oh, God.

Oh, God, please let it fade.

This won't last. I tell myself it can't, of course. It started in the wrong place and keeps going into even more wrong. Something like this, with me and Will, this up, up, up, this crazy chaos, this inferno…things like that don't last.

If I stop it now, I think, while the seconds tick by and I stare and stare at my work as though it should mean something, yet I can't make the numbers line up. If I stop it now, very soon, before I know it, all that's left will be memory. And over time, the smell of him will go away. The taste of him.

I put my fingers to my mouth and let my tongue stroke over the tips. I can still taste him. I lift my shirt to breathe against the fabric where he held me close; I can still smell him.

He is all over me like a stain.

This can't last. I will end it, or maybe he will, when he discovers someone new and real, not me, the bright and shiny, the star always out of reach. Will's going to find someone new; I expect him to. I tell him and myself I want him to, but we both know I am a liar, the worst sort, the kind who smiles with the lie clamped tight between her teeth.

This will end. It has to. Very soon, I think as I refresh my email in case there's a message from him. Check my voice mail in case he's called. This will be over very soon, and I will go back into my life and try somehow to make it work.

I will get away with this.

I press my fingertips to my eyes to hold back the tears; nobody can come in here and see me weeping at my desk. Sobbing like a lunatic. But the pain rears up and grabs me by the back of the head to pry open my mouth. It kisses me breathless while it drips venom through every vein, and though I wish this pain could make me numb, it only sets me on fire. I hold back the sobs with the heel of my hand against my lips. By biting my tongue. I breathe and breathe.

What if I could be happy with Will? Really happy. Not settling. What if I have waited my whole life to find this person who fits me like the missing piece of my puzzle? What if my entire life has led me to this point, not to teach me a lesson about appreciating what I have, but to help me let it all go?

I finish for the day. I go home. I make dinner, which Ross and I eat while he talks to me about his work and I nod without really listening. Jac calls, talks to her dad. Talks to me. I pay some bills. We watch a movie. Ross reminds me about a long list of things that need to be taken care of, all of which I've already arranged to do, but I nod and nod and let him talk. When he goes to bed, I pretend I'm engrossed in the book on my lap, but I haven't read more than a paragraph in hours. I can't focus. Can't concentrate.

I haven't talked to Will in two long days—he's busy with his son and I've had a lot going on around here. Our real lives got in the way of the fantasy one, which is to be expected, but I don't like it. I miss him from someplace low in my gut, and yes, it's sexual, but it's also more than that. He's become a part of my day. The best part.

Two in the morning and I haven't read another word. I've reorganized my cookbooks and cleaned the fridge and done a lot of online holiday shopping to get it out of the way, even though Christmas is months off. And still the weight of missing him is in my gut, weighty as a pile of stones that stack and stack until they block my throat, too. Two in the morning is the worst time to need someone.

Balance, I remind myself. It's only been a couple days. *He's not ignoring you. He hasn't disappeared. Balance, Elisabeth. Don't be that girl who shows up with mascara tracks on her cheeks, asking, "Am I pretty? Do you think I'm pretty, really?"*

I should go to bed. I should not, at the very least, text him. But of course that's exactly why I do, knowing he won't answer because he's asleep.

Have a great day....

But he does answer me a few minutes later.

You're up late.

Yes. So are you.

Working on some edits. Got a bunch of last minute client requests.

The conversation continues in that stuttering, stilted manner, until I break down and ask him what I really want to: Lunch tomorrow? (Today)

Can't. Sorry.

When?

No answer. Not for several interminable minutes, then not for another hour. I sit and stare at my phone, then methodically go through and delete all the messages. Then all my recent calls.

This, to quote Eminem, is the part where the rap breaks down.

Because now I'm unable to sleep, and upstairs, Ross's alarm goes off, and he comes down to find me pretending I got up early to make him breakfast before he leaves for yet another business trip to someplace I can't recall. And because I realize for the first time what it means to be having an affair, how it consumes everything. Every thought, every action, the slices of toast I put on his plate, the kiss he gives me at the sink, everything is overlaid with the steady, constant thump of the same thought, over and over.

What would you do, if you knew?

"You're the best wife I ever had," Ross says at the platter of scrambled eggs and bacon I present. It's a joke, an old one, and I laugh because I'm supposed to. I'm the only wife he's ever had, but surely even being the only, I can't be the best.

Chapter Twenty-Eight

I'm not expecting Will to call me the next day, right before lunch, but when my phone rings and I see that it's him, I answer right away. I have to. I think I'm physically incapable of ignoring him. I can't stop myself from smiling, even as I hate myself a little for being so relieved. "Hi!"

"Hi." He sounds off, and immediately, I'm on my guard.

"You okay?"

"Tired. Didn't get a lot of sleep."

I make myself sound sympathetic. "Yeah. Me, neither."

"Got my work done, though."

"Good."

There's a pause. I hear traffic and the intake of breath. He's smoking.

"What are you doing now?" I'm stupid for asking, but there's still hope, always hope, that he's calling to meet me for lunch.

"Getting ready for a cover shoot."

"Science fiction?"

"Romance," Will says.

I picture a couple embracing. "Sexy. Sure they want you to take the picture and not be in it? 'Cuz you'd totally sell a million copies, especially if you had your shirt off."

I'm trying to tease him. He'd have laughed, before. He doesn't laugh now.

"Yeah."

I break. "Have lunch with me, Will. Just a sandwich. It won't take long...."

"I can't." He sounds irritable. "I told you."

"Then why are you calling me?" I bite out the words.

"Because if I didn't, you'd get all bent out of shape," he snaps. "Christ, Elisabeth. Back off, okay?"

I'm silent.

"Look," he says. "If you want to pick something up and come over about two, I'll be done by then."

"Only if you want me to. I'm not trying to force you."

"I said you could, didn't I?"

This is exactly the argument I never wanted to have, and I hate it. But I take the sandwich to his apartment, and I arrive at two on the dot so he can't accuse me of being too early.

I don't kiss him when he lets me in. We eat the food with minimal conversation. Will takes the plates and puts them in the dishwasher while I use his bathroom, taking an extra long time to wash my hands so I can be sure I won't cry when I say goodbye.

"Thanks for lunch. I'll call you," I tell him at the door, even though I have no intentions of doing that.

"I wanted to ask you to come with me to this thing I got invited to," Will says suddenly. "It's a bring-a-date sort of thing."

Before I can ask him when it is, and mentally check my calendar, he goes on. "But then I realized I couldn't ask you, because you probably couldn't go, and if you could, it would be because you made up some excuse about what you were doing."

"Will..."

His look is guarded, no expression. A blank. "I wanted to

be with you, and I couldn't. So I got pissed off. I don't like wanting what I can't have."

Well, I think, *who does?*

But he wants me, that's what I hear, and although it should make me feel better, it only makes me feel worse. I don't want him to hurt. I never wanted that.

"Should I leave?" I think I mean his apartment, but once the words are out, they could mean anything.

"Yeah. I think you should."

My hand on the knob, I look at him over my shoulder. I want to be dignified about this. At least I want to try. "Should I not call you again?"

He doesn't answer for half a minute, and my heart breaks slowly, piece by shattered piece.

"No. I'll call you when I've had some time to think."

Fuck dignified. I'm too proud. "Don't say it if you're not going to. I'd rather you just tell me you're not going to talk to me again than try to save my feelings or something like that."

His expression softens, still guarded, but not so blank. "I'll call you."

I nod stiffly and let myself out. I hold my shit together all the way back to the gallery, where I lock myself in the bathroom and press my hands to my face to stifle the sound of the sobs I'm expecting to tear me apart—except they don't come. Everything about me is bone dry.

Chapter Twenty-Nine

He does call me, but the conversation is bland as baby food, no flavor. The ocean is muffled and distant, the gulls silent when he says my name, and the smell is of old seaweed and fish, not fresh salt air and sand. I'm the one who makes excuses to end the call, but I think we're both relieved.

His text is simpler—a picture of the Brooklyn Bridge with late afternoon sky and clouds giving it an eerie feel. The work is lovely, even without any editing, and I tell him so. The next message is of his face, eyes covered by black Ray-Bans, cigarette dangling from the corner of his mouth. I take a picture of my shoes, a pair of spectator pumps I picked up from a thrift shop. We trade these snapshots back and forth for the rest of the day without saying another word. Sometimes we use the emoji emoticons for our phones to make rebuslike messages that become more and more complicated, until one of us give up and has to ask for a translation. I've sent him one that I'm sure will make me the winner of this silly game…except that Will doesn't reply.

There really are only so many times when the same thing can continue to sting, so I push away the irritation and finish up my work. Naveen raps on my office door just before I'm ready to go home. His huge grin is supposed to charm me, but I know him too well. My guard goes up.

"What?"

"Business trip. You and me."

I laugh out loud, the first time all day. It feels good, to be honest. "You and me. Uh-huh. Where? What?"

"It's a buying trip. Philly."

"That's hardly a business trip for me, Naveen. You want to stay at my house?"

He shakes his head.

"Ah." I cross my arms as I lean on the edge of my desk. The toe of my spectator pump taps. "What do you need me for?"

"Some business, for real. She has a collection. I want you to help me put a value on it."

I give him a suspicious look. "That's not usually what I do."

"But you have a good eye. And you are officially a buyer for this gallery, and you do handle the invoices and receipts."

"And everything else. I still don't get why you need me. Can't you use one of your appraisers?"

He gives me a look. I sigh and shake my head, but there's no resisting him. Especially when he comes to hug me, nuzzling a little too familiarly at me until I slap him away. He kisses my cheek.

"I told Puja I'd be with you. She's going to call you."

"She's suspicious?" That would be a first.

He doesn't say anything for a moment, which is answer enough. "I need you to cover for me."

"I could do that without going with you."

"I trust your opinion," Naveen says honestly. "She has some great stuff, but some of it's junk. You'll give me an honest answer about it."

I sigh and check my calendar. "Fine. Ross will be out of town again, anyway."

"Thanks, Betts. I owe you. If you ever need…" He pauses. "Well. You know I'd do the same for you."

"You won't have to." It comes out sour.

Naveen looks into my eyes, uncharacteristically quiet, though I can see he's thinking hard about what to say. He kisses my cheek again, softer this time. He rubs my arms up and down. "I mean it, Betts. Anytime. Anything you need."

I could break down then. Sob on his shoulder. I could let him counsel me through this; God knows I've listened to him agonize over a lot of relationships over the years. The only one he's never complained or confided in me about is the one with his wife. I could let Naveen comfort me, except I don't deserve grief.

I smile. "I'm fine. What time, where, what am I doing and how much do you want to spend?"

On the train ride home, I tuck my phone in my bag and pull out a book to read instead. I used to spend this time with Will. And for a long while, I sit with the book in my hand and stare out the window, instead.

Would this be worse, if I knew he didn't want me at all? No.

Because I know I have hurt him just by being me. Oh, God, all I wanted was… I just wanted…

I didn't know. I didn't want this to happen. I didn't seek this, it found me, and he was there, right there all the time. I didn't do this alone.

I am not the devil. I am not some temptress, leading him to sin. I never made him do anything he didn't want to do. He was there right with me, every step, even sometimes urging me. Leading me. We did this together, so why do I feel it's my fault, all alone?

Pull me close. Push me away.

And I understand, oh yes, I know why he has to step back and put up a wall, but that doesn't make any of it better or easier. If he found someone else, my heart would break, but this is worse. This is worse because I know he wants me.

But he won't take me.

Chapter Thirty

Date night.

It was my suggestion, one that seemed to surprise Ross. He said no, at first. Didn't want to go out, had to get up early for work. Didn't like any of the movies I wanted to see.

I convinced him.

Once upon a time I had fallen in love with this man, and I'd married him. We have children and built a life together. There's value in that, no matter what else has happened or what I've done. I'm not in love with my husband anymore, but I'm trying to remember why I once had been.

It's easier than I deserve it to be. Ross can be charming, when he tries. Considerate. Even generous. He takes me to dinner after the movie and plies me with wine and regales me with funny stories from his travels. He's treating me a little like he treats his clients—and I know that, but it's an effort from him and I appreciate it.

We talk about the girls, who've both grown up so well. Ross is proud of his daughters, as am I, but watching him talk about Jac's new job and Kat's recent work with her favorite charity, I can see exactly how much they mean to him.

When I reach for his hand across the table, he takes it.

When he reaches for me in bed, I let him.

★ ★ ★

Late at night, Will texts me when I'm asleep. I see I have a message when I get up to use the bathroom—too much wine with dinner. I think about not answering it, but 2:00 a.m. is still the worst time to miss someone. I go downstairs and thumb his number across the keypad. He sounds tired when he answers, but I know he wasn't sleeping.

"I want you to be here, right now," Will says without even saying hello. "And you're not."

"No. I'm not." I don't say I wish I was there, too. There doesn't seem to be much point. I'm not. I could be, if he'd given me the chance to make it happen, but even if I was there now, it wouldn't be enough.

Silence.

I curl into a ball on the lumpy recliner we relegated to the basement when we refinished the den upstairs. The girls used this room for their sleepovers and parties and, let's face it, their boyfriends. It's damp down here, and chilly, even during the summer. The blanket I pull over myself has cartoon princesses on it and smells a little of the dog we used to have.

"Where are you?" Will asks.

"At home."

"Are you alone?"

"No," I say again. "I'm not."

"What does he think when you get out of bed in the middle of the night to talk to me?" I hear the click of Will's lighter, the hiss of his breath.

"He doesn't notice."

"How can he not fucking notice?" Will says, angry. "What are you going to do when he does? What would you tell him if he said, 'Who the hell are you talking to at two in the morning?'"

I've thought about that, of course. What I'd say. What I

should say or do, but haven't and probably won't. "I don't know."

"Well, maybe you should fucking think about it!"

I'm at a disadvantage, because I can't yell. I have to swallow my words, make them soft, though they're nothing close to sweet. "What do you want me to say? If you don't think I should be talking to you in the middle of the night, maybe you shouldn't fucking text me!"

"You don't have to answer!"

"No," I tell him, soft and slow and low and bitter and angry. "I guess I don't."

More silence. I'm curled so tight that everything aches, but I can't force myself to shift and make myself comfortable. I want to hurt.

"But I always do," I say eventually, when he doesn't say anything.

"You shouldn't."

"Is that what you want, Will?" I'm weary of this. All of it. Even the brightest fires leave nothing but ash behind. "Because if that's what you want, I can make that happen."

"I just want you to be here with me. Now. That's what I want."

"Well. I'm not," I snap. "I don't like it, either, but unless something changes, that's how it is."

Will's voice is raspy. "Is something ever going to change, Elisabeth?"

Even in the damp chill of the basement, I'm suddenly flushed. Not with passion, but a sick sort of anticipation. I have to think very carefully about what to say, how to say it.

"Are you asking me to leave my husband?"

"No."

I'm angrier now than I was before. "If you have something to say to me, if you want something from me…"

"I don't."

I am tired, I am depressed, I am sad and lost and on the edge of a cliff I don't want to jump off but might just have to. And though I know better than to poke the monkey, because when you do, it flings poo, I poke, anyway. Hard.

"A month from Friday, I'm going to be with Naveen, some buying thing. I'll be out overnight here in Philly. Come meet me."

"I don't think I can."

Of course he can. Even with his kid, his responsibilities, Will spends most of his time alone, and there's plenty of time for him to rearrange whatever schedule he has to accommodate an overnighter out of town. Every time we've been together, it's been me making the effort, me taking a trip into the city, arranging my schedule.

"You make things important. Or you don't. I can see you in a month. Overnight. I can't be there now, but I can be with you—"

"Sorry," Will says in a cold, neutral tone that's not sorry at all, not one bit. "It's not going to work."

He's right, of course. What about this could possibly work? Me and him, nothing alike, the only thing we have in common is how good it feels to fuck each other until we are raw and hobbling. There's nothing to us aside from...

Everything

Aside from everything.

I swallow, and swallow again, all the anger, the disappointment, the tears. Sharp as razors, that's what those words are against the tenderness of my throat, but I keep my voice as unemotional as his. "Fine. Whatever. I can't make you do anything. You do what you want to do. In four weeks, I'll be with Naveen at some stupid swanky club in downtown Philly, authorizing him to spend money he doesn't have on stuff to impress some woman he thinks he's in love with. You can be there or not. I won't ask again."

"What about between now and then?"

"Every day," I tell him, "you will miss me either a little less or a little more. Until one day you will wake up and realize you don't miss me at all, or you will find yourself incapable of living without me."

"And then what," Will says. "Then what?"

"Then," I say just before I disconnect, "come find me."

Chapter Thirty-One

"Come with me."

I pause with my toothbrush at my mouth to look at Ross, next to me at his own sink. "What?"

"Come with me to South Carolina. The weather will be great. The hotel's nice. You can lounge around the pool...."

I spit, rinse and spit again. "Ross, I have to work. I can't just take off for South Carolina with you. If you'd asked me a couple weeks ago, maybe."

"Just call Naveen. He won't care." For a moment Ross's brow furrows. "You can get him to give you anything you want."

"What's that supposed to mean?" Surprised, I shove my toothbrush back into the holder and put my hands on my hips. "Ross?"

"It means that if you want to come to South Carolina with me, you could."

We stare at each other. I'm not sure what to say. Ross has never asked me to go on a business trip with him before, even back in the days when I'd have wanted to go.

"I know you think my job's not that important," I say carefully, "but I made a commitment to Naveen to be there for this sale this weekend, and it is part of my job. I can't just blow it off."

Ross frowns. "Maybe you should just quit."

"Why on earth would I quit?" I can't believe we're having this conversation.

"To spend more time with me," Ross says, and pulls me close. "When I retire."

I'm so surprised by this that I let him kiss me. "Are you planning to retire?"

"Well…yeah. Of course."

"Soon?" It's the first I'm hearing of it, and while I know I'm supposed to be excited by the idea, all I can think of is what I'll do with him when he's here all the time.

Ross kisses me. Shrugs. Pulls away to finish splashing his face with cologne. "Sooner than you think. Everything's always sooner than you think." He turns and winks, giving me the smile that made me fall in love with him all those years ago. "Sure I can't change your mind?"

For one fleeting second, one breath, one tick-tock beat of my heart, I almost say yes. But I think he knew I really couldn't come. I think maybe that's why he asked, because when I shake my head, something like relief gleams briefly in his eyes.

"I'll call you when I get there," Ross says.

"Safe travels," I tell him.

He forgets to kiss me when he leaves.

I've met a few of Naveen's women over the years, but this is the first time he's ever formally introduced me to one. She's pretty but not beautiful. Short, not petite. And busty, yes, but also plump in a way she shields with well-tailored clothes, but which can't be completely hidden. She's so not like any of the rest of them—including me—that all I can do is marvel while trying not to show my surprise.

Francesca supposedly doesn't know I know about her and Naveen, at least that's what he told me. Part of this package is not only providing him with official cover, but also pretending to her that I don't know what they're really up to. I didn't ask him why it's so important, but I do my best to smile and nod when he introduces us, and when she starts showing us around the pieces she's trying to sell. Naveen doesn't want to keep any of these. At least I thought the plan was to pick up the bulk of her collection and resell it immediately without even showing it. There's always a market for "art" that doesn't challenge anyone, in corporate settings that want something a little fancier than the usual portraits of pears.

The arrangements are all made quickly, with little fuss, and I'm not even annoyed in the end. Maybe it's because the actual collection is surprisingly eclectic. There are a few truly delightful pieces, well worth the prices she's asking, and the others are all at least resalable. Or maybe it's because I see the way he looks at her. His hand at the small of her back. The way she leans to listen to him when he points out something with one of the sculptures. I've never seen Naveen so...happy.

"It's done, then?" he asks when she's settling up some things with the people who will pack the art for shipping.

"All done. Are you satisfied?"

He looks across the room at Francesca and then at me. "Yes. Thanks, Betts. You're the best."

From my purse comes the loud, familiar ping of a text message.

I already know it's Will before I thumb the screen to check it. It's been three weeks, six days and twelve hours since the last time we spoke. I thought I'd convinced myself I would never hear from him again, but the instant that chime rings, I know I was waiting for it all along.

Hi

Oh, you son of a bitch, I think, even as my knees go weak with relief. Naveen is chattering, something about going to dinner. Something about drinks. Will I be okay, will I need a ride home? Do I want to come with them?

At home, I have a dark and empty house waiting for me. Ross is out of town until Monday. Naveen is already making moves to take his lady love away someplace private. So I do the only thing that feels right. I thumb a message into my phone.

You can be here in two hours.

Chapter Thirty-Two

"You okay?" Naveen presses another drink into my hand.

It's my third gin and tonic, and the first two went down like water. We had dinner at some bistro, and though I could tell Naveen was anxious for me to leave, his lovely lady friend was solicitous and generous and kind. I can see why he loves her. She is everything he always avoided in the past.

It's been an hour and forty-five minutes.

Now we've moved to a club down the street. There's an Irish pub on one side, where we are standing at the bar, with a dance floor through a set of arched doors, and a sports bar on the other side. You can move from one to the other, but Naveen's itching to get out of here. I don't blame him.

Another text pings through—Will, giving me the update on his travels, how close he is. How much longer it will be until he gets here. Naveen hasn't asked me who it is or why I told him I'm not going home, but he won't leave me here alone until he's sure I'm okay.

Just got off the train. Cab. 15 min?

Everything inside me goes tight. I swallow the rest of my drink and put the empty glass on the bar. To Naveen I say, "You can go on. I'll be okay."

"Are you sure?" Francesca asks, looking around the bar. "Are you waiting for someone? Is…he…here?"

So delicate and appreciated, and we share a look that says she knows I know the truth, and appreciates my discretion, too. "Not yet."

I hug Naveen. Kiss his cheek. Whisper in his ear, "Go, I'll be fine. Go and have fun."

He holds me close for a second or two longer than I intended, saying against my cheek, "Be careful, Betts."

Funny advice, coming from him, and it makes me close my eyes and take a deep breath. I squeeze him hard before stepping back. "Go."

Ten minutes pass. Another text from Will. He's not quite sure where to go and the cabdriver has let him off down the street. I call him.

"Where are you?"

He names the corner of two streets a block or so away.

"Keep walking," I tell him. "I'll wait outside."

South Street in Philly on a late July night is crazytown. *Throng* is a good word to describe it. I stand with my phone pressed to my ear and navigate him toward me while I search and search the crowd for the first glimpse of him. Unfamiliar faces pass me. I keep looking.

"I'm in front of a lingerie store," Will says. "It has a gimp suit in the window."

He's close. "Keep coming. You're one block away."

I see him before he sees me. He's looking, though. Scanning the crowd and the storefronts as he dodges and weaves through the foot traffic.

"I see you," I say.

And then he sees me, too.

Recognition lights his face and he puts away the phone, tucking it into the pocket of his pants. Like Neo going after the Woman in Red in the *Matrix,* he battles the opposite-moving crowd, until at last, at last, Will is in front of me, and all I can do is stand there.

I want to kiss him, but there's still a sting from this long month of nothing and waiting. I'm too proud, I guess. Or too determined not to get stung again. But still, he's here. He came. No matter what happens after this, nothing else matters.

Will kisses me, hesitant.

"Kiss me harder," I say against his mouth, and he does.

We pull apart.

Will opens his arms. "So. Now what?"

I look over my shoulder, then back at him. "Let's go dancing."

Chapter Thirty-Three

The room is lit in lines of blue and green, and though most of the rest of the club is jammed elbow to elbow, crotch to ass with strangers grinding and writhing, this room is much smaller and almost empty. At least this part is, the raised step with benches built in against the wall. I sit with a sigh, and Will sits next to me.

DJs don't spin anymore—but I do. I spin even though I'm sitting, because Will's thigh presses mine, the warmth of his calf rubs my bare skin, and he jiggles a little to the beat of an eighties classic. When the music changes, shifting into the familiar opening strains of Michael Jackson's "Beat It," he gives me a grin.

"Show me your sweet moves," I say.

And he does.

Nobody's ever danced for me that way before, all silly and goofy. It's heart-stoppingly sexy because it's not all smooth and concentrated, the way the guys in the corner are dancing, with the girls bending over to shove their asses into the guys' crotches. Will just dances as if it doesn't matter what he's doing, and I watch with my smile growing wider and wider. I can't stop smiling, and I clap my hands and bounce a little on the smooth vinyl bench.

And then, just then, in that moment with the lights that are blue and green and gold, and the music pumping, I know that I love him.

I am in love with him, and I think I've known that for a long time, but now I can't stop myself from admitting it. I love the way he dances for me, trying to make me laugh, not caring if he looks a little like a fool. He is adorable and charming, and the breath leaves my lungs and my heart forgets to beat, moment after moment.

I love him.

I love him.

I love him.

You never fall in love with anyone the same way you fell in love with someone else. It's always different, every time, if you're lucky—or cursed—enough to have it happen more than once. But I've never been uncertain about love, not any of the times I found myself in it. Love is always real, even when it doesn't last.

I love him, and I want this night to go on and on forever. I want this song to never end, but of course it has to, and he slides onto the bench beside me. He's laughing, but I can't find the air to laugh with him. All I can do is kiss him.

More slow kisses, feather brushes of lip on lip, the quick and furtive slip of his tongue inside my mouth.

"Kiss me harder," I'd said earlier in the night, but this is not hard. It's slow and sweet and soft, and I can't get enough.

"Let's get out of here," Will says, linking his fingers in mine. The squeeze of his hand is perhaps meant to be casual, but there's a weight of meaning in it.

"Yes," I say. And again. "Yes, yes, yes."

The alcohol didn't intoxicate me. His mouth does. His hand on the small of my back, tugging at my dress to keep me from stepping into the street. The way he hails a cab and opens the door, waiting for me to slide inside before he gets in after me. The press of his knee on mine. I am drunk on Will.

The streetlights seem elongated and wavering, the view from the pilot's seat of the *Millennium Falcon*. Traffic lights are a rainbow. The driver's music is low and something foreign I don't recognize, and he barely says a word to us, not even glancing in the rearview mirror. Maybe he's had too many drunk and horny couples in the back of his cab and he knows better. More likely, he just doesn't give a fuck beyond getting us to where we want to go. I give him the address of a hotel close to the train station, because it will be convenient for Will in the morning.

We don't kiss or touch except for the inconsistent press of our calves, the occasional brush of our fingertips, each of our hands on top of our knees. Everything is surreal. Nothing seems right. Am I dreaming this? And if I am, I don't want to wake up.

"Salvador Dali," I murmur.

Will turns his head. "What?"

"Dali," I say. "All of this…everything is like Dali. It's all Dali."

Will laughs and takes my hand as the cab slows in front of the hotel. "Melting clocks?"

"No." I can't explain it. I wave my free hand and turn to him. "Just that nothing seems real, that's all. Why are you here?"

He leans close and kisses me, his reply too low for anyone but me to hear. "Because you wanted me to come."

The cabby coughs then, expectant. Will pays him. We get out of the cab. The hotel is fancier than I remembered, not the sort that rents rooms by the hour, but they do accept cash and there is a room available. The elevator is the sort that requires the key before it will go beyond the lobby, and I fumble with it, though everything has begun shifting toward clarity. Will puts his hand over mine to guide the keycard into the slot.

"You have to slide it in slow," I say, the words a giddy mouthful, tasting of caramel. "In and out."

The hotel is old, the elevator ornate, with lots of brass. The light is warm and yellow and makes everything prettier than it ought to be. The door closes, and Will backs me up against the mirrored wall. I can see myself in the ceiling and over his shoulder.

His mouth is greedy on my neck, that sweet spot he always manages to find. His hands roam my body, never lingering, but managing to hit all the right places in just the right order. We're on the tenth floor, and by the time the elevator stops again, he's already got his hand up my skirt and his fingers inside me. Thank God there's nobody waiting to get on when the doors open.

The room, as it turns out, is immense. There's an alarm clock on the bedside table with a connector for my iPhone, which I plug in so I can put on some music. I set it to shuffle, and the first song that comes up is one we danced to earlier tonight. It's like a sign.

Unbuttoning, unzipping, we move together. Beneath his striped shirt he wears a formfitting black T-shirt that makes me want to bite him. My dress slips off easily over my head. His pants end up somewhere on the floor.

The desk turns out to be the perfect height for me to sit on the edge, with Will between my legs. I pull him by the front of his T-shirt to get at his mouth, every kiss punctuated with my murmured plea. "Fuck me, fuck me, fuck me...."

I'd let him take me there on the desk, but Will has other ideas. He breaks the kiss and steps away. He gives the bed a significant look that makes me laugh and also sets me on fire.

"What?" I tease. "You don't want to just fuck me right here? Phew, I guess the shine is off the penny."

"I want," Will says slowly, "to make love to you on that giant bed. All night."

His words dry my throat so that I have to swallow hard to find my own. "The night's almost over already. We'd better hurry."

"I'm not going to hurry. I'm going to take my time."

We look at each other without saying anything, both of us smiling like idiots. My heart is so full I can't believe it can possibly still beat without bursting right out of me. My desire for him is so fierce I'm afraid to stand, because I know my knees will be too weak to hold me, but there's more than that. This great and bursting thing inside me is love.

"I want to take a shower, first." Fucking on a desk without taking off all your clothes is one thing. Making love all night in a bed requires a whole different sort of preparation, and at the very least I want to rinse my mouth. I stand. Hold out my hand. "Come on. Let's see if the shower's as nice as the bed."

It's nicer, as it turns out. Marble tiles, detachable shower-head with different settings. Even a steam option. We look at each other.

"Wow," Will says.

"Hey, when you ride with me, you ride in style." I turn on the water, watching the steam wreathe the room for a minute. My head's still spinny, but the Dali feeling's gone. In its place is a hard-edged clarity, bright as diamonds.

This is happening.

Will reaches a hand over his shoulder to pull off his T-shirt, leaving him in gray boxer briefs. I'm still in bra and panties. I want to get on my knees in front of him. I want to lick him from his perfect feet all the way to his beautiful prick. I want to get my mouth on every part of him. A fuck noise slips out of me involuntarily, something hoarse and raw, and it makes him laugh.

With a deep breath, I strip out of my underwear and get under the water, which is so hot it stings, but feels so good at the same time. There's plenty of room for both of us, especially when we move at the same time to pull each other close. Water makes us slippery, the shower gel I squeeze from the bottle even slicker. Suds tickle, the water cascades over us, and we're kissing, kissing, kissing. His touch tickles. I could stay in here forever, but I keep thinking of that big bed and his promise to take his time.

The towels are thick and fluffy, as lovely as everything else in this room. One for him, two for me so I can rub my hair dry. It's dripping and heavy over my shoulders, and I'm sure it looks like a wreck, but then he's pulling down the comforter to expose the vast expanse of crisp white sheets, and laying me down on the bed. I no longer give one tiny fuck about my hair.

We tangle ourselves. Arms and legs. He kisses me with a hand rubbing just right between my legs, and I'm already so close I come like a strike of lightning.

Will groans at the pulse of my body around his fingers. He looks down at me, mouth wet, and smiles. I thread my fingers through his hair at the back of his neck and force myself to look at him even though the pleasure is so great it's all I can do to keep my eyes open.

"I love watching you get turned on," he says.

All the other times have been frantic and fast. But now he kisses me some more. Mouth, chin, jaw, throat. He moves his mouth over my breasts, taking his time with each one, all while his fingers keep their steady, circling pace on my clit. Over my ribs and my belly, and though I want to cringe, I refuse to do so. Back to my mouth for one more kiss, but then he pulls away.

"I want to watch you again."

"I'll see what I can do," I say, a little breathless.

It's hard, though. Letting go while he watches and I do nothing but let him build this pleasure inside me. The first orgasm was hard and sharp, and I'm not even sure I can come again. And of course, the more I think about it the more likely it is that I won't.

But Will is patient, Will is kind, he's generous. He nuzzles my neck while his fingers work their magic, and the feeling builds and grows until finally, at last, his name slips out of me on a sigh. When, blinking, I can focus on his face again, he looks serious.

"Elisabeth—"

All at once, I'm not ready to hear what he might say. Not if it's anything like what I want to tell him, and not if it's something else. I stop his words with a kiss, silencing the rush of the ocean even as the smell of salt and sand still lingers.

Fuck me, fuck me. I've said it a hundred times to him if I've said it once, but that's not what I say now, here on this great big bed with the clean white sheets. It's not what I say when I'm finally naked with him.

"Make love to me."

There are a whole bunch of positions in the Kama Sutra, but there's a reason the missionary position is one of the most popular. He covers me with his body, fitting as if he was made for me. He shivers a little on that first thrust, the way he always does, and as always, I am charmed and thrilled and moved at how my body can make him feel so good.

It's the longest we've ever taken. Slow motion. I wrap my arms and legs around him. We move together as the sun comes up and paints the room in another layer of light. Will buries his face against my neck and shudders against me, and all I can do is hold him as close as I can. I don't ever want to let him go.

The music's still playing through the alarm clock speakers, and I know I should roll over and turn it off, but I can't rouse myself enough to do more than reach to turn the volume down. I haven't been paying attention to what was playing, but now the simple sounds of a guitar and a man's voice begin. I know the song, of course; I'm the one who downloaded it. But I haven't listened to it in a while. He's singing about letting the world fade away, about how only heartaches have given him sight, and I totally, completely and utterly understand exactly what he means.

"Will," I murmur.

Will makes a sleepy mumble and turns to face me, pulling me close. "Hmm?"

I tell him everything. About the smell and taste and sound of his voice. The colors I see when he says my name. I've told him little things before, small details here and there, but this is the first time I've ever described this to him so honestly.

"You are my ocean," I tell him, wishing for darkness that could make this easier to confess, but grateful the light allows me to see his face as I watch him understand what I'm trying to say.

He kisses my mouth. Pushes the hair from my face. "Not the mountains."

He remembers.

We sleep, and I realize it only when the bed shifts and I startle awake. Will's sitting on the edge of it, forearms on his knees, shoulders hunched as he scrubs at his face. When he pads naked into the bathroom, I take the time to finger-comb my hair. It's still so early my brain refuses to admit I'm not asleep. I hear the toilet flush, then the rush of water in the sink. I need to pee.

We cross paths without saying anything, him back into the bedroom and me into the bathroom, where I close the door and take care of everything that needs taking care of. I find my bra and panties and put them on. I rinse my mouth at the sink, wishing for toothpaste. In the mirror, I check for raccoon eyes, but thanks to the miracle of modern cosmetics my waterproof mascara is still intact. There are circles under my eyes, though, from lack of sleep, and I splash my face carefully with water even though it won't do any good.

Back in the bedroom, Will's almost fully dressed. My heart pangs. I want to crawl back into bed with him and make the world fade away, but that's not the way reality works.

"Hey," he says. "I have to get going. I have some stuff I need to do today."

"Of course. Sure. I should get home, too." I pull on my dress and find a hair band in my purse to make some sort of order of my hair. He's still standing there when I'm finished.

"I can't find my other sock," he explains.

I want to laugh and cry at the same time, mostly because his look of consternation is as charming as everything else I ever discover about him. "It has to be around here. Did you look under the bed?"

He lifts the dust ruffle, but the bed's the sort that sits on a platform, and nothing can be lost beneath it. He's clearly annoyed, so I don't laugh. I look under the desk, the chair. I look on the other side of the bed and, finally, peeking beyond the armoire, I discover his single sock and hold it up, triumphant.

"How'd you do that?"

"I just kept looking until I found it," I tell him.

This is what it would be like, I think suddenly. Me and Will. Sharing a bed, a bathroom, looking at his sleep-rumpled hair in the morning. Having to help him find his socks. Domestic and normal and everything you already know you kind of hate.

But it doesn't feel as if I'd hate it with him, it feels exactly the opposite, and even though I know it's all fantasy, I am overcome with emotion strong enough to make me sit on the bed. I can't look at him. I can't leave with him, both of us sneaking out in the clothes we came in with, hailing separate cabs in the rising light of day.

"I'm going to, um….you go on ahead," I tell him. "I need to finish getting ready."

But I can't let him go without saying goodbye, so I walk him to the door, where we stand and stare at each other as if we should be shaking hands instead of embracing. He does, in fact, try to leave that way, and at the last minute I refuse to let this be the way we part. He sees it on my face, that look, and he pulls me close to kiss me. Once, twice, passion beneath sweetness, and even though it's brief, the kiss takes my breath away.

I hold on to him longer than is necessary, but then I let him go. Of course I let him go; there's no other choice. He has a life, and so do I. No matter what I want, the sun has come up and the world will not fade away.

When the door closes behind him, I put that song on repeat and listen to it ten times in a row while I shake and cry, pressing my fingertips to my eyes until I see color bursts of red and green and gold. Until I can force myself to breathe.

Chapter Thirty-Four

When I let myself in through the front door, I'm not expecting anything beyond the possible hum of Maria's vacuum and the sanctity of my bed for another few hours of sleep. My eyes are grainy, throat raw. If I feel like shit, I can only imagine what I look like.

"I didn't think you'd be home until later." Ross, his suit rumpled, is in front of the fridge with a carton of orange juice in one hand. No glass. He looks appropriately guilty.

I'm so happy I took the time to shower and make some semblance of order to my hair and face before I came home.

"You know how Naveen's kids are. Up at the crack of dawn. I figured I'd duck out early and get home. Lots to do today." The lie tastes like butter and is as smooth. "I didn't think you'd be back until tomorrow."

"Finished early," my husband says. "Got a different flight."

We stare at each other across the kitchen, and I can tell he's waiting for me to say something. About the juice, about his schedule, I don't know what. But the truth is, I have nothing to say.

In our bedroom, I strip out of my clothes, taking one surreptitious minute to lift the fabric to my face and breathe in the scent of Will's cologne. It's faint and fading away, and I can't get enough of it. I shove my panties and bra to the bottom of the pile and go naked into the bedroom, where I dress myself in plain white cotton underwear. Sweatpants. I pull my hair on top of my head. I don't look in the mirror.

"What are you up to today?" Ross comes up behind me and, unexpectedly, puts his arms around me. He juts his chin into my shoulder blade.

Every part of me tenses. "Not much. I thought I'd organize my office a little bit. Get caught up on some paperwork. I need to get to the grocery store. Do you want anything special?"

His hands are moving over me. Rough and possessive. He presses between my legs. "How about some of this?"

I can't.

But I do.

And I give it everything I have, every talent or skill I've ever learned about how to lick and suck and caress. I know this man, every part of him. How to make him squirm. How to make him explode.

I try to take the same from him, because Ross knows my body, or at least he used to, and sex was one thing that was always good between us, even when the rest of it wasn't. But no matter what he does, how he touches me, all I feel is a growing sickness in my guts that becomes an actual physical nausea by the time he's collapsed on top of me, panting and sweaty. I've never once felt guilty about being unfaithful to my husband, but this feels like cheating is supposed to.

In the bathroom, forcing myself to sip water, I clutch at the sink with one hand and try to keep myself from puking. Ross, typically, doesn't notice as he gets in the shower, talking the entire time about his business trip and the golf game he picked up for later in the day, and oh, by the way, the girls are coming home for dinner tonight, so I might want to get something good for dinner when I hit the store later.

"Wait, what?" I splash my face with water and try to imagine turning around and saying "I'm leaving you."

I'm leaving you.

He leans out of the shower. "Yeah. Message on the machine from Kat. She and Jac are both coming home with what's-his-face and the other one."

Their boyfriends, part of their lives for years, now. "Jeff and Rich."

"Yeah. They're all coming home tonight for dinner." Ross closes the shower door. "How about your lasagna, Bethie? You haven't made that in a long time. You make the best damn lasagna."

I'm leaving you.

But I can't say it, just like that. Not mere minutes after I had him inside me and he was saying my name over and over again like a prayer when he came. Not with our children on their way toward us right this minute for some unexpected reason.

"Sure," I say aloud. "Lasagna. That sounds great."

Chapter Thirty-Five

I haven't been able to say it, but I have decided to do it. Leave him. And with that, everything is brighter. Somehow sharper. I'm looking at the world through a new filter, and feel off-kilter. Giddy, my stomach sick, and yet so much lighter I find it hard to believe I could ever have been anchored to the ground.

I'm not happy, not exactly. But I am hopeful. Relieved. And, eventually, as the kitchen fills with all the delicious smells of the lasagna that's Ross's favorite, and chocolate chip cookie pie that Jac loves, and the special garlic bread with cheese Kat always requests, I'm at last calm.

When Ross comes in to snag a sliver of pie the way he always does just before we sit down to eat, I don't shoo him away as I've always done. I take a knife and cut him a piece, put it on a plate. I hand him a fork.

"Life's short," I tell him when he looks surprised. "Eat dessert first."

I do not hate my husband, but I am going to be so, so glad to leave him.

Dinner is cacophony. Jac and Kat, their boyfriends. Me and Ross. His parents, surprise guests who won't stay more than an hour after dinner's finished, even though Jac asks them to, specially.

That's a little suspicious, but I don't think about it as I'm filling the dishwasher as full as it can get and eyeing the sink and counters full of dishes, estimating how many more loads to go and if I should bother hand-washing some of the pots and pans now, or wait until tomorrow. I'm voting for tomorrow when Jac peeks into the kitchen. She's started wearing her hair differently, framing her face, and I'm just about to tell her how much I like it when she sighs.

"Mom, c'mon. Come in and sit, have some coffee and dessert."

"That was my plan." I straighten and turn on the dishwasher, listening for the familiar hum. She's looking at me oddly and shifting from foot to foot. When she was a toddler we called it the pee-pee dance, but I'm sure Jac's grown out of her pants-wetting habit.

She doesn't wait for me to finish but takes me by the elbow to hustle me into the den. She has indeed managed to convince her grandparents to stay, though they don't look happy. Not that they ever do. Ross is deep in conversation with his dad, both of them looking so much alike it's eerie. Kat sits on the arm of the couch, her fingers linked with Rich's. He's talking to Jac's boyfriend, Jeff.

It's the perfect picture, and the last one, I think with sudden clarity. This is the last time we will all be together this way. Even if Ross and I come together at the holidays for the sake of the kids—an idea that seems both impossible and necessary—it won't be the same. It will never be the same as it is right now.

I take it all in, every detail. Every sight and scent, every sound, every flicker of candlelight and glitter of laughter. *This is the last time,* I think, and I want to remember every single second.

"Mom, Dad. Nan, Pop and everyone." Jac's stopped the

shifting, but her grin's a little too wide, too manic. Everyone turns at the sound of her voice, so loud above the soft mutter of classical music coming from the stereo. "Jeff and I have something we want to tell you."

Jeff looks put on the spot, but stands to wrap his arm around Jac. He's a nice kid. They've been together since their freshman year, so it's not a surprise when she announces that they got engaged a week ago. Amid the applause and congratulations, though, there is a surprise.

"Everyone." Kat doesn't talk as loudly as her sister, but nevertheless we all pause in our well-wishing to look at her. "Rich and I...well, we have some news, too. We got engaged last night!"

Jac squeals and hugs her sister, dancing. "I knew it! I knew it!"

Kat, laughing, tries to get out from Jac's grip and can't. "I didn't want to step on your news, but..."

"No!" Jac's eyes shine. My daughters have always gotten along as sisters do, better than some and not as well as others despite the fact they shared the womb, but there's never been any doubt that they love and support each other. "It's perfect! We can have a double wedding!"

There is more hand-shaking and backslapping and cheek-kissing. In the midst of this, I find myself standing with my girls on either side of me. White light flashes. A picture. Then Ross is next to me, and we're posing together, too.

"Merry Christmas," my husband says. "Guess what we're doing instead of going on that cruise."

"Congratulations," I say to Jac as I hug her. "I'm so happy for you."

Jac is buzzing, fluttering, to and fro-ing, while her sister sits quietly with her fingers linked in her soon-to-be-husband's.

She's not my huggy daughter, but I hug her, anyway. She clings to me for a moment longer than I expect.

"So happy for you," I whisper in her ear.

"Mom, don't cry."

I swipe at my face, embarrassed. "Oh, you know me. I get all broken up over Hallmark card commercials."

I excuse myself to go into my bathroom, where I sit on the toilet with the lid down and my face in my hands, and I press the heels of my hands to my eyes to keep myself from dissolving into sobs. Minutes pass. I can't make myself get up.

"Hey." Ross knocks lightly on the door before he comes in, which isn't like him. Toilet privacy isn't something he's usually concerned about. "You okay?"

I should get up. Wash my face. Stop crying. I do get up, moving like an automaton. I go to the sink. Run the water. Stare at it. Stare at my face.

"It was coming for both of them—it's not such a shock." Ross sounds worried. "I was only kidding about the cruise, Bethie. We'll be okay."

It's not the cruise or the shock or the cost of two weddings.

It is the taste of joy and pride and happiness for my children, and it is undercut with the bitter, rancid taste of my personal grief. I can't share this with him, or anyone. Even I can't be that selfish.

So I straighten my shoulders. Draw a breath. I put a smile on my face, and I force myself to focus on the happiness and push away the selfish sorrow.

"Yes," I tell him. "We will be fine."

Chapter Thirty-Six

That life and this.

This life.

That life.

The one beneath is drawn in solid lines and bold strokes; it is a picture drawn in permanence with ink. It's a tattoo. Indelible.

The one on top of it is sketched on vellum in soft brushes of charcoal, easily smudged. It covers the one beneath, but can't hide it.

That life.

This life.

It looks as if you can have both. I mean, they're both right there, one on top of the other, and it looks as if they'll blend.

But they never will.

So, you take this thing.

You take this thing you want,

and you put it in a box

and you close the lid.

You can let your fingers trace the cracks, the places where the light gets in, the dark gets out, but the lid stays on. You don't look inside. You don't look at this thing you want so much, because you can. Not. Have. It.

So there's this box, you know, with the thing inside, and you could throw it away or bury it or shoot it into space; you could set it on fire and watch it burn to ashes, but really, none of that would make a difference, because you cannot destroy what you want. It only makes you want it more.

So.

You take this thing you want
and you put it in a box
and you close the lid.

And you hold the box close to your heart, which is where it wants to go, and you pretend it doesn't kill you every time you feel yourself breathe.

Chapter Thirty-Seven

Stolen minutes. That's what we have. When it becomes harder to find them, all the more precious.

I always dress carefully for Will…the jewelry, the panties and bra, the exact curl of my hair, thickness of liner and shade of lipstick. Always, I take such care. Dressing for a lover.

I've taken even more time now because this is the last time I will see him in person. Always I've made certain that what we do never overshadows anything else, and now with wedding plans and travel and work and my life, my messed up, messy life, there will be no more time for Will.

I wear a black dress. Not new. A favorite, though. It clings to me and flatters curves. It dips low in the front to show off cleavage.

It ties at the hip and he'll be able to slide his hand inside, if he wants.

Oh, God. I don't want Will to ever stop wanting.

Under the dress, a teal bra with a leopard print stripe along the edge. Teal panties. Leopard print garter belt—again, not new, and not my style, usually, but the pieces seemed fun when I picked them up so long ago. The stockings are sheer and black, with lace tops. None of this is new, but putting it on layer by layer, covering my body, all I can imagine is how it will feel when he takes it off.

In all the long months we've been doing this, we've never had a date. How could we? Every time we meet, we pretend it's for some other reason.

He doesn't know the reason now. All I said was "I need to see you," and this time, he gave me no argument. He just agreed. So here we are in a nice restaurant neither of us has ever been to, in a town someplace between us in which we've never met, but where I had to be for another of Naveen's auctions.

Will's dressed up, too.

Dark dress trousers, a dark blue shirt with faint silver stripes. His shoes are black and shiny, not the boots or sneakers I've always seen him wear. He's combed his hair. Shaved. When he leans to kiss my cheek, chaste as any casual acquaintance, I catch a whiff of his cologne.

He did this for me, and it makes my knees weak.

The waitress, seeing my dress and Will's suit, or maybe the way we can't stop staring at each other, asks us if it's a special occasion. "A birthday?" she suggests, bright-eyed and intense, her smile more a baring of teeth than a grin. "An anniversary?"

It's a special occasion, yes. But can it properly be called an anniversary when it hasn't happened yet? The anniversary of a death…while we are still alive.

"I'll have the steak," Will says. "Elisabeth will have the lamb."

Startled, both at his use of my name and the way he orders for me—he ordered for me? Should I be affronted or aroused?—I hide my grin behind my hand.

"What?" he asks when the waitress is gone. He reaches for my hand, and I let him take it.

Our fingers curl together right there on the table for all the world to see.

"Maybe I wanted the chicken," I say.

At first he looks apologetic. Then slowly, he smiles. Shakes his head. "You didn't."

"I didn't." Our grasps tighten. Palm to palm for a second. Oh, God. His touch, even this simple, subtle touch, still makes everything inside me melt. Liquid. I am soft as butter. Soft as clouds.

The food comes on pretty plates with fancy garnish. As always with him, my appetite is not for food, but he cuts into his steak and offers me a piece, which I take from his fork as his foot rubs my calf under the table. I share my lamb and the slab of potatoes that have been ground and seasoned and pressed into a block and sliced, then fried. Everything is delicious, but none of it as lovely as the flavor of his laughter.

Coffee, dessert. We each order and share tastes. And finally, when I can't put it off anymore, I say, "I have to tell you something."

Two things happened when I was sixteen.

First, Andrea's parents split up. Her mom moved out, leaving behind four kids and an angry, embittered husband who had no idea how to run a house. Nobody had clean laundry or packed lunches or got to where they needed to be on time, and they spent hours alone in their big, increasingly filthy house while their father worked. And why? Because Andrea's mom had developed what her father referred to as "a little love affair with the slots."

In private, Andrea told me that it would've been better if her mother had run off with another guy. Maybe her dad could at least get over that. What he couldn't forget or forgive was the thousands of dollars her mom had lost in the casinos on all the trips she'd taken with girlfriends to Atlantic City, or the money she'd spent in secret on shoes and clothes and spa treatments, running up their credit card bills to insufferable, unpayable amounts. Andrea's mom had left the family destitute with her addiction, and though she'd moved into a one-bedroom mobile home and had taken two jobs in order to support herself, she didn't stop the trips to Atlantic City and Vegas. She couldn't quit. Her addiction tore their family apart. To this day, Andrea had very little to do with her mom—not because she was angry or hated her, but because the woman had failed her when Andrea needed her, too many times. She'd ruined her daughter's trust.

The other thing was that Becky Lazar's mother killed herself. Becky sat in front of me in English lit, and we'd gone to school together since kindergarten. That sophomore year we had the same lunch period and had migrated to the same table because she was friends with a couple kids who were friends with a few of mine. We weren't close, didn't hang out after school or anything, but we'd become friendly. I liked her. She was smart, with a dry sense of humor, and once she'd lent me lunch money when I'd forgotten to bring mine.

I'd met her mom only once, a few months before, after a performance of the school musical. Becky'd had the role of Eliza Doolittle in *My Fair Lady*. She had an amazing voice. I'd gone to the show with Andrea not because either of us were into musical theater, but because she had a huge crush on the guy playing Henry Higgins. Also, it was an official school activity, so Andrea's dad, who'd gotten a little out of control with rules, wouldn't restrict her from it. We giggled our way through the entire show, when Andrea wasn't sighing with the heartache of crushing on a boy who'd never give her the time of day. And after, when the cast members gathered in the lobby to sign autographs and receive flowers and generally bask in their tiny, high school level of fame, Becky waved us over to meet her parents.

Her dad was tall, with a permanent frown and a crease between his eyebrows. Her mom was petite, and out-of-fashion in a floral print dress, and hairstyle that looked like it hadn't been changed since she herself was in high school. She didn't say much, just smiled and nodded at us. But she did smile, and that was all I could think about when Kathy Bomberger told me what she'd done.

"Where's Becky?" I'd asked, sliding my tray onto the table. "She sick today?"

Kathy looked surprised. "No. Didn't you hear?"

Becky's mother had run a garden hose from the exhaust pipe of the family station wagon into the cracked-open driver's side window, and left the car running in the closed garage. Becky's younger brother, a fifth grader, had been the one to find her. She'd done it in the middle of the week, on a school night, and all I could think about was that smile. She'd seemed happy enough, that one time I met her, but obviously she hadn't been.

That was when I really learned that smiles can hide a lot of secrets.

I learned a lot of things that sophomore year that followed me into adulthood. The burgeoning power of sexuality, the importance of personal responsibility, how simple it is to break a heart. And also, how easily a mother can destroy her children.

"When I had my children," I tell Will, after the rest of this story is finished and he's listened quietly, his green-gray eyes never leaving mine, "I vowed that I would never, ever fuck them up the way Andrea's mom did. Or Becky's. I'm not saying I believe in sacrificing everything for your kids or anything like that. It's important for them to know their parents are human beings. But I did vow I would be there when they needed me. That I would never, ever let my selfishness make a mess of them."

I draw in a breath. Then another. I want to kiss him, but there's a table between us.

"My daughters are both getting married. A double wedding, something I never thought I'd be doing. They're twins, but I always tried to make them their own people. But that's what they want, so that's what they're doing. They need me, and their dad, to be there for them. They deserve that. They deserve—" My voice cracks and breaks finally, and I have to look away from him. "They deserve a mother who hasn't dropped her basket. So if I have to white-knuckle my way through this, to make sure my kids are taken care of…if I have to…keep it all together for just a little longer… Well. Then that's what I'll have to do."

"I understand."

"A year," I tell him. "I have to make it through this next year."

I look at him then, not sure what I expect to see. Not tears, of course. Disappointment, maybe? Will he ask me to reconsider, to stay? Will he say we can work it all out?

Will he tell me that he'll wait?

"You should find a real girl," I tell him, not for the first time.

"Are you breaking up with me?" Will puts a lilt into the words, making them light so I can laugh and shake my head.

"Oh, Will."

He leans back in his chair. "I understand, Elisabeth. I do. You have to be there for your kids, and this isn't right, anyway. We both know it."

I know it. I don't care. "Yes. Of course."

So formal. Now we're done. So this is the end, and all the pretty pieces of me are dying inside.

I let him pay the check.

Outside, the sun's gone down but the late summer heat weighs us. We walk along the quaint street, looking in the windows of antique shops filled with junk. The sidewalk's made of cobblestones that threaten to snag the heels of my shoes, and I use it as an excuse to hold his hand. And then we're at the parking garage and there are no more excuses to keep this night from ending.

In the backseat of his car, we sit inches apart. The heat is unbearable, a sauna. The light, orangey-white, creeps in and makes it all too bright when I would rather have shadows.

I don't know who moves first, just that his mouth is on mine and it's still so sweet. So fucking good I can't stand it, and I open for him. My mouth, my arms, my legs.

My heart.

We've done more than this, but somehow this furtive, somewhat frantic kissing is more erotic than anything we've ever done. I am greedy for it, and him, and I want to imprint every second, every breath, into my memory forever. Because I am leaving him. Ending this.

"We have to stop," I tell him.

Will's mouth is still on mine. "I know."

We kiss again.

Again.

How can I stop this? How can it end? When everything I am and have become is wrapped up in him, when I breathe from one second to the next because I know each breath brings me closer to the time when we'll be together?

He is on his side of the car. I'm on mine. We look at each other across the brief expanse.

"This is ridiculous," I say. "Like teenagers making out in the backseat."

His hand curls against the back of my neck. We kiss. His hand slips over my panties, touching me just right, always just right, and before I know it, before I can stop it—not that I want to stop it, I do not, I want it to go forever on and on—before I know it, I am breathless again.

Mindless.

"Give me your tongue," Will says, and I do.

I will give him anything he wants.

He doesn't know this and I can't tell him, because it's not fair. It's a responsibility he doesn't want. And because I love him, a burden I can't bear for him to carry.

My hands are in his hair, his cupping the back of my neck while the other moves slowly, slowly, slowly between my legs.

How many ways are there to describe pleasure? How many different words can express how it feels to come in the backseat of a car on a hot summer's night, and the only reason you can breathe is because someone you love is offering you his mouth and his own breath?

Green and gold, the sound of bells, the smells of sunshine.

My orgasm is more than the rush of blood and twitch of muscles.

My mouth moves against his. "Do you want to make me come?"

"Yes."

We whisper though nobody's around to hear us.

"Just a little more," I plead, not caring that I beg. "Just a little more."

He thinks I mean the stroke of his fingers against me, and I do. But I also mean all of this. Everything. I don't want this to end, for this to be the last time.

"Please," I whisper into Will's kiss. "Just one more."

These are the words we say, one after another: *I want to eat you like a peach, eat you all up. Put your hand under my shirt, kiss me while you touch my stomach. You wanted me to touch you. Oh, God, yes. Fuck, yes, I want you to touch me now. I want you to burn for me.*

I want to tear you apart.

The air is so much cooler outside the car, where we stand with inches of distance between us, as though that can take away what we spent an hour doing. I still taste him. I'm sure I smell of him, and of sex. My hair's a mess. I don't care.

"Are you okay?" Will asks.

And this is what I think: *No, I'm not okay. I'm stuck in a place I don't want to be, and I don't see any way to get out of it without hurting everyone around me. And I hurt you, too, just by being me. By all of this. So I make a change and hurt everyone in my life, or I don't make a change and I hurt you instead, and no matter what happens, I hurt.*

No matter what I do, there is casualty.

"I have to go," I say. Ross may or may not be home, but I promised Jac I'd go over some wedding plans with her via video chat. Oh, technology. "Goodbye, Will."

Will nods. And, so formal, so distant, we do not touch again.

Not even one last time.

Chapter Thirty-Eight

I am okay.

This is what I tell myself to get through the day, when I make the motions of living. Cook, clean, laundry, pay the bills, take out the trash, unload the dishwasher. I have done all these tasks and can't remember doing them.

In the shower, in the dark, I put on the songs that make me think of him. I know I shouldn't. This is masochism. This is as self-harming as if I took a razor to my wrists. This is worse, because if I slit my wrists I would die, and I am still very much alive.

I go to my knees in the shower, in the dark, and the music plays and the water is hot and it pounds on my naked skin, and I press my face into my hands.

I grieve.

I have never mourned the loss of anything in my life as much as I mourn for the loss of what I didn't really have.

I had thought I might cry, of course. The music. The dark. The shower. But what I do is not crying. I break and shake and shatter; I am undone.

I am torn apart.

When have I ever wept this way? Even as a child, an infant, never. Everything with him has been a list of nevers. This is another. Because even though the shower is my favorite place to cry, it's never been like this, so fierce and raw and hard that I can't breathe.

Of course I can't breathe; isn't that how it's been with him since the start? I gasp and choke, I clutch at my face, my fingers dig deep into the meat above my heart, and I open my mouth and cry and cry and scream.

The sounds of grief and pleasure can be so much the same. Am I crying or coming? Who would be able to tell? I'm not sure *I* can determine the difference. The rush and rise and force of this feeling is no pleasure, not like an orgasm, but the relief of it spilling out of me is almost the same.

There is a pain in my heart, a real physical pain. Because my heart is breaking. It is broken. I press my hand against it, and imagine the beat of it has stopped—but it hasn't. It goes on and on, and each time it is sharp and stabbing, a knife beat.

Afterward, still dripping, I look in the mirror and do not know my face; I have made myself a stranger. I didn't know it was possible to cry so hard you give yourself a black eye, but there it is, the visible proof of my grief, the dark red burst of blood in the soft places of my skin.

I am not okay.

Chapter Thirty-Nine

Every day I wake up thinking this will be the day I stop thinking so much about him, and every night I go to sleep with the ache still as firmly entrenched in my heart as it was the day before.

It is almost impossible to fully grieve in the presence of others. When you need to break down, you always have to do it alone. My pretty breakdown takes place in public bathroom stalls, where I stifle my sobs with the back of my hand and force myself to breathe. It happens without warning, when Jac talks of wedding dresses and bridesmaids and the cost of carved roast beef instead of chicken Cordon bleu, and I pretend to sneeze, complaining of allergies to explain my red eyes.

I'm on a different sort of train now. Jac is the engineer of this one, her sister and I along for the ride. Kat has her own ideas about what sort of wedding she'd like, but she's letting her sister call the shots.

"You don't have to do what she wants, you know." I tell her this in the dressing room of the bridal boutique, where she's trying on another gown we both know she won't like. My Kat's not a frills and flounces kind of girl.

She looks in the mirror at the beaded bodice, letting her fingers run over it. "This is pretty, Mom, don't you think?"

"It's beautiful."

She eyes the price tag and gives me a wry grin. "It's five grand."

We both burst into laughter that has Jac pounding on the dressing room door. I put a hand over my mouth to keep in the laughs that threaten to become sobs; I close my eyes when Kat leaves the room to show her sister the dress she will never, ever buy.

These are my girls, my life. So I pull my shit together and watch them parade around in dresses the way they used to when they were small and playing princess. They are beautiful. They are my pride. They are the best thing I have ever done.

Jac, typically, finds three dresses she can't decide among. Kat stands quietly in front of the triple mirror, studying her reflection and smoothing the fabric of a simple satin gown in a vintage style. But when I ask her if she wants to buy it, she just shakes her head.

"No, Mom," she says. "I'm not sure about it."

"Then you shouldn't get it."

Kat, face solemn, nods. She smooths her hands down the front again, then gives me a small smile. "It's pretty, right?"

"It's beautiful, honey. Very you." I haven't checked the tag on this one, but what is money for if not to spend? "But you shouldn't settle. Not when it should be something so special. You should make sure it's what you really, really want. And even then," I say with a small laugh, "you'll probably look back on it in twenty years and wonder what on earth you were thinking."

She turns to me. "Do you?"

I think of my wedding dress. I'd wanted to wear my grand-mother's 1940s suit with its padded shoulders and peplum, the sleek skirt. My mother had talked me into a mermaid-style dress, a monstrosity of lace and satin that had never fit quite right no matter how many times we'd had it altered. I haven't looked at my wedding pictures for a long time.

"Yes. I'd have picked something different. So you should make sure," I say, looking across the room to where her sister is now twirling in front of the mirror in a fourth choice, "to pick something you really really love, at least right now, because that way even when you look back and can't believe you picked it, you'll remember how much you loved it when you did."

Kat, like me, is not a hugger, but she hugs me now. Tight. "Thanks, Mama."

Jac comes over with a hand on her hip. "I didn't find anything I really liked. Oooh, Kittykat, that's nice."

Kat and I share a look. I gather both my girls to me, squeeze them hard. "Dinner," I say.

Ross calls as we're leaving the boutique, and though it's supposed to be girls' day out, he meets us at the restaurant. How could I tell him not to come? They're his daughters, too, and he sees them even less than I do.

We go to one of our favorite places. I haven't been there since my birthday, and I'm suddenly starving for their good Greek salad, the gyro platter. We order too much food. And because we took a cab to the store and Ross will drive us home, drinks, too. It's still strange for me to have cocktails with my daughters, who will forever be tiny and precious to me even though they're all grown up.

It's the best time I've had in a long while, the four of us laughing and retelling our favorite stories. This is what I love best about our family, all those shared inside jokes. Vacations, holidays, school plays. The good times, and the bad ones, too. All our lovely misadventures that have made us the unit we are today. The girls don't live with us anymore, but we will always be a family.

How can I think of breaking this? And thinking that, I break. In the bathroom, in the stall, I cover my mouth with my hands. Press the heels of my palms to my eyes. I shake and shake, sickness like a hurricane rising in me, and the world spins.

Outside the stall there's laughter and the sound of rushing water, so I shake myself until I can stand. I wash my hands. I splash my pale face, avoiding the sight of my own eyes. I press my lips with color, my hand steady and unfaltering.

The best thing, I think, and the hardest thing, are the same.

Chapter Forty

I am the architect of my own unmaking.

I check my email ten times in as many minutes. Refresh. Refresh. My cell phone stubbornly doesn't chime or ping or ring with an incoming message of any kind. No email, no text, no instant message, not even a fucking "thumbs-up" on my stupid Connex status.

I delete him from my contacts so I won't check again. I delete everything, every way I've ever had of contacting him. I put my phone in my purse, which is on the shelf in the closet, and I close the closet door and walk away from it.

I want him.

I want him so much it makes me shake, as if I've had too much coffee or run a race or gone without food for days. That's exactly how it is, as if I'm starving, only it's not food I want and need and crave, but Will.

I want him the way I want a cold drink on a hot day or a soft place to sit when I've been standing for too long a time. I never took up the habits of smoking or liquor or drugs. I've never had an addiction, but I think I understand now what it must be like. I've never wanted anything as much as I want him.

More than anything else, I want him to want me.

I know this is crazy, insane. I know it's wrong. And as I

pace, biting my thumb and feeling my stomach roil with tension, I don't care. The phone in the kitchen rings. I can't answer it. It won't be him; he wouldn't call me at home. I'm sure he doesn't have the number, though it wouldn't be difficult at all to look it up, if he wanted to. But he doesn't, I think, as the ringing stops and the silence is louder than any phone could ever be. But not as loud as the sudden thunder of my beating heart as it fills my ears, and I put a hand on it to make sure it doesn't beat right out of my chest.

I can't stop thinking about the taste of his skin. The smell of it. How smooth it was beneath my fingertips when I traced every rib. My fingers curl, remembering the jut of his hip bone and the thickness of his cock. I close my eyes and hear the soft hiss of his breath when I stroked him, up and down. When I sucked him until he came in my mouth.

It's been two months. Summer's long gone. Winter's on its way.

I've spent my entire life surrounded by colors, sounds, smells that don't "match." But now the world is gray. No color. If there is a song, the notes have all gone sour. The space without Will is immeasurable, and I cannot bear it.

No color. No music. No scent. I'm in a void, formless, nothing even to press against. Nothing to anchor me to this life.

How will I live without my ocean?

There's nobody to share this with. I could tell Naveen, allow him to be the shoulder on which I weep, but I'm too aware of how he came to me once with this same pain, and how I'd been so harsh. Too, there's the thing with Naveen that we never talk about, that unfinished business we've both agreed to leave forever undone.

No, I carry this alone.

It's my pain, and I gorge on it, the blood-copper taste of it, the slicing, bitter sting. The venom. I glut myself with it, and

I do it all in the stolen moments I have when I'm alone. In a bathroom, washing my hands. In the upstairs hallway as I carry a basket of laundry, and suddenly the floor tips and I stagger so that my elbow bangs against the framed pictures on the wall. Memories captured and held under glass. A trip to Disney, swimming lessons, weddings, graduations, christenings.

Our wedding.

The dress I didn't love but wore to please my mother. My brother's wife in emerald-green, Ross's sister in the same color, identical dresses for very different women. And Ross in a black tuxedo with a vest and tie, his hair long in the back. So impossible now, looking at it, that we were ever so young.

That we were ever so in love.

As the nights come earlier and colder, I go to bed beside Ross at the same time, instead of waiting for him to be asleep by the time I slip between the sheets. Some nights he rolls toward me, hands roaming, and I give up to him. Some nights I crawl toward him over the bed and use my mouth and hands to get him hard. Make him come. So that I can pretend everything is fine, that this has not been undone. We have more sex than we've had in years, and yet I never come.

As snow falls outside and the holidays come and go, I make mistakes at work and have to redo everything, over and over again, obsessively fixing invoices and order forms and invitations to shows. I take calls from Jac, who's increasingly frantic about the planning, and make them to Kat, who's uneasily silent about the entire process. I watch Naveen moon his way around the gallery, sneaking away for lunchtime trysts I'd be jealous of if I were capable of feeling anything beyond this dull nothing.

"How much longer?" he asks me one day in late February, when I've spent the morning arguing with caterers and easing Jac out of a bout of hysteria because the shipping for the monogrammed chocolates she wants for the tables is more than the candy itself. He's caught me at the coffeepot for my fourth mug of the day. I will never sleep tonight. "Until I get you back?"

It's the wrong question to ask, but maybe the right time. The coffee I don't even want sloshes when my hand shakes, and I put the mug back on the counter. I take a breath to give him some lame answer, but all that comes out is a slow, sighing sob.

We've been friends for a long time, so when Naveen pulls me close, I let him. I fit nicely against him, my face in the curve of his shoulder. He smells good. His voice, murmuring soothing phrases that don't make much sense, nevertheless smells of cotton candy and caramel apples. Naveen's voice is a carnival, and I need one.

"What's wrong, Betts? Tell me, love." He nuzzles the sensitive skin of my neck, and I'm done for.

Once, long ago, in a dark dorm room with The Cure playing low, Naveen kissed me. I hadn't been expecting it then, and can't say I'm expecting it now, but maybe this time I'm the one who kisses him. I can't be sure. All I know is that our mouths meet, tongues sliding, his warmth against me where lately I've felt only cold. His hands rest on my hips, then slide upward to curl around my ribs just below my breasts. We kiss on the mouth and then he's sliding his lips to my throat again. There's the press of teeth.

His hair curls like silk against my palm when I cup the back of his neck.

We do not fuck.

When he looks at me, finally, it's with an expression I don't want to see. Regret.

"Betts, I'm—"

"Don't." I extricate myself from him to straighten my

clothes. The coffee from my mug's spilled all over the counter, and I look for a cloth to wipe it up.

"I'm sorry," he insists on saying.

My shoulders sag. I hold on to the counter, not looking at him. "Shh, honey. Don't."

"No. No, I'm sorry. That was really shitty of me—"

"I said don't!" I lower my voice at once, though we're the only ones in the gallery today and there's nobody to hear. "I don't want you to be sorry, Naveen. Please, God. Don't...be sorry."

And then I laugh and laugh until I cry, because Naveen is my dear friend and I love him, and more than twenty years ago we almost-but-not-quite fucked and now here we were again. Almost-but-not-quite.

When I cry, he holds me. It's a different kind of release, but maybe one I needed more. I wish I could let it all go. Ugly snot crying. Sobs. But I can manage only silent, trickling tears against the front of his shirt while he strokes my hair.

"What is it, love?" Naveen doesn't ask who.

I look at him with wet eyes, streaked mascara. He's seen me worse than this. "It...hurts, Naveen. That's all. It hurts so fucking much."

And then he folds me in another hug to whisper into my hair, "Yes, love. I know."

Chapter Forty-One

I move Ross's toothbrush to his own side of the sink. His beard hairs are scattered across my washcloth, which I left hanging in its neat and tidy place on the hook next to the hand towel, but which somehow has managed to "conveniently" fall into the puddle of soap leaking from the dispenser he keeps promising to fix.

The sinks drips.

Drip.

Drip.

Drip.

How many months since I first asked him to fix it? How many times have I suggested we simply fucking call a plumber?

"No," Ross always says, affronted by the idea that somehow some other man could fix what he broke. "I'll get to it."

But he doesn't get to it, ever. Instead there are business trips and golf games and baseball games on TV. There are excuses. Always excuses, when all I want is for the fucking sink to Stop. Fucking. Dripping.

I am not incompetent. I am not useless. How did I get to this point, where I need to wait for Ross to do something for me?

How hard can it be?

I go on Google. YouTube. There are dozens of instructional videos about how to fix a dripping faucet. I watch. When I can't find the tools I need in the horror that is the toolshed, I go to the hardware store. And then, armed with a wrench, a pair of pliers, a new washer and rubber gasket, I fix the fuck out of that dripping faucet.

Washing my hands, I catch sight of my reflection. My hair has fallen over my eyes, clings to my cheek with sweat. It was both harder and easier to fix the sink than I expected, but infinitely more gratifying.

At least until I'm giving everything a final wipe down and putting away the tools and leftover supplies I used into the small canvas tool bag I also bought myself. That's when Ross breezes into the bathroom and proceeds to unzip and pee without so much as a hello. He lets out a long, ripping fart that fills the bathroom with the heavy scent of shit.

If everyone treated their spouse or partner with the same respect they'd give a friend sharing a hotel room, a lot more marriages would be saved.

Then again, there are always people who would tell you how considerate they are. How generous. How they care more for others rather than themselves. They're the worst ones.

Ross glances at me as he pushes past to the sink, where he washes his hands. Soap drips from the dispenser I haven't yet fixed. Water splashes the freshly cleaned mirror when he shakes his hands, ignoring the hand towel. Then he uses my washcloth, the one I use on my *face,* to finish drying his hands. My gorge rises. *My face.*

He tosses the washcloth onto the rumpled pile at the side of the sink. I snatch it up and throw it into the laundry basket.

He notices me looking. "What?"

"I fixed the faucet."

I can see instantly that he doesn't believe me. I'm waiting

for the pat on the head. The patronizing smirk. Ross twists the water on, then off. No drip. His brows knit.

"I told you I'd take care of it."

"But you didn't," I point out, reasonably enough, my voice a calm lake, unruffled by so much as a breeze.

"I told you I would," Ross repeats, as if this will make a difference. As if by saying it again he can...what? I don't even know.

I keep my focus on the tools I'm fitting into their slots, each into its place. "But you didn't. And I did. What's the big deal?"

He doesn't answer. He turns the faucet again. On. Off. On. The water runs. He turns it off and I stare, triumphant when it doesn't so much as sneak out a single drop of water.

"Make sure you put all my tools back where they belong," Ross says.

I overlooked the splattered mirror, the disgusting use of my washcloth. But at this, my fingers twitch and clench. "They're not your tools. They're mine."

"What do you mean, yours?" He moves as though to touch the tool bag, but I back up a step, holding it close. Protectively.

"I mean they're mine. I went to the store and bought them."

"Why would you do that?"

"Because I couldn't find what I needed," I explain, patient on the surface. Churning underneath.

"I have all of that stuff in the shed."

"I looked in the shed. I couldn't find anything I needed." It's my turn to repeat, though I know it won't make a differ-ence. Ross won't hear me. "So I went out and bought them."

He puts his hands on his hips, fingers touching his leather belt. I bought him that belt. That yellow polo shirt, the khaki pants. I bought him the shoes on his feet, the briefs I'm sure he's wearing. All he ever had to do was reach into his closet and pull out the clothes I bought for him. Washed and dried and ironed and folded for him.

"That was a stupid waste of money," Ross says flatly. "In case you didn't notice, we have weddings to pay for. Two of them."

Two weddings he's done nothing to plan. That burden falls solely to me, like the years of science projects, dance rehearsals, dentist appointments and boyfriend drama. And I'm more than aware of the cost of things, since I'm the one who pays all the bills.

"I didn't have what I needed." I repeat the words slowly. Carefully. "So I went out and got it."

My husband, the man to whom I have pledged my life, gives me a look so full of scorn it stings like a nettle caught in tender flesh. "It's not like you'll ever need them again, Beth. I mean, you are kind of useless when it comes to fixing things."

If there's ever been a moment in my life when I've come close to killing someone, this is it. Love, when it goes, can sometimes burn to ash.

And sometimes it can leave nothing.

Chapter Forty-Two

I've lived in this house for twenty-two years, and don't think I've ever known the full length and width of the kitchen before. Not this way, as I pace and try to occupy myself with cleaning crumbs from toast I didn't make and splashes of coffee I didn't drink. I empty the fridge and freezer, scrub away spilled blobs of ice cream, and toss packages of brussels sprouts I have to admit I will never cook. I organize the condiments by the size of their bottles and think, stupidly, *There. Now he'll never be able to find the ketchup.*

Ross isn't coming home tonight, or tomorrow, or the night after. He might be home sometime the day after that, if he comes to the house instead of going to the office from the airport, but I didn't ask him his plans, because I don't care. He could stay a month and I won't miss him, and this, like the bag of brussels sprouts, is something I finally have to force myself to admit.

I stand in my kitchen and look at everything around me, and I wonder how in the hell I got to this place. What happened to me? To my life?

I turned around, I think. *And there he was.*

And nothing has been the same since, and it will never be

the same. It doesn't matter that I ended it in the backseat of his car with his fingers against my thigh and his tongue in my mouth. It doesn't matter that I have a responsibility to my daughters, that they deserve a mother who can keep her shit together. It doesn't matter that it's over, because it happened, and I am forever changed.

The pain and weight in my chest aren't new; I've felt this stab before. For a period of a few months several years ago, I was convinced I was having a heart attack. The good part was that it convinced me to stop smoking, to eat better, to start working out, so I wouldn't be that woman people talk about in hushed tones, the one who keeled over in her thirties from an unexpected heart attack.

No, now I'll be the woman they talk about behind their hands, the one who up and left her husband after twenty-two years.

The pain is from costochondritis, an inflammation of the cartilage connecting the ribs and sternum, and there's no cure for it except rest and sometimes anti-inflammatories. It hurts more when I breathe and less when I stop, an irony I do not miss. I press my fingertips to the underside of my left breast, my eyes closed, and wish away the pain. The fact is, it feels as if someone's taken a spear and stabbed it through my chest and out my back.

Through my heart.

And then I am folding like a house of cards, onto my knees on the hard kitchen floor, one hand still trying to make my heart stop hurting and the other pressed to my mouth to keep myself from sobbing out loud. There's nobody to hear me but myself, but I don't want a repeat of the day in the shower. I don't want to lose myself that way again. Yet here I am, lost.

I am lost.

I am selfish. I am greedy. I'm incapable of being anything

else, and I get myself off the floor. I get my phone. My spear-stabbed heart leaps when I see the tiny red "1" indicating a message, but I can't make myself see who it's from because it's still Schrödinger's cat. At this point, it's both from Will and not, and I will never know until I check it.

In the bathroom, I set my phone on the counter and wash my face. I touch up my makeup, which is stupid because it's six o'clock in the evening and I'm alone. I turn my face from side to side, studying features so familiar they've become alien, like saying a word over and over again until it no longer has meaning. I force myself to count to ten, then twenty, then again. To a hundred. To a hundred and fifty while I clean the toilet and shower and tub even though Maria does a fine job and they're not dirty. I refold the towels. I organize my cosmetics drawer.

And finally, at last, when I can stand it no more, I check the message. It's not from Will, it's from Andrea, canceling our lunch date tomorrow, which is fine with me because that means I now have nothing on my Saturday schedule and can sleep in. I should fill the tub, read a book. Go to bed early. I should do the right thing.

Of course, I don't.

One word, that's all I type, but my fingers are so unsteady on the phone's touchscreen that I have to type it three times before it stops autocorrecting.

Hi

I wait, breathless, to watch the tiny letter *D* for delivered become an *R* for read. I hold the phone in both hands, willing him to answer. Waiting, waiting, waiting. And then—

Hi

It should feel anticlimactic, after all that breath-holding, but I'm just so fucking relieved that he answered me I don't care what he said. How are you?

Fine. You?

We are strangers, circling and cautious, and I hate it but understand it, too. I'm the one who ruined this, and I'm the one who should leave it alone, but I can't. I don't want to.

Fine, I type. Just settling in with a book. What are you up to? Anything fun?

Nothing. Nothing. Nothing. The minutes tick by, and even though I can see that he's read the message, the bastard, he's not replying. I can't cry about it. All I can do is fume and wait. And just when I've given up and turned on the shower, intending to do what I know I should, shower and go to bed with a book, the small *ping* alerts me to his answer.

I'm at Trinity.

Blue lights, green lights, the steady thump of music. I remember Trinity. We went there dancing once. My throat closes, eyes burn. I'm just about to turn my phone off completely when another message comes through.

You can be here in two hours.

Chapter Forty-Three

In slow motion, I push through the crowd, ignoring men who leer and women who scan me up and down, checking out the competition. I'm not here for them. I squeeze past a gaggle of bachelorette party princesses and some guys in suits ogling them.

And there, finally, is Will.

He leans against the railing with a drink in one hand, his attention on the dark-haired girl in front of him. She's young. She's pretty. She wears her vintage style like armor. The victory rolls in her hair, the red lipstick and arched, plucked brows, the historical tattoos all up and down her bare arms and on her chest. She's not unique or edgy, not really, and she knows it. I can see it in the way she shifts closer to him even when she looks away, as though she doesn't care what he says. When I was young and uncertain of myself, I used to do the same thing.

He leans closer as I watch, to say something in her ear that makes her tip her head back in laughter. He lingers a little too long, his face hidden by hers. He touches her bare shoulder at the same time.

I hate him.

I want him.

He looks at me then, and I think he knew I was there all along. Will doesn't smile or beckon me closer. He lets his fingertips graze the girl's naked skin from the curve of her neck all the way down to her wrist, and his fingers brush over hers before he takes away his hand.

People come between us. I stand still. I'm not sure I can make my feet move toward him, but I can't stay here, buffeted by the crowd, my feet trampled by drunk girls who can barely walk in stilettos when sober. The cold splash and tangy scent of beer on my hand from someone's spilled cup is what pushes me forward, finally.

"Elisabeth!" As though he's surprised to see me. It's a game, and not for my benefit but hers. Will moves closer, to pull me into an unexpected embrace I allow because I can't refuse it, even if I'm already on my way to being angry with him. "Chelsea, this is Elisabeth."

Chelsea tilts her head to look at me, and her smile is wide and warm and inviting. She doesn't shake my hand, but she does lean a little closer to me. "Hi!"

I look from her to Will and back again. "Hi. Nice to meet you."

Will's arm slips around my waist, draws me close. Hip to hip. "What're you drinking?"

I glance at the girl in front of us. She has a glass of something fruity. I look at him. "Dirty martini."

He appears faintly surprised, then nods and leaves us. We look at each other the way women do when there's a man between them, only I'm being careful not to be a bitch, and she seems more curious than anything.

"So...how long have you known Will?" She sips her drink. Her lipstick is perfect.

"A few months. You?"

"I just met him tonight," Chelsea says. "A friend of mine hooked us up. He takes pictures, right?"

"Yes. He does."

"He's good," she adds. "I mean, I saw his stuff. I'm looking for some work. I want to do pinup stuff, get into some fetish magazines. Stuff like that. Naveen says—"

"You know Naveen?"

Chelsea pauses, arched brows knitting. "Yeah, he was here a while ago. Do you?"

Before I can answer, Will's back with my drink. He presses it into my hand, and the glass is cool and slick with condensation. The taste is sharp. Tart. I let it linger on my tongue, and watch him follow the motion of my throat when I swallow.

I finish the drink and set it on the railing. To Chelsea, and without looking at Will, I say, "I should let you two get back to talking about pictures."

But when I turn to go, Chelsea stops me. "Don't leave on my account. Hey, I love this song. You guys wanna dance?"

Suddenly, it's all I want to do.

We find a place on the dance floor and move to the music. The drink went right to my head—not an excuse, just the truth. I'm buzzed. I let the music push and pull me, closing my eyes for a moment when the swirl of lights threatens to make everything spin. When I open them, Will's behind me with his hands on my hips, but I saw how he looked at the girl in front of us.

I move and he moves, and he's between us. We aren't the only threesome on the dance floor, because the DJ's playing that Britney Spears song "3" and all at once the entire room has tripled up. The whole crowd moves. Writhing, grinding, thrusting. Someone's on my ass and I'm pressed to Will's back as he dances with Chelsea. I can see her face over his shoulder. She's smiling at him, and I'm the one who put her there.

I told him to find someone else. I just didn't want to be here when he did.

I shouldn't have come.

"I'm leaving." I have to shout for him to hear me, and he probably doesn't catch anything but the mumble of my voice, but he can't miss that I'm pulling away and pushing through the crowd. Or at least I would be, if the group in front of me didn't have me gridlocked. I suffer the random grinding from a guy in a suit, his tie pulled loose, before I manage to step to the side and find a clear space.

A hand on my arm turns me, but it's not Will. Chelsea frowns. "Hey, don't go."

"I really...I need to get out of here." The room is too hot. The drink was too strong. Everything's too bright and pulsing, and my heart's beating too fast. The pain is back, but when I hold my breath I feel even worse.

"Me, too!" she cries. "C'mon, let's go!"

Will comes with us, the three of us on the sidewalk outside in seconds, where the air is marginally cooler and I can breathe a little easier. He puts his arm around me, pulling me close to look at my face. He frowns.

"You okay? What's the matter?"

I shake my head. What could I tell him? "Drank too fast."

"I'll call a cab," Chelsea says, and I'm more impressed with her than I was at first because she hails us a ride without hesitating. When we all slide into the backseat, her knee presses mine on one side, Will's on the other. To Will, she says, "What's your address?"

By the time we get to his apartment, I'm no longer woozy from booze, and the pain in my chest has let up. But I'm not at ease. This is not what I wanted the night to be. But here I am, drinking a gin and tonic in Will's kitchen while Chelsea and he talk about magazines I've never heard of, like *Stockings* and *Garterbelt Monthly* and *Betty.*

And then Chelsea's stripping out of her vintage frock down to a very cute set of authentic vintage underclothes—bra and panties and garter belt with seamed stockings. Her lipstick is still perfect, but her eyeliner's smudged. Her hair's a little mussed. She strikes pose after pose and Will takes her picture while I watch.

All I do is watch.

Chelsea's eyes go sleepy-lidded, sultry. She might've been a little uncertain in the club, but in front of the camera this girl is all self-esteem. She unhooks her bra, lets the straps fall forward with the material cupped to her ample breasts. Pouting mouth. Vintage poses get increasingly more explicit as Will murmurs encouragement and Chelsea complies. She doesn't get entirely naked, which of course is sexier than if she stripped down all the way, but she does unhook the garters to slip out of her panties to stand in the belt and stockings. She's trimmed but not shaved bare, and she kneels on the chair, legs spread to show a glimpse of her pussy, and looks over her shoulder with a cheeky grin—but not at the camera.

At me.

"Take Elisabeth's picture," she says in a low voice.

Will doesn't stop snapping shots even when he answers. "Elisabeth doesn't want her picture taken."

"Why not?"

"She doesn't like it," he says, and I'm unaccountably irritated that he thinks he can answer for me.

Chelsea gets off the chair and pads toward me in her stocking feet, her near nudity as nothing to her, while it makes me blush. "Come take a picture with me. It'll be hot."

I shake my head. I shouldn't be surprised when Chelsea kisses me, but of course I am. Her mouth parts mine. Her tongue is small and sweet, and flickers in and out so fast I don't even get a taste of her, but I hear the flutter of birds' wings. It surprises me more than the kiss, that sound. Her hands slide up to cup my breasts through the silky material of my dress, and all I can do is stand there, stunned.

She looks over her shoulder at Will. "Sure we can't convince her?"

Will's expression is impassive for a second before he smiles. Shrugs. He holds up the camera, not to his face, just showing it. Then he puts it carefully on a side table. "I don't know. It's up to her."

Chelsea looks at me. We are so close I can see the beads of clear glue sticking her false lashes to her lids, and the rim of her contact lenses around her irises. Her breasts push against me, and I'm not sure where to look or touch, or if I want to shove her away or pull her closer.

Will is watching us when she kisses me again, this time longer. More searching. She presses her body to mine and I'm still not sure where to put my hands or if I want to stroke my tongue along hers. I've never kissed a woman before. I've never had one touch me like this, her small hands confident as they move over my body.

"No?" Chelsea says when she pulls away, and glances again at Will. Then at me. Her brows rise for a second as she looks considering. Then she tugs me by the wrist toward him until we stand face-to-face.

Chelsea puts one hand on the small of my back, her other on his. She pushes us together two stumbling steps. "Kiss her."

He does. I have no trouble figuring out where to put my hands or how far to open my mouth for him—Will's kiss is as familiar to me as anything I've ever done. His hand slips into the hair at the base of my skull and tips back my head when his mouth slides along my jaw to nuzzle my throat. The hand on the small of my back pushes me against him. His cock's hard—his kiss is hard, too. He nips my throat. He pulls my hair. Something like a gasp eases from my parted lips.

Chelsea's touch disappears for a moment, and in the next the bright lights Will had set up for the pictures go out, one by one. There's light coming from the kitchen and from the streetlamps outside the windows, but we've fallen into shadow. Will groans against my skin.

I look at Chelsea. She's sitting on the chair, watching us with bright eyes. Her legs are spread. I can see everything.

I won't lie—there is something sexy about knowing she's watching us. Something forbidden. I can still feel the soft press of her against me, the flicker of her tongue. I can hear the flutter of wings.

But I don't want to do this with an audience. I might be a bit of a voyeur, but exhibitionism's not my thing. And though I'm no longer worried that Chelsea has supplanted me, I don't want her to be part of this.

Her fingers toy with her clit and dip inside her pussy for a second or two, but when she sees me looking, she closes her legs and cocks her head. We share something with a look, no words necessary. With a small nod, she gets up and begins to gather her clothes.

Will looks up from my neck when the front door closes. His mouth is wet, his eyes a little glazed. His face, when I press my cheek to it, is flushed and warm.

"She left," I say, in answer to the question he hasn't asked.

The taste of soap coats my tongue. It's the flavor of disappointed anger. I think of the way he was looking at her before he knew I was there, and there's no denying it. I'm jealous. That he told me to come, knowing I would see him with another woman, makes me more than that. I'm furious.

I kiss him, too roughly. Our teeth clank. Chins bump. I break the kiss by pushing him away.

Will frowns. "The hell's wrong with you?"

"You're what's wrong with me. You." I stab my finger into his chest.

He captures my hand and holds my wrist, keeping me from poking him again. "What's that supposed to mean?"

"Nothing." I tug, but he won't let me go.

We're both breathing fast. My heart beats fast, too. My nipples are hard, and the ache between my legs begs for him to touch me there. But I won't give him the satisfaction of knowing that. Instead, I lift my chin, defiant.

"It's late. I should go." It's an echo of that first time we were together. I didn't mean it to be, but as soon as I say it, his mouth quirks into a half smile.

He keeps my wrist imprisoned in his grip. "Yeah. You should go."

I snap myself free of him. I can't banter. I can't grin. I can't flirt. "Stop it."

Will's gaze flickers. "You're pissed? About Chelsea."

"Shouldn't I be?" I need my purse and can't find it. I run my fingers through my hair, knowing I'm a mess. My lipstick is far from perfect.

"No."

I stop my fussing. We stare at each other without blinking. "You knew I'd be there. You told me to come. I said I was on my way."

"I didn't know she'd be there. Naveen texted me, said he had a girl he wanted me to meet. I told him where I was."

"Did you tell him I was coming?"

Will looks guilty.

"Why would you do that?"

"I didn't think about it," he says, but I suspect he's lying. Maybe only a little, but it's enough.

"He can't know, Will."

Will's gaze remains steady, unblinking, his mouth no longer quirking, but straight and almost grim. "I didn't set any of it up, Elisabeth."

Seagulls scream at the sound of my name in his voice. "I saw you looking at her."

"Of course I was looking at her! She wanted her picture taken!"

We are toe to toe like fighters in a ring. My fists and my jaw are both clenched. A trickle of sweat rolls down my spine, and when I lick my lips, I taste salt. My throat is tight.

"You wanted to fuck her!"

"Of course I want to fuck her," Will says after a long, long pause. "I'm not blind."

His words punch the air out of me. The pain in my chest flares, and I press a hand to my sternum, but the stab won't go away. I have to breathe, but I can't because it hurts.

"Fuck you."

He grabs my arm when I turn, and doesn't let go even when I give him a look that could burn concrete. "You told me to. Just remember that. You told me—"

"That doesn't mean I want to see it!" I shout. "You didn't have to shove it in my face!"

"You want me to be alone? Is that it? You won't be with me, but you don't want me to be with anyone else?"

That's exactly it, the truth, caustic and stinging like the bite of rubbing alcohol. We struggle. His grip's too tight, and when I manage to yank my arm free he's already snagging my other arm and keeping me from backing up more than a step. I'm pulling, he's coming after me, the two of us are shouting accusations I can't even follow because the words all taste like gasoline and smell like sulphur. I could get away from him if I stepped on his foot or kneed his crotch or bit him, any of the dozen self-defense moves I learned in the course the girls and I took at the local YWCA years ago, and I'm just about frantic enough to try one of them when he must see something in my face, because he stops shouting and pushing at me.

"You're so pissed off at me right now, you hate me. You probably want to punch me in the face." His grip slides from my upper arms to my wrists. He shakes my hands lightly. His eyes never leave mine. "Go ahead."

"I'm not going to punch you in the face—"

"Slap me, then," Will says steadily.

"I'm not going to—"

"I wanted to fuck her," he says. "I wanted to fuck the bartender, too. You didn't see her, but she was smoking hot, with a huge pair of tits, her nipples poking out of her T-shirt like they had my name on them. I wanted to fuck the girl standing behind you when you walked in. She had on a short dress and an ass that would not fucking quit."

"Stop it."

"I look at women every day," he says. "I think about what it would be like to be inside them, think about what their pussies must taste like. Sometimes I think about getting off between their tits. That would be so fucking hot."

I'm shaking, but I can't move. "Shut. Up."

"I went to the bookstore the other day and thought about bending the salesgirl over one of those couches, fucking her right there in the store. She was this tiny little thing, couldn't have been more than a hundred pounds, and I wanted to eat her pussy until she screamed—"

I have never slapped anyone, ever. My hand cracks his cheek hard enough to turn his head and make him stumble a step or two. Will doesn't even put his hand up to cover the perfect imprint of my fingers on his skin. I am horrified at the single, sliding drop of crimson at the corner of his mouth. He licks it away. We both say nothing.

And then slowly, slowly, Will goes to his knees in front of me. He buries his face between my legs, the heat of his breath scalding me through the gauzy fabric of my skirt. His fingers skate up the backs of my bare calves, then beneath my skirt to my thighs.

I touch his hair, lightly at first, barely skimming it. A moment later, when he nuzzles my cunt, finding my clit with his nose and the point of his chin, my fingers sink deep in his hair. I can't keep the cry locked in my throat, and it's rough and raw and would be embarrassing if I gave a single tiny fuck about anything but how good his mouth feels on me.

Will pushes up my skirt inch by inch and pulls my panties to the side to find my cunt with his mouth. My knees are weak, but I anchor myself with my hand in his hair, his palms on my ass holding me close while he licks me. He shifts one hand behind my knee, urging me to hook my leg over his shoulder.

Oh, God. I want to come, I'm so close, but he eases off, teasing me. I can't stay this way forever. I'm going to fall. I'm going to melt.

Orgasm hits me like a truck, and pleasure becomes the only thing I see. Feel. Smell. Taste. His mouth on me is magic; there is nothing else but the flick of his tongue on my clit and the pressure of his fingers on my ass, keeping me standing. And somehow, before I've quite finished, pleasure still coursing through me, Will hooks the chair toward me. We move together, in sync, him not pushing and me not fumbling. I turn and put my hands flat on the chair seat, then my forearms. Ass in the air, legs spread, open to him as he undoes his jeans in the time it takes me to catch my breath.

He doesn't even take my panties off, just keeps them pulled

to the side when he pushes his cock inside me, taking his time for this first thrust, but after that slamming into me from behind, hard and deep. He fucks me so hard the chair moves, though I grip the sides so tightly my fingers ache. My head hits the wooden slats of the chair's back as he pounds me. It hurts. Everything hurts, and I'm coming again, and the pain and pleasure have tangled so tightly there's no more telling the difference between them.

When it's over, I'm on my knees, my cheek on the seat of the chair. I'm boneless and aching all over. Will's on his knees behind me, his face pressed to my back, his arms around my waist. This isn't comfortable, not at all, but I don't want to move. I'm not, in fact, sure I can.

He draws in a shuddering breath finally, and shifts. We end up in a tangle of limbs, me between his legs, curled against him, while he strokes his hand down my hair. We breathe together, and I soothe myself with the beat of his heart. It's not much more comfortable than the other position, but I don't want to move now, either.

I do, though. I push away to gently touch the mark I left on his face. I think it will bruise. He'll carry it for a while, anyway. I kiss the corner of his mouth where the blood was, and he pulls me close again.

"I didn't think you'd show up tonight," Will says.

Outside, the traffic beeps and blares, even this late. In here, I press my face to his chest and listen to the thump of his heart. I tip my head to get my lips on his throat, to feel the pulse just below his ear.

"I thought we were finished with all of this," Will tells me.

I say nothing.

"I was unfaithful," he says next, and I don't know what that means. Unfaithful how? Can it be cheating between two people who aren't committed, who've never made that agreement, who can't even be together because one is married? My confusion lasts another few seconds until he continues. "A lot. I cheated on my ex. More than once. All the time, as a matter of fact. Not even because I wanted to, or because I was unhappy. Just…sometimes, because I could."

This is the sort of confession that should push me away, but I cling tighter to him instead. I shut my eyes, curling close as if I can be absorbed into him. Disappear inside him.

"She left me, and it was my own fault. She hates me, and that's my fault, too. Married people shouldn't fuck around," Will says. "Someone always gets hurt."

This time, I move. I touch his face again. "I'm sorry, Will."

He turns his head to kiss my hand before he takes it away and holds it tightly, our fingers linked. "I hated when you told me to find someone else."

"I thought I meant it," I say. "But I don't. I'm selfish and greedy. I'm sorry. I'm so sorry."

Our kisses are feverish and sloppy, bitter tasting.

"I want you to be happy," I say into his mouth. "I know you're going to find someone else. I don't want you to be alone forever. Just…just for a little while longer…"

It's the worst thing I could ask of him, the most awful, selfish and greedy thing, and I hate myself for saying it as soon as the words leave my lips. And still I cling to him, and still I kiss him. I take his face in my hands and I kiss and kiss and kiss.

"We're together and then you go away. I'm here alone," Will says. "And I think about how much…I want…and can't have. Slapping my face hurt way less than that."

But you can have, I think. *You can have everything.*

Sometimes you say things because they make you feel better. Sometimes you say them because they make someone else feel better. *"I love you"* stays locked behind my teeth because there is no way saying it aloud will make either of us feel anything but worse. I don't say it, because when you love someone, really love them, you don't want anything you do to ever hurt them.

"I know why you told me to find someone else," Will says, and I understand exactly how he could want a slap to the face rather than something like this. "But I hated it."

"I don't want you to hate me, not ever."

"I could never hate you," Will says. "But I don't want someone else."

"You should. You will. Someday." *Before I'm ready for you.*

He says nothing. I kiss him again, doing my best to memorize the shape and taste of him—as if I could ever forget. I unfold myself from his embrace and stretch my creaking muscles, every part of me stiff and sore and bruised. Will stands, too.

"I shouldn't have come tonight," I tell him. "I said we needed to end this, and I didn't hold up my end of it. I'm sorry for hurting you."

And then the words rush out of me. I can't hold them back. I don't want to lie, and not saying anything feels like a betrayal.

"I want you to be happy, Will. Because I love you."

He looks startled. Then pleased. But before he can say anything, I shake my head to keep him quiet.

"But this is wrong. It's not a question of if this will end badly," I say, "but of how badly it will end. I don't want to be bad for you. I don't want to hurt you. You deserve better than this, Will."

"You're breaking up with me. Again." He tries to sound light, but neither of us is even close to laughter.

If I speak, I'll burst into braying, ugly sobs, so all I can manage is to nod. I want to kiss him again, but if I do I will never leave this apartment. I will never go home. I won't drop everything; I will simply open my hands and let it all fall.

I swallow the ball of tears in my throat and force out words.

"It will only hurt at first. Only for a while. Eventually, it will all be okay."

"Do you believe that?" Will asks.

"Yes," I tell him, even though I don't. "I need you to do something for me."

"What. Anything. You know that."

"I need you to tell me that you don't want me. That you don't love me."

Will says nothing. He won't look at me. I study the curve of his jaw, the hair that pushes in front of his ears, and the scruff of his unshaved cheeks.

"I need you to tell me you don't want me, Will." My voice breaks and I catch myself so I don't break down. "Please."

Still without looking at me, he shakes his head.

"You have to." My voice gets hard and heavy, bordering on cruel. "You have to tell me you don't want me or love me or need me. Because I can't leave you if you don't."

I want him to say "Then don't leave me."

Mostly, I want him to look at me, but he does not. Will keeps his face turned from mine, his shoulders hunched and his fingers tap-tapping nervously on his knee. I swallow against the shards of emotion slashing at my throat. I taste blood.

I think of asking him to tell me he loves me instead. That he wants and needs me. That he can't bear to live without me. I imagine sinking to my knees in a slow-motion, movie-drama moment set to some sad song; I think I might bury my face in my hands while I kneel at his feet and beg him…yes, fucking beg him, to be my reason for walking away from everything.

But I don't beg.

He won't say it.

I won't ask.

And that's when, finally, I walk out the door and don't look back.

Chapter Forty-Four

So now it's over, that's what I think, as I sit and stare and stare out the window, but see nothing. It's really over this time, because it has to be. Because he told me that it makes him sad, because it hurts him, and this is no longer some kind of game, it's not something I can pretend is not going to end badly.

It's as if a weight lifts off me, when I think of it, of not trying to find the time to be with him. Of being able to focus and concentrate on my work, the things I need to do in my life. Without Will, I will have so…much…time.

Without Will, I have an empty place.

Knowing it was empty for a long time before I met him makes this no better. At least before I met him, I didn't know what I was missing. Now I do.

It's bullshit, I think. All shit. All of it.

Happiness is overrated. Maybe we are not built for it. Maybe the best we can hope for is to be…content. To be resigned. To muddle through life and be grateful for the good, and work through the bad. Maybe that is what I will have for the rest of my life, this good life to which I am resigned, for which I am grateful.

Fuck you, universe, for letting me glimpse what might have

been joy, if only he wasn't so afraid. If I wasn't so stubborn that I had to be sure I could make it on my own, that he was not my reason, that I would not allow him to be my reason.

Chapter Forty-Five

There is silence in my house.

The weight of words unsaid. I didn't ask Ross to move out, or to sleep in the guest room, and I haven't moved my things out, either. We still share a bed. Him on his side. Me on mine. There's plenty of room between us.

I haven't told Ross that I want to leave, but every day I look at the real estate websites for houses. Every day I calculate the expenses of dividing our assets. I walk through this house I love so much, room by room, and touch everything we own, and I decide what I would leave behind and what I can't live without. Decorative vases and candlesticks and cooking utensils with stupid functions, like the pomegranate de-seeder I'll never use, ever. There is so much that doesn't matter. And so much that does.

If he notices, my husband doesn't say anything. He goes about his business the way he always has, while I do the laundry and pay the bills and buy the groceries and keep on schedule this life we've built. I don't greet him at the door, but then I haven't for a very long time.

If I stay, this could be the way it is for the rest of my life.

But before the rest of my life can happen, I have two daughters to marry off. They move home in the last week before the big day, so I can be on hand to help with last-minute details, and because both of them have ended the leases on their apartments before they move in with their future husbands. Jac will go to Boston, Kat to Colorado. I am going to miss them both so much I refuse to think about it—after all, neither of them has lived at home for the past four years. But it will be different. Everything is different, now.

Every day the wedding planning brews to a magnificent, perfect storm of mania from Jac and curious calm from Kat. Jac is alternately glowing and fuming. Kat, on the other hand, is quiet and contemplative. Jac bursts into tears and tantrums, but her sister merely moves through each day, as we get closer and closer, with shadows under her eyes and in the hollows of her cheeks.

So I ask her, one day when Ross and Jac are both out, "Kat. What's wrong?"

She doesn't answer at first, and I think maybe she'll lie to me, but my sweet girl turns to me and says, so matter-of-factly I know she means every word, "Mom, if I have to marry Rich, I swear to you I will end up in prison for murder."

She looks at me as if she expects me to tell her there's too much invested at this point, one week away. The dress, the ceremony, the honeymoon. The guest list. But instead I take both her hands and say, "Then don't do it."

Kat doesn't break into tears; maybe, like her mother, she's cried too many and has none left now. She draws a breath, blinking rapidly. "I don't love him, Mom. But I think he loves me...I know he loves me. So how do I tell him I can't go through with it?"

I don't ask her why she can't. I don't try to talk her into going through with it. I like Rich well enough; he's always seemed like a nice guy. He and Kat have been together for a long time, since their sophomore year of college. But Kat's my girl, and I have no loyalty to him.

I squeeze her hands. "My advice…just tell him."

"It's going to hurt him."

"Yes," I say. "I'm sure it will."

"What if I'm making a mistake?" Kat cries.

I give my daughter the advice I wish I could take for myself. "The world won't wait for you to change, not ever. You either take a chance or you stay in one place while everything else goes on."

Kat draws a deep breath, but there's some color back in her cheeks. "Dad's going to shit a brick. And Rich… Mom. I don't know how I'm going to do it. He's going to be so mad. And all the guests…"

"Half of them are coming because of Jac, anyway. Don't worry about it. It's a week away—they can all still cancel their hotel reservations. And Rich is going to be mad and hurt and upset, but better it happen now than next week. Or next month. Or next year. Or in twenty years," I add quietly, and squeeze her hands again.

She nods, then hugs me. "Thanks, Mom."

I rub her back the way I did when she was small and upset about something. The days of fixing boo-boos with a kiss are long, long gone, but it's nice to know I can still make her feel better by being her mother.

"I'll go talk to Rich," Kat says after a minute, "but…would you talk to Dad? And Jac. Oh, God, she'll be ballistic."

"Absolutely. It'll be fine."

It's not quite fine, of course. Ross is angry and shouting about the money, the waste, and Jac's in hysterics about her sister's breakup—and not about the favors or guest list or seating arrangements. I feel a little bad that I'd expected her to be a bridezilla. I should've known she'd take her sister's pain as her own. That's how it's been since they were kids.

We gather in the kitchen, Jac and her Jeff. Kat, without Rich, who she says took the news surprisingly well and confessed his own doubts—a much better outcome than she'd expected. And Ross, still angry and blustering, but beneath that, truly concerned for the well-being of his girls. I see that in him. The worry, and not just about the money. It reminds me that he's always been a great father, and, for the most part, a good husband. At least the best he could be, and that's the most anyone should ever ask for.

We are a family in the good times, and we're a family in the bad times, too. We will always be a family, I think. No matter what else happens.

And later, when the girls have gone to bed and the house is quiet, I say, "Ross. I need to talk to you."

Chapter Forty-Six

I came in on the train and then took a cab. Cold spring drizzle trickles down the back of my collar and down my spine, but my skin is heated and feverish and the chilly water feels good. I've taken care to cover my hair with a scarf to keep it looking at least a tiny bit less bedraggled, and my mascara's waterproof, though not solely because of the rain. I'm dressed for the weather in my woolen overcoat, thick stockings, warm boots. Winter sometimes still clings, even in March.

I called him first, of course I did. I wanted him to be ready for me, not surprised. I wanted to give him the chance to tell me not to come, and part of me expected him to say just that. But he didn't.

Will greets me at the door, and I drink up the sight of him as greedily as I've ever gulped down a glass of water. The *plink-plink* of water from my umbrella is very loud before he takes it from me, to tuck into the large vase by the door. He takes my coat, solicitous. Polite. My scarf, which he hangs next to the coat, though he hesitates and glances at me before he does. It's the same scarf I once used to blindfold him. Of course we both remember.

He offers coffee, tea. Wine. And though I'm thirsty, still so thirsty, I decline with a shake of my head, and move past him to the space beneath those tall windows where the gray light turns everything to pearl.

I take off my clothes, piece by piece. The boots, the stockings. The dress, which buttons from throat to hem. In satin and lace I stand in front of him, and then I take those off, too. Hiding nothing.

Will takes up his camera. Eye to the lens. The whir and snap of the shutter tastes brittle and dry, like dust. His voice, murmuring instructions, saying my name, is the ocean.

He will always be my ocean.

Taking picture after picture, he moves around me. Posing. Adjusting. And then finally, just touching me, over and over. He puts the camera down and his mouth finds the spot at the back of my neck. The slope of my bare shoulders. He moves along my skin with the sureness of familiarity, but with hesitation, too. His fingertips trace the knobs of my spine. The length of my arm to my wrist. He takes my hand, and our fingers link, and I don't care anymore that I'm naked and insecure, because in front of him, I feel beautiful.

This is it. The last time. I tug open the buttons on his shirt and draw it off his arms. His belt, his jeans. I kneel in front of him and nuzzle the soft, fine hairs on the insides of his thighs, while my fingers find the waistband of his briefs and pull them down. I take him in my mouth.

I map him.

Every part of Will, with my mouth and hands, tongue and teeth. I pay attention to every beautiful inch of him because this is the last time I will ever touch him, and I want to have this with me for the rest of my life. The inside of his elbow, smooth and sweet. The back of each of his knees. Ankles, bony and hard under the pressure of my teeth.

Every finger, knuckle by knuckle.

I press my lips to the pulse in each wrist. His palms. The

scoop of his collarbones has me undone and shaking, and I nuzzle the hollow at the base of his throat until I stop. I kiss the line of his jaw. His cheeks. I cup his face against mine and flutter my lashes against his skin, over and over, while he laughs softly, and then I kiss his closed eyes.

I thread my fingers through his hair. I study the curve of his ears, the slope of each shoulder blade, with my fingertips and then my mouth. I kiss his spine all the way to the base, and then the sweet spots of each dimple above his ass.

I take everything, and I make him mine.

I want to never forget it. His smell, the taste of him, everything about him. I love him so much it is like dying. The pleasure, like dying. And I want to die with it, but I won't. I will just go on and on, even though it kills me, like nothing ever has, and oh my God, I wish I could be with him forever.

You could call this a lot of things, but I will always call it love. Even when the pace gets frantic and grasping, when I rake my nails into his skin and he bites me hard enough to bruise, even when he turns me so he can take me from behind and pounds into me, flesh on flesh. When the headboard creaks from how hard I'm gripping it, and when he yanks my hair until my head tips back. When he tells me how much he hates me for staying away so long, and all I can do is murmur his name, over and over, each time a little louder, like a plea.

And yes, yes, yes, even when I beg.

The universe gives us what we need, but not always how we want it. Spent and gasping, I lose track of how many times I tip into orgasm. There's too much pleasure. Too much pain. And at the end of it, when he buries himself inside me and my name sighs out of him with the rush and hiss of waves on sand, all I can do is hold on tight and love him as much as I can.

"What do you want me to do with the pictures?" he says

after a while, when we've dozed to the spatter of icy rain against the windows.

Night is falling.

"Keep them," I say. "They're for you. If you want them."

Will shifts in the tangle of sheets, his hand splayed on my belly. "Do you have to get back?"

There's nothing to get back to but an empty apartment I haven't yet filled with things I love.

Without answering the question, I turn to face him, our heads together on the same pillow. He's so close to me that even in the dimming light I can see the shimmer of gold in his greenish eyes. "Remember when we didn't know each other?"

"Yes," he says. "I remember."

"Will...do you think we could ever really be together? For real, I mean."

He doesn't pull away, but his expression goes guarded. "Yes. I've thought about it."

"You don't think it would work?"

He hesitates. "I think...I wonder if maybe you just think it would work better with me because you don't like where you are. I think we'd work for a month and then we'd fuck it up. And then what?"

And then what.

"At least we'd know," I say. "At least we'd have tried. Could we? Try?"

Will says nothing, and I kiss him so we can both pretend there were words. I kiss him until my mouth is numb, and when he curls against me, his face against my chest, I stroke his hair until his breathing slows and he falls asleep. Then I get up slowly and quietly and dress, and I leave without a note or another word, because the kindest thing you can do for someone you love is to never tell them how much they have broken your heart.

Chapter Forty-Seven

I take another train, and at the end of it, I stand and stare at the ocean.

The water comes in. The water goes out. The ocean always changes, and yet it's eternally the same.

For an endless moment all I am is the ocean. All I have become is the sea. It kisses me with salt, and I wonder if I will always taste tears when I think of him.

Yes.

The memory of his voice will always taste like salt and smell like sand and wind and the cry of gulls.

Some people live their entire life and never once feel how I felt every time he looked at me. So yes, this hurts. And yes, I feel as if I might die. But I won't. And somehow, I find a way to let it all go…just let it go. No regrets. No grief. It will always hurt a little, down deep in that secret place, but it's become a pain I can handle. Besides, if it didn't always hurt, just a little, it wouldn't mean as much.

At my feet, the water leaves behind shells and seaweed and rocks. Black and beige and white and gray. Among them is one I need; all I have to do is look. And there, half buried in the sand, hidden in a way it would have been so easy to miss, is the one I'm looking for.

Heart-shaped rock.

The universe gives us what we need. I wipe away the sand and trace the rounded edges. It is the most perfectly heart-shaped rock I've ever found. It would be the best one in my collection. So of course I throw it as far out into the water as I can.

Someday.

Not a demand, but a wish.

Please.

And with this, with that, the colors all come back. The wind whispers music and the sound of birds is the tinkle of bells, and the way my heart beats is a steady one-two thump that works the way it's meant to.

The well of my heart is a very deep place, and at the bottom, it's dark.

He was my ocean, and I didn't know if I would drown until I learned how well I could swim.

I could write without music, but I'm so very glad I don't have to. Included is a partial playlist of the music I listened to while writing *Tear You Apart*. Please support the artists by buying their music.

"Tear You Apart" —She Wants Revenge
"Oh No" —The Commodores
"Missing You" —John Waite
"You Won't Let Me" —Rachael Yamagata
"One More Night" —Maroon 5
"Crazy" —Stars Go Dim
"Everything Changes" —Staind
"Against All Odds" —Phil Collins
and
"Nicest Thing" —Kate Nash

In addition, *Tear You Apart,* the novel, can be experienced as a "rock opera." Listen to the songs in order. They tell a story.

<u>*Tear You Apart,* the Rock Opera</u>

"Where Have You Been" —Rihanna
"Starry Eyed" —Ellie Goulding
"A Girl Like You" —Edwyn Collins
"Glad You Came" —The Wanted
"What Would Happen" —Meredith Brooks
"I Get Off" —Halestorm
"Addicted" —Kelly Clarkson
"In Your Room" —Halestorm
"Birthday Cake" —Rihanna
"Beat It" —Michael Jackson
"Kiss Me" —Ed Sheeran
"You Shook Me All Night Long" —AC/DC
"A Kiss Is Not a Contract" —Flight of the Conchords
"I'm a Machine" —David Guetta, Crystal Nicole & Tyrese Gibson
"They Bring Me to You" —Joshua Radin
"Starring Role" —Marina and the Diamonds
"I Don't Want to Fall in Love" —She Wants Revenge

"Radioactive" —Marina and the Diamonds
"Weakness in Me" —Katherine Crowe
"Distance" —Christina Perri
"Stealing" —Gavin DeGraw
"Almost Lover" —A Fine Frenzy
"Always Have Paris" —The Apers